RAIDING PREHISTORIC

FOURTH IN THE WEST OF PREHISTORIC SERIES.
ERIK 'TRACER' TESTERMAN

SEVEREDPRESS

RAIDING PREHISTORIC

ISBN: 978-1-922861-54-2

For my readers, without you none of this would have been possible. Thank you and God bless.

RAIDING PREHISTORIC

The Shaynee brave was looking for a cow to steal when he saw the large plume of smoke rising in the distance.

Curious, he slowed his spotted pony and stared.

The smoke was in the direction of Huck Berry's ranch, and it looked bigger than the usual wasteful white man fire.

Kicking heels to the flanks of his mount, he rode towards the twisting pillar of smoke, and soon heard faint pattering shots of gunfire.

Warily, he considered slowing, but curiosity got the better of him, and he headed into the nearest patch of forest instead. The rest of the way, he'd approach quickly but under cover and unseen.

By the time he reached the edge of the trees near the ranch, the shooting had stopped, and the house was engulfed in flames. Several men were throwing corpses over the backs of riderless horses. On their dark suits, tin badges flashed in the morning light.

Pink Men, the Indian thought bitterly.

Squinting through the leaves of the underbrush, he watched as the riders rode away in the opposite direction, down the wagon trail and into the forest towards town. Behind them, they pulled the small three horned beast the white man had been raising. The trike bellowed pitifully and pulled against the rope only to be tugged down the road against its will.

Once the group of Pink Men were out of sight, the brave pushed his pony through the forest brush and into the open.

There were two bodies in sight. One looked familiar. And the horses in the corral that stamped their hooves and shifted about nervously, he knew them well.

Reaching the packed dirt yard, the brave slid from his pony and ran to the downed man.

It was Huck Berry, and he wasn't moving.

The brave looked at the horses again, then back at the house. Large amounts of smoke were billowing from the windows as flames lapped at the roof. He hadn't seen the Pinkertons take anyone with them but there were four horses in the corral and only two bodies in sight.

Without thinking, he ran onto the porch and hit the closed door with his shoulder. It was barred from inside and withstood his strength.

But one of the windows... the shutter was cracked open.

Taking a deep breath, he leapt through the billowing smoke coming out of the window and dropped to the floor on the other side. He landed painfully on several fired cartridge shells that rolled on the floor beneath him.

The brave could hold his breath a long time underwater, but inside this burning inferno, the smoke stung his eyes and leaked into his nose as he clamped shut his lips. The heat was unbearable on his exposed skin, and he fought the fear that he would burst into flames himself.

Reaching his arms out, he slid across the floor on his belly like a snake, searching for anything of importance.

He found a discarded rifle. Pushing it aside, he crawled further into the house.

He touched something warm. Not from fire. But from life.

A slender bit of flesh, soft and supple, but long... an arm, he thought.

Grabbing it, he pulled and threw himself backwards towards where he thought the door was while tugging the dead weight with him. Flames and smoke made it impossible to see, and his lungs screamed for him to swallow a fresh breath of air.

Fighting against his body's urges, he moved against the wall until he felt the rough door against his back. Squinting upwards in the semi-lit darkness, he found the board barring the door. It was on fire. Bracing himself for the pain, he slammed the heel of his fist upwards against the burning piece of wood, knocking the door free and open.

Tumbling outside, he reached back in, grabbed the still form under the arms and pulled.

He dragged a white woman out with blood smeared across her chest and shoulder.

Skyla, he thought. He felt her chest for movement and found it. She was still breathing, barely.

The roof collapsed in a shower of sparks and flames.

There was no going back in for anyone else.

Grabbing her around the waist, he lifted the wounded woman over a shoulder and carried her away from the fire and smoke towards where his pony stamped its hooves impatiently.

Gently laying her down in the grass, Otto swept dark hair away from her soot covered face and looked back towards where Huck Berry had fallen by the corral.

The body was gone.

As was Carbine.

***

My body felt like it was on fire. Carbine's galloping sent wave after wave of pain through my body until it felt as though it would consume me from within.

But hatred kept me going.

Skyla.

Charles.

Bo.

All dead.

And it was all my fault.

Coughing up a wad of bloody phlegm, I spat to the side and checked my weapons.

I had only my *Eighty-Six*, Bowie knife, and shotgun tucked away in my bedroll behind the saddle. It wasn't much, but it didn't matter.

Vengeance called me.

And I was answering.

Riding around a curve in the trail, the Pinkertons appeared before me. They were walking their horses nonchalantly while leading several horses with bodies tied to the saddles. The so-called detectives didn't have a care in the world now that their evil work was done. Sara shambled along behind them, her three horned head dropped low and defeated.

Gritting my teeth, I pulled the *Eighty-Six* into my shoulder, waiting for the ivory beaded front sight to drop on the closest detective's back that held the rope to my trike.

For Skyla.

I pulled the trigger.

The man arched upright and toppled off his horse. Before his corpse hit the ground, I thumped my heels against Carbine to keep him running.

In confusion, the surprised Pinkertons milled about, turning around to see what was happening behind them.

The next detective, I hit in the chest with another large .45-70 round fired from my rifle.

I racked the lever on the weapon. This time I was close enough to fire without aiming. Blood splattered on the horse's neck as a third Pinkerton slumped forward lifelessly and slid from his saddle.

The next Pinkerton I passed; I jammed the rifle barrel into his face like a mounted knight with a lance. A strip of flesh ripped away from cheek to ear. His scream was just empty noise in the background as I focused on the next man.

Passing my rifle to my left hand, I drew my Bowie and hurled the blade at him. The practice with Skyla's old butchers came in handy as the blade whipped past his horse's head and sunk into the detective's belly.

Screaming, he fired his pistol without aiming, hitting another detective's horse, before grasping feebly at the massive knife jutting from his stomach and falling from the saddle.

The wounded horse bucked, throwing his rider to the ground before racing away into the forest.

Passing through the group, I jerked on Carbine's reins and spun him around to face the survivors.

There was only one with any fight left in him.

The man thrown from his wounded horse.

Detective Thompson.

The leader of the Pinkertons.

The large man pushed himself onto all fours, breathing heavily as though the wind had been knocked out of him.

I jumped Carbine forward, bumping my horse against the detective's side and knocking him back down.

He lay sprawled on the road, coughing painfully and clutching his chest. The fight in him was gone.

My entire body was racked with pain. I knew that faintly, but all I could feel was the pounding of blood in my ears and the hatred that I knew was twisted on my face.

Reaching behind me, I jerked the hidden sawed-off shotgun out from between the rolled blankets then stepped down from the saddle.

Stalking forward, I watched the lead detective crawl onto his knees.

With a hand raised towards me in a plea for mercy, he began to push himself to a stand.

I fired the first barrel into his left leg.

Pink mist, bloody chunks, and pieces of white shattered bone sprayed from the buckshot's impact.

Screaming hoarsely, he toppled back over, grabbing at the mangled remains of his lower limb.

I stopped in front of him and waited as the screaming turned to a low whimper.

"How, Jed?" he cried out painfully as tears rolled down his face. "I-I killed you."

I unloaded the second barrel of buckshot into his chest without answering.

He could ponder my survival on his way to hell.

Turning, I looked around the trail. There were a lot of bodies strewn about. The man with my Bowie in his belly was still dying though. And the Pinkerton whose face I nearly ripped off was busy trying to disappear into the forest.

Pulling a pistol from the nearest corpse's holster, I fired a shot into the back of the escaping Pinkerton, pitching him face first into the muddy wagon ruts.

He didn't move again.

I surveyed the area. Bodies. Lots of bodies. And a handful of horses standing around as though unsure of what to do. Sara was tugging at her rope, pulling it free from the dead man's grasp.

The anger in me was burning off, and I felt sick, battered, and exhausted.

I dropped to a knee and let the shakes take over me.

Everything hurt.

Everything felt like it was on fire.

I felt like I could scream, shout, cry, mutilate the bodies around me, or just put a bullet through my own brain. I was pulled in a dozen different directions all at once. Anger, grief, sadness, loneliness, rage, and fear… the emotions ran the gauntlet all at the same time.

Vomit spewed out of my mouth onto the grass beside the trail. I let myself fall to the side of the splattered pile and lay there, breathing heavily as tears streaked down my face.

Sara nudged her beak against me as though to offer comfort and I placed a trembling hand on her small horns to steady myself.

But of everything, all the thoughts, all the emotions, all the pain, there was one thing that forced me to wipe the tears away and crawl back onto my feet.

Revenge.

***

After retrieving my Bowie, I took the tin detective badge from each of the corpses and left the bodies where they lay.

Painfully easing myself back into the saddle, I let Carbine walk back to my ranch at his own slow speed.

My house was still burning when we arrived. The roof had caved in on Skyla and Charles' bodies, and I tried not to think of what I'd find once the fire died down. Yet, the thoughts lingered, and I felt fresh tears roll down my bearded cheeks.

Stepping out of the saddle, I hobbled to an overturned bucket by the barn and sat facing the fire. Carbine walked away, reins dragging in the grass. He snorted at me as if disgusted with my weakness.

But I didn't care. My world was turning to ashes in front of my very eyes. With my foot, I dragged my pistols from where they'd been dropped in the ambush. Picking the Colts up, I knocked the dirt off and holstered one while staring at the other.

It'd be so easy. Just a trigger pull.

And I'd be with Skyla, forever.

I felt another tear trickle into my beard. Damn, but I wish I could.

But I couldn't.

Skyla wouldn't want that from me. And besides, if I did that, Reydan would win. He'd continue his miserable existence until someone else put him down like the rabid, feral creature he was.

And that was my duty.

That... That my friends would want from me. To avenge them.

Sara lay down in a pile of discarded hay and rifle shell casings from where Pinkertons had shot into the house. She bellowed softly for Skyla, before resting her horned head on the ground and watched the fire burn with me.

Pulling the dragon scale lined vest back, I lifted my dark blue shirt to look at my side and chest. There was a hideous amount of red swelling and early stages of bruising going on. Gingerly, I touched my side. From the searing pain that shot through my body, I'd reckon the bullet cracked at least one rib. And the front of my chest, dead center, where Detective Thompson had tried to finish me off... I got lucky there; the bullet caught the edge of the vest, and the scales sliced me open pretty good but still managed to deflect the pistol round.

By all means, I shouldn't be alive. If it hadn't been for Skyla's thoughtfulness and the dragon scaled vest...

Wincing, I dropped the shirt edge and my eyes flicked to where Bo lay. The old ranch hand had become a good friend and confidant of my past. Now he was crumpled by the bunk house, undershirt soaked in blood, an unfired rifle lying where it'd fallen from his lifeless hands. He was no less dead than those inside the house but passed away more mercifully than being burned alive.

I blinked through red-rimmed eyes.

Kill Reydan.

That thought was running over and over through my head. But I knew I couldn't go riding into Granite Falls and gunning him down, as much as he deserved it. And where the hell my father was, I didn't know. He was supposed to have killed the man by now. Had he accomplished that deed, this wouldn't have happened.

Instead, Reydan had taken everything from me.

And I was going to return the favor.

But first, there were some things I needed to take care of … things I didn't want to.

Exhausted, I leaned my head back against the barn and closed my eyes. Just for a moment.

"Huck Berry."

I blinked rapidly, unaware that I'd passed out.

Standing in front of me with a disgusted look on his face was Runs With Dogs, one of the Shaynee braves, with a white and brown paint pony behind him. I didn't know how long I'd been out, but judging by the flames on the house, it couldn't have been more than an hour.

"What?"

"Come with me."

"Piss off," I waved a hand around me. "You see this? This is my life. Gone. Burning to ashes with my Skyla somewhere inside."

"Come," he repeated with annoying insistence.

Growing angry, I drew a pistol and cocked back the hammer. "Go away or die."

"Skyla lives."

Nearly dropping the gun in surprise, I looked at him as a slow glimmer of hope suddenly rose inside me.

"She's alive? How? She's…." Gripping the butt of the gun firmly, I gestured at the house with the barrel. "No! She's dead! She's in there!"

"Otto save her."

"What … What? How?"

"Come." He shrugged. "Or stay." The Shaynee warrior grabbed his pony by the mane and jumped onto its bare back.

Trembling, I stood and looked for Carbine. He was a dozen feet away, nipping at some long grass by the edge of the corral. In a daze, I walked over to him and pulled my battered body into the saddle. With a soft whistle at Sara, the trike lumbered to her feet and came as called.

Touching heels to his flanks, I rode after Runs With Dogs as my head spun.

***

When the Shaynee village came into sight, I kicked Carbine's sides, leaving the Shaynee brave and Sara behind as I raced my horse down the plain towards the large grouping of teepees that stood along the river's edge.

Indians scattered and dogs barked as I rode to a quick stop at the outskirts of the village.

A lithe Indian was waiting for me with an upraised hand.

"Where is she, Otto?" I shouted at my blood brother as I leapt off Carbine, looking around for her.

"Bad hurt. Come with me." My blood brother walked away in long strides, leading me to an undecorated teepee. It looked newly constructed, made from fresh hides, yet unmarked or painted in Shaynee symbols and drawings.

As I reached for the flap covering the opening, he grabbed my arm.

"No. No go in."

Spinning out of his grasp, I shoved the scarred Indian away.

"Like hell I won't!" I moved to crawl into the teepee.

A pair of braves grabbed me from behind with iron banded grips. Swearing every Shaynee curse word I could think of, I kicked and fought as they dragged me away. One brave got a solid elbow to his jaw, and I stomped on the other's foot with the heel of my boot to a satisfying howl of pain before Otto finally had enough and smacked the decorated stock of his rifle into the back of my skull.

The blow didn't knock me out, but it knocked me down. Hard.

After a moment of collecting myself, I looked up angrily at the scowling braves surrounding me and slid my hands towards my pistols.

"By God, get out of my way or I'll kill you all," I swore. Skyla was mere feet away inside the teepee, badly wounded he had said, and nothing was going to keep me from seeing her.

Chief Toko moved in front of me. Kneeling, he placed a calming hand on my shoulder and looked me in the eyes with an uncharacteristic frown on his usually lively craggy face. "Skyla bad hurt." He shook his head, "Do not interfere with the spirits or Arthur inside as they work."

I gulped hard and let go of the Colts. Looking down at the ground I tried to take some deep breaths, but every lungful felt like fire as my cracked rib shifted.

"You no look good. Otto thought you dead," Toko said, as he and my blood brother slipped their hands under my arms and helped me up.

"Come." He pointed at a large painted teepee nearby that I knew from previous visits was his. "We wait for spirits to decide."

"Decide what?" I asked groggily while tenderly feeling the lump swelling on the back of my head from Otto's rifle stock.

"If Skyla live or die," he said solemnly.

***

It'd been a long day and was becoming a longer night as I sat in that teepee with Chief Toko and Otto. The two of them tried to make small talk, about the Vikings, the kraken and Toothed One that we killed, even about Arthur's time with them over the past few days. The trained surgeon turned writer had helped many of their people. But I had nothing to say as I worried that the Shaynee spirits would let my love die.

I knew a lot of people didn't think much about the Indian's pagan gods of corn or weather or buffalo or whatever. But right now, I knew that as long as the Shaynee believed their heathen gods would help, they'd help. Otherwise, they'd stop any tribal treatments and let her wounds run their course, and then it'd be solely up to Arthur to keep her alive.

Otto did tell me about how he saved Skyla and about her wounds. A pair of bullets to the chest and shoulder and a lot of suffocating smoke inhaled. It was astounding that he had been in the area.

I was angry at myself though.

I'd been so certain that she was dead and focused on killing the Pinkertons that I didn't try to save her. I didn't even notice Otto's horse in the yard when I crawled into the saddle and set off after Reydan's men.

But I'd have plenty of time to kick myself later, I thought. If she survived.

While the tribe's healer and medicine man worked on her with Arthur's assistance, I sipped on the bowl of broth and beef that one of the Shaynee women had brought us and contemplated what I would do if she died.

Honestly, the dark thoughts of my revenge scared even me.

But that didn't mean I wouldn't do it.

I would.

And I'd leave a wake of blood and body parts behind me.

After hours and hours of sitting, I began to nod off again. At first, I chastised myself for daring to fall asleep while Skyla was fighting for her life. But Chief Toko noticed and gave me a comforting pat on the back.

"Huck Berry. Sleep. Skyla in good hands."

"No. I can't. Not while the spirits decide." Or while Arthur worked, I left unsaid.

"They decide without you one way or other. Sleep. You need it for what comes next."

Otto pushed some more sticks into the fire in the center of the floor and grunted in agreement. "You were dead, Huck Berry. I saw with my eyes. Rest now. Death takes price on man's body."

Giving in, I carefully laid down on the buffalo and deer hides that lined the ground of the Shaynee Chief's teepee. It took some gentle wiggling to get into a position that didn't hurt. But within seconds, I was asleep.

I dreamed of fire. Lots of fire. A great dragon from Prehistoria had made its way to our side and was breathing flame on myself and Skyla as we tried to race away across the open prairie. On the back of the dinosaur rode Reydan White, laughing as he pointed his ivory tipped cane in our direction. The flames weren't touching me, but they were burning Skyla and her horse away as she screamed my name until she was nothing but a heap of ashes and burned bones.

At some point, someone removed my vest and shirt and folded them neatly beside me. When I woke, there were bandages and poultices wrapped around my torso covering the bullet inflicted bruises and cuts. Gingerly, I touched them with my fingers as I sat up. The places still hurt. And would for some time. But I was pleased to see the strange purple ferns from the other side had made their way to the Indian village and were being put to good use to help heal. I was willing to bet the braves had looted plenty from the apes we killed from when we slaughtered them at the former site of Fort Jipson.

Chief Toko grinned from across the fire as he twisted what looked like a rabbit leg on a sharpened stick in the flames. "Spirits decide that Skyla live. She want you."

Grabbing a buffalo hide, I quickly wrapped it over my bare chest and wounds. Ignoring the pain, I crouched down and slipped out of the flap opening.

Rushing across the frost tipped grass in bare feet, the moonlight overhead seemed to stream between clouds and illuminate the very teepee I was headed to.

Ducking down, I crawled inside.

Skyla lay on a pile of hides beside the Shaynee healer, her face pale and covered in sweat. She smiled at me slightly and slowly raised her hand.

Grabbing it, I slid beside her, ignoring my own pain and being careful not to jostle her.

"Hey," she said weakly.

"Hey back." I kissed her on the forehead. It was hot with fever.

"I got shot."

"I know, I'm sorry. It's all my fault."

Her hand jerked mine up and down. "No! No, it's not. It's Reydan's."

"I'm the reason though."

A tear ran from the corner of her eye and slid down her face. I gently wiped it away.

"I thought you were dead," she said. "I saw you fall, and Thompson stood over you and fired his gun." Another tear rolled down her face and into her dark hair. "You didn't move. We kept shooting and shooting. Then I got hit helping Charles bar the door." Her hand squeezed mine weakly. "Where is he?" she asked. "Where is Charles?"

Unable to meet her eyes, I looked at the fur and hide lined floor of the teepee and silently shook my head.

"Oh, no, no! And... Bo? Did he make it?"

I rubbed a hand over my face then shook my head again.

She began sobbing.

Gently cupping her cheeks, I touched my forehead to hers and closed my eyes. Charles and Bo had been good men. And they'd been taken from us.

I swore to myself that no more of my people would die, only Reydan and whoever stood in my way.

***

"Skyla cannot move. She needs rest. Lots of rest," Chief Toko warned me as I stepped into Carbine's saddle. Skyla was in a deep sleep. Arthur warned me that it would be hours, maybe even days, before she woke again. Unspoken was the fact that she may not ever wake if her blood became poisoned or infected from her wounds.

"I know. And as a blood brother to the Shaynee, I need you to protect her while she heals."

He nodded solemnly. "This we can do."

I looked down from my horse at the Chief of the Shaynee and nodded my thanks. With their pledged protection, I could rest easy knowing that she'd be cared for.

I had to get going while there was still plenty of light left. There were some things that needed to be tended to before I began my rampage.

"Thank you," I told him sincerely while turning Carbine around. Tapping my heels to the dun mustang's flanks, we rode away from the village, away from Skyla, and back to my ranch.

As I rode Carbine out of the river bottom and onto the plains, I thought about the grim task that awaited me. Some things a man simply must do, even if he doesn't want to.

A couple hours later, I was lifting charred roof timbers from the remains of my collapsed house and looking for Charles.

I found his nickel-plated Schofield revolver first. The gun had been fired empty and broken open, as though he dropped it in the middle of a reload. A moment later, I found burnt, curled fingers from his outstretched hand nearby beneath more fallen timbers and ashen shingles. The flesh was cracked and knurled, peeling away from pale white bone.

I stared at the exposed hand and pistol of the Stratten family butler for a long time. Charles had been a good fellow, even if he was British. The man had lived through a lot and had been a solid protector for Skyla and a friend and confidant for me.

Across the yard, his horse, Sir Lancelot, stood at the edge of the corral, watching me solemnly as though he knew what I'd found.

Damn Reydan.

Damn him to an eternity of torment and agony in hell.

Steeling my resolve, I began pulling burnt boards off my friend's body. It was as bad as I thought it'd be, and I pulled my bandana over my mouth to keep from inhaling the ash. Using a canvas tarp from the barn, I wrapped my friend the best I could. With a grunt of pain, I cradled what was left of his corpse and began stumbling through the remains of my house to where the wagon waited with Carbine.

Once I was free of the entangled ash covered debris, I gently laid his body beside Bo's in the back of the wagon.

Climbing into the seat, I adjusted my rifle and shovel beside me. There was work enough for both tools ahead of me.

I flicked the reins.

We rolled across the yard, crossing a small creek, and into the open pasture, before coming to a stop by a grassy hill crowned with a single white cross on its crest.

Jim's final resting place.

Bo would like to be buried beside him. He really liked that kid. And Charles... well, I didn't know where he'd like to be buried, he'd never mentioned any place as being a particular favorite of his to me. So, I reckoned this would have to do. He would have understood.

Taking the shovel in hand, I started digging.

The ground was cold and hard, and my ribs burned and ached as I chipped away at the frozen dirt with the metal blade. But I kept going, occasionally relying on my Bowie to pry rocks out of the way. It was nearly dark by the time I finished the two graves, and I barely had the strength to pile rocks on them. For a pair of crosses, I'd nailed together some unpainted trim boards left over from the barn. They deserved better, and I swore to myself that I'd come back and give them a proper headstone with their names carved.

Kneeling before the trio of crosses to catch my breath, all I could think about was how I should have killed Reydan a long time ago. Once

I discovered who he was, I never should have stopped trying until he was dead. To think I could live a somewhat peaceful life alongside my mortal enemy was a fool's gambit that others paid for with their lives.

I didn't have any words to say over the graves. I was never good at that sort of thing.

But Jim, Bo, Charles… all good men. And now, all dead men.

And Skyla and I almost joined them because of a blood feud that started decades ago. On the day that Reydan and his Union Raiders rode to our house and left me, as a child, for dead.

Climbing into the buckboard of the wagon, I released the brake and turned Carbine back towards the barn.

Wolverine Wade Mackin and Ashley James were waiting for me when we arrived. Their wagon was stopped by the corral, and the pair stood watching me as mine rumbled into the yard and to a stop.

"What happened?" Ashley asked, quickly crossing over and grabbing me tightly by the arm as I slid down from the buckboard.

"Reydan sent the Pinkertons," I told her wearily.

Wade's mustache twitched as the famous Westerner frowned. "We saw Thompson and his detectives' corpses on the road."

"Where is everyone?" Ashley looked up at me, worry etched across her face.

"Charles and Bo are dead. Skyla is with the Shaynee," I looked away, unable to meet her eyes and swallowing hard. "She's bad hurt."

Ashley gasped, pressing a hand to her mouth in shock.

Gripping me tightly by the shoulder, Wade spun me around. "Tell us what happened," he said angrily.

***

Sitting in the barn, the interior lit with a pair of lanterns, I finished telling them of the attack.

Wade nodded slowly. "When you all didn't show up for the wedding, we decided to come check on you." He rubbed his mustache and goatee thoughtfully. "I just wish we'd been here sooner."

Reaching through the corral that'd been built inside the barn, I rubbed one of the proto's heads gently. The tiny dinosaur grunted and shoved his horned face and bone shield into my hand.

"Sorry we missed your wedding," I replied absently.

"Oh, the hell with that," Ashley said. "It's time for Reydan to die!"

"I agree." Wade stood up and grabbed his heavy single shot Ballard rifle. "Where do we start killing, Jed?"

Looking down at the proto, I ran my fingers along its small bump of a horn above its beak. "I need you to take these protos and Sir Lancelot with you to Cheyenne. I'll take Smoke back to the Shaynee for Skyla, but I need you-"

"Take Charles' horse and the dinosaurs?" Wade roared and kicked a center post with the heel of his boot in a fit of rage. In a testament to Jim and Bo's construction, the barn didn't so much as shake. "Are you giving up, Jed?"

I rubbed my eyes. "No. I'm not. But I'm not about to risk anyone else I care about because of my past."

"Jed, Reydan hasn't outplayed us," Wade pleaded. "There's still a lot we can do. We can go to Governor Hale, or President Cleveland, if we must. But we can get justice."

"Forget that. Let's just shoot the bastard!" Ashley stood, towering to her petite five feet and change with her famed *One of a Thousand* rifle in hand.

"He will be dealt with!" I shouted suddenly, silencing the newly married couple. "On my own terms. And no, my terms don't include the legal avenue. I'm an outlaw, remember? This is what I used to do."

Ashley didn't look shocked, and by the way Wade scuffed his boots on the ground, I knew that he'd told her. That wasn't a surprise. Honestly, I'd have been shocked had he not told his best friend, partner, and now wife about me.

I put my hands on my hips. "Look. You two have a good thing going with your New West show, I'll not have you throw it away over me." Jabbing a finger at the little protos, I continued. "I want you to take them and take care of them. Because I can't and they deserve it."

"And what about Cato and the army of Pinkertons between you and Reydan?" Wade growled.

"The Pinkertons are just pawns. I'm only going to kill the ones that get in my way or come after me."

"And Cato?"

I pulled my hat off and ran a hand through my black shaggy hair as I thought of my long-lost brother. "I don't know what to do with him. I reckon I'll make something up as I go. But if he crosses me in a bad way, he dies."

Ashley sat down, her back leaning against the wall. "With Thompson and his men not showing up, I'd say Reydan knows you're still alive."

"Yes. You need to step careful, Jed." Wade gestured towards my vest. "And make sure you keep that on. The fewer people who know about it, the better. It's an ace up your sleeve."

I touched the vest gently. There were some tears in the leather, but the dragon scales underneath had survived the bullet impacts. Although several scales were cracked slightly and would likely need replacing. But if it hadn't been for the vest given to me by Skyla, I'd be a dead man and the Pinkertons the victors.

Ashley looked warily out through the crack in the door towards the moonlit darkness outside. "Do you think Reydan will send more Pinkertons? There's only three of us, and Wade has his silly single shot rifle. Which means there's really just two of us."

Wolverine Wade scowled at his new bride while patting his heavy barreled Ballard rifle. "You just line them up, dear. I bet I can punch through two of them with one bullet."

"I don't think they'll come anytime soon, but still…" I said quietly, not enjoying the couple's usual banter about their differing styles of rifles. The condition of Charles' body was not something I was likely ever to forget. Neither was laying him and Bo in their graves.

Ashley quickly caught on and leaning over, put a hand on my shoulder. "Sorry, Jed. I know you've been through a lot."

Standing, I picked up the *Eighty-Six*. The rifle gave me a reassuring feeling as the solid weight of the wood and steel comforted me. "Let's not stay here tonight. There's a place about half a mile away we can shelter at. I know it's cold out, but I'd rather not be trapped in here should anyone come back to finish the job."

***

In the depths of an aspen and spruce pine forest, beside a small stream and tucked in amongst a jumble of large boulders, we risked a fire. It was cold out and getting colder it seemed with every passing week. But the heat reflected off the stacked rocks behind us and back onto our bodies, and we managed to stay warm.

Wade fed a handful of broken sticks into the hungry flames. "What are you going to do, Jed?"

"Come morning, I'm going to go after them."

"Things have changed," Ashley warned as she rubbed her hands near the fire. "When we left Cheyenne to come find you, there were notices being put up. The only people allowed to cross through the Shimmer are folks who enlist. Governor Hale and Fredrick have requested a civilian detachment for the military. Calling them Rough Raiders and asking for anyone who's a fighter and willing to get paid to go to war against the apes."

I lifted one shoulder in an uncaring shrug. "Doesn't matter. Reydan White is on this side."

"No." Wade jerked his head side to side slightly. "Not anymore. He crossed back over."

"Shit!" Slamming my canteen down on the ground, I rose and angrily ran a hand through my hair. "He's got to come back though," I muttered to myself hopefully.

Ashley glanced at Wade. Her husband nodded. Reaching into her saddle bags, she pulled out a folded newspaper. "This is today's paper, we picked it up on the way to your place." Without looking up, she passed it over to me.

Feeling a lump forming in my stomach, I unfolded the newspaper. It was the Cheyenne Herald. The title read, "RAIL TYCOON LEADS WAR AGAINST PREHISTORIC APES!" in large block letters across the top. Quickly skimming the article, I read that Reydan was back in Whitesberg, refusing to leave Prehistoria until the apes had been defeated and the land open and available to settlers as promised.

I was about to fling the paper into the flames when the last couple of lines of the article made me pause abruptly.

"Reydan White survived an assassination attempt yesterday with no injury thanks to the quick guns of his bodyguard commonly known as the Black Plague. One shooter was killed and the other made good their escape."

My old man had made his move after all. That would explain why my ranch was hit. Reydan probably thought the attempt to kill him was orchestrated by me and sent his men for revenge. I slapped the newspaper against my leg and gritted my teeth. Damn all the luck.

Everything was working against me.

Wade and Ashley were staring at me, waiting for me to say something… anything. But my mind was too busy racing as thoughts and possibilities were thought of then discarded just as quickly.

There only seemed to be one course of action.

But first…

I tossed the paper into the fire and grabbed my saddle up from where I'd been using it as a backrest.

"Jed-" Wade started to protest.

"What are you doing?" Ashley asked.

"The paper said Reydan survived an assassination attempt." I shook the dirt and fallen leaves off the bottom of the saddle.

"Yes." The married couple looked at each other before turning back to me. "We thought maybe it was you."

"No. But the article said one of them is dead, and the other escaped. I need to find out who escaped."

"Why?" Wade stood and dusted his hands off against his pants "What does it matter? I'm sure that bucket of hog slop has plenty of enemies looking to get even. He owns a railroad for crying out loud, that makes him one of the most despised men in the country."

"These shooters weren't trying to kill him because he stole land or tricked them out of mineral rights. They were trying to kill him for what he did to me."

"Jed," Wade said slowly, his mouth turning to a frown as he thought through the words he was about to say. "Who were the shooters?"

With a soft sigh, I dropped the saddle back down on the ground and sat on it. "One of the shooters is… or was… my father." I looked up at the pair of them standing across the fire with looks of shock on their faces. "Yeah, I guess I never told you how I became an outlaw. After being nearly whipped to death as a child, my father and I searched the South for the Union Raiders who did it. We found most of them, but never the man who ordered it." I spat into the fire and shook my head. "Not until I came here."

"Reydan," Wade said bluntly.

"Yes. Then my father showed up. I told him about Reydan and he went after him. It was just piss poor luck that he didn't succeed, and Reydan thought that I did it. So, he sent Thompson and his Pinkertons after me." I looked at the ground and shuffled the toe of my boot through the fallen leaves. "I'm the reason Charles and Bo are dead, and Skyla is laid up with a pair of bullet holes in her and probably damaged lungs from smoke inhalation."

"It's not your fault," Ashley cautioned, as she stepped around the fire and squatted down beside me. Resting a hand on my back, she rubbed comfortingly.

"We were always destined to butt heads again, and this wasn't the first time he came after me. I should have paid attention and killed him already."

Wade sucked his teeth for a moment, then picked up his canteen and emptied it over the flames. The fire extinguished with a hiss as thick white smoke billowed from the drowning embers. "Let's get going then. If your old man is still alive, he may need a hand to stay that way."

I swallowed the lump in my throat and rose to my feet, grateful to have friends like these. "Okay. Let's find him."

***

"We should check the Doc's first," I told the others as we rode down from the large, grassed valley and into the booming town of Granite Falls. Oil lamps were still burning, illuminating the fronts of stores and the boardwalk and packed dirt and broken gravel streets. Even at this late hour, there were still a few dozen people in sight. Most of them inebriated from the looks of their movements. I bet the Bucket o' Blood was making a financial killing these days.

"Wouldn't that be kinda obvious?" Ashley quipped out the corner of her mouth sarcastically.

"I'm sure Reydan's Pinkertons have been all over that place," Wade added.

I felt a smile tug at my lips. "We will see."

Leaving Main Street and its lit lamps, we quickly rode down an alley towards one of the back streets. This town was overrun with Pinkertons, and I didn't need another shootout with them. I didn't feel the urge to gun down every suited, badge wearing hypocrite that I came across... just the ones who got in my way. And the less of them that got in my way, the better my odds for survival.

Once on the darkened back street, I felt some of the tension leave my scarred back and shoulders. I'd be harder to recognize in the dark shadows. Especially on this street. This street skirted the edge of China Town. And that was not an area anyone but the Chinese were interested in visiting these days.

Ever since the Chinese staged a protest for better pay and treatment from the railroad, and who were then promptly gunned down by the Pinkertons for it... they hadn't cared much for white folks.

Shame, really.

They had some mighty fine food.

Noodles and chicken, that's where it's at.

"This way," I told Wade and Ashley, doubting that they knew where Doc's place was. Turning Carbine's head to the side, I walked him down another side street.

During the Battle of the Apes, after I'd first discovered the Shimmer and the ape army crossed over, Granite Falls had been a small town of maybe five hundred folks and just thirteen buildings along Main Street. Now the town was on the verge of becoming a small city, I thought with annoyance as we finally reached Doc's house.

It was a decent looking place. Not too expensive, but not too shabby either. Just... orderly. The man had a whitewashed picket fence with a small garden and large stepping stones leading to the door placed in slap board siding. Being the sort to have callers at all hours, there was a painted sign nailed on the fence stating to tie your horse up out back and don't let them eat the damned vegetables or the bill would triple.

I'm not kidding. It said that.

Riding to the back of the house, I slipped out of the saddle and carefully tied Carbine to the hitching post. Wade and Ashley followed suit. From the looks on their faces, they thought I was wasting time. But I knew things they didn't.

And we had to start our search somewhere.

Lightly rapping on the back door with my knuckles, I waited a minute then repeated myself, a bit louder this time.

"He might be out?" Wade suggested.

As if to mock him, a burst of light came from the cracks in the shutters on a window as a lantern was lit.

"Nope. He's here," Ashley drawled.

Moments later, the door edged open a bit as an eye peered through the crack. Then the door was pushed open wide.

"Jed," Doc said simply.

"Doc." I gestured at Wade and Ashley, "This is-"

"I know who Wolverine Wade is. I'm not blind. And I suppose this must be Ashley, his new wife." Doc shook their hands with a boyish grin on his craggy old face.

"Do you know why I'm here?" I asked, curious.

He peered up at me from beneath bushy eyebrows. "Knowing you, I suspect someone's been shot."

"Yes, and we're hoping you can help us locate him."

"Ah." His smile vanished. "I already told the Pinkertons, I haven't seen anyone."

"Doc, we're not with them," Wade warned.

"Still. Haven't seen anyone." He began to close the door.

I shoved my boot in the way and the door jammed against it abruptly. He glared at me through the small gap.

"I just need to know which man it is. Tall, lean fellow named Travis, or big guy, kind of looks like me, named Eugene."

"Un-huh. And out of curiosity, who are these fellows to ya?"

"One is my father. The other ain't."

His head shifted back and forth as he tried to look around and past me. "Anyone else out there other than you three?"

"No."

"C'mon in then. It's getting cold." He pulled the door open and held it for us to enter the building.

We stepped through and the door closed behind us.

"Hello, Orville."

Spinning, the three of us faced the corner the opened door had concealed. My father stood there, a pained expression on his face, a crutch under his arm, and a revolver in hand. He looked weak and wobbled a bit as he holstered the gun.

Doc grabbed him by the waist and helped him sit. As he settled into the chair, he winced and coughed painfully.

I looked down at him. "Guess Travis is the dead one then."

"Maybe me too, son."

Doc frowned at the two of us. "Gene should be resting. So, Jed, whatever you've come to say or do, say or do it quick. I need to get him lying back down and healing... if he can."

My father raised his hand to silence him. "It's alright, Doc. A bit of sitting might be good for me."

"How the hell would you know that?" Doc exclaimed, throwing his hands up in frustration. "Did you go to medical school? Or did you learn that stitching a cow up in a barn somewhere?"

Gene glared at the doctor, before finally giving him a slight smile. "Alright, help me back to my hidey-hole and we can talk."

Reaching down, I grabbed him under one arm as Wade took the other. Doc snatched his crutch away and headed towards where I knew the kitchen to be.

"Hidey-hole?" Ashley asked, confused.

"Most Docs worth their salt have a room large enough to hide a man," I told her while Wade and I lifted my large framed father to his feet. Steadying him, we walked together into the next room.

A cupboard had been pulled aside, exposing a waist high bed of sorts, with space underneath for storage. A decent-sized man could lay down on the bed and be closed in, and there was a nook above the bed with a pair of small tallow candles still burning and giving off a faint light. With effort we managed to help my old man onto the bed; he barely fit with probably an inch from his socked feet to the end of the secret space.

"Pretty homey in here," my father chortled weakly, apparently amused at his secret hide out.

"Better than a jail cell," I told him. "That's if the Pinkertons let you live long enough to see handcuffs. And I doubt that."

"Me too," he replied as he shifted slightly and set the pistol on the blanket beside him within quick reach.

"How many bullets did he take?" I asked the Doc.

"Two. I got one out before he passed out." He frowned. "The second, well, I can't find it. It's still somewhere in his chest. Hopefully not doing any more damage..."

Ashley spoke up from behind me. "I'm still confused. Doc, you've got a secret hiding place for wanted men?"

He looked down at his feet, as though a bit embarrassed before finally looking up. "Hippocratic oath."

"What's that?" she asked.

"An oath taken by those who practice medicine." He coughed then straightened as he recited, "I will remember that I remain a member of society, with special obligations to all my fellow human beings…" He glared at Gene and then me before adding, "Including ones who stray from the moral path of God at times."

"We appreciate that, Doc," my old man told him sincerely.

"You do the usual?" I asked my father quietly.

"What's… the usual?" Wade asked with a raised eyebrow.

Gene spoke up from where he lay without looking over. "The usual is when we operate in an area, we seek out any doctors who might be able to assist us should things go sideways. Then we slip them a few coins to stay ready for us with the promise of more afterwards."

I nudged the Wolverine Slayer. "Basically, we bribe the Docs to save us from death."

"Hippocratic oath my-" Ashley started to say, but her husband raised his hand.

"Healing doesn't come free, does it, Doc?" Wade said sympathetically.

The old healer shuffled his feet on the wood flooring with a nod. "Nothing wrong with paying a man for plying his trade."

"No sir," I told him sincerely. "There is not. We greatly appreciate you and your discretion."

Doc looked relieved. He tipped his head at us. "Speaking of discretion, I'll be in the other room if you need me. I suspect you all have some talking to do."

"We do." I reached out and shook his hand. "Thank you."

He nodded and left the kitchen, sliding shut the partition door between the rooms to give us some privacy.

I pulled a chair away from the kitchen table for Ashley, then another for Wade. When he raised his hand to pass, I sat myself down in it instead.

"What happened?" I asked my father bluntly.

"We cornered Cato as he left that damned metal railroad contraption of Reydan's. I was going to try and talk to him while Travis kept watch…" He sighed painfully. "Then Reydan stepped out behind him. I just… seeing that sonuva bitch standing there after the wake of bodies and carnage he left across the South… after knowing what he did to you…" He took a deep breath. "Next thing I know, I'm drawing my pistol. All I could think of was putting a bullet through that bastard's skull." He stopped, shaking his head slightly from side to side.

"Let me guess, Cato stopped you?" I asked quietly.

"Yeah, Cato. He's quick, Jed. I've never seen anyone so quick. He put two bullets through my chest before Travis started shooting at him from behind the corner of the railcar. I managed to get out of the crossfire before Cato took Travis out. Then, as all the damned Pinkertons in town started moving towards that cursed railcar, I managed to sneak my way over here." He waved his hand around the small cupboard he was hiding behind. "And here I've been since. Just trying to get healed up."

He carefully pushed himself upright and peered at me. "Now, what are YOU doing here?"

"After your shootout, they hit my ranch. Killed Bo and Charles and burned the house."

He grabbed me suddenly with surprising strength in his hand and asked in a quiet panic, "Skyla? What happened to Skyla?"

I blinked as my eyes suddenly moistened and looked away. "She's alive. For now. She caught a couple bullets before they set fire to the house. She and Charles were holed up in it trying to fight them off."

"Where were you?" he asked, quietly and without judgement in his voice.

Opening my vest, I raised my blue shirt. "Layin' dead in the yard."

Ashley gasped at the sight of my chest and Wade leaned over to get a better look. The large round bruises were a mottled red, yellow, and purple. "They tried to kill me first." I gingerly patted my black vest. "This ain't just for looks though."

He looked curiously at my black vest. "Where do I get one?"

"I'll see what I can do," I promised while letting the blue fabric fall back down over my chest and pulling the vest closed over it.

The partitioned door behind us slid open without warning.

Looking over my shoulder, I expected to see Doc.

Instead, I saw Cato standing there, pistol in hand pointed at me. From beneath his black hat, his brown eyes watched our movements. Wade's hand rested on the butt of his Remington, but mine wasn't anywhere near my pistols. Ashley, well, she just looked shocked.

"Don't," Cato warned, his deep voice harsh and unforgiving in the small room.

"Sorry, Jed," Doc's voice came from behind Cato, small and plaintive sounding. "I tried to stop him... but..."

I stared at my boyhood friend, feeling anger rising like bile in my throat. This man shot my father. This man threatened to shoot Skyla. And me. And everyone else I cared about.

Cato slowly pointed his pistol towards the floor and lowered the hammer gently. With a fluid motion he slid it into his right holster strapped to his belt and tied to his thigh.

"Cato," my father's voice was weak and trembling as he raised a hand in surprised greeting.

Lurching forward a step, I threw a right hook and caught the Black Plague below the ear with my fist.

His dark hat flew off and he stumbled against a row of shelves. Glass bottles of various fluids and such cascaded onto the floor, shattering with a satisfying amount of noise.

I vaguely heard the Doc shouting in complaint as I went at the black gun man with fists flying.

I got two solid hits in, one to his stomach and another to his face before the Black Plague recovered and shoved me bodily across the small room. Ashley leapt out of the way as I tumbled through the spot that she'd occupied a moment before.

"Get him, Jed!" she cried as I slammed against the door jamb and knocked Doc sprawling.

Before I could move, Cato hit me with a right jab to the face that felt like John Henry swinging a sledgehammer. My skull bounced off the wall with a nasty thud that danced stars across my vision.

Thankfully, Cato took a step back to give me a moment and I spat a stream of bloody phlegm onto the floor from where I'd bitten my cheek.

"Easy now, gents," Wade cautioned with a pair of raised hands. "You both got some licks in. No need for things to get heated."

"Like hell! Let's finish this," I growled as my father tried to protest from his position on the bed. Ripping my belt buckle open, I let the gun belt with its pair of pistols and Bowie knife fall to the floor in a clatter.

Cato's lips pressed into a thin line as he unbuckled his own and turned to set the gun belt aside.

Taking advantage of his distracting movement, I lunged forward and hit him in the side with a balled-up fist.

He grabbed me around the waist and shoulder, and we clinched, each trying to use his body weight to control the other.

"You always were a cheat," Cato hissed into my ear.

"You always were a whiny bitch," I spat back before head butting him.

He staggered, eyes squinting in pain. A trickle of blood ran down from his broad nose.

I threw a kick at his knee.

He dodged my booted foot, then hurled a liquid filled bottle that survived the collapsing shelves at my face.

The brown bottle shattered against my upraised arm, showering me with bits of glass and a rather pleasing liquid that smelled of whiskey and sage.

"Who's the cheater now?" I growled while slipping across the increasingly wet floor to get the gunman.

Cato missed a savage uppercut that was intended to take my head off, and we both fell to the ground in a pile. Boots kicking and flailing, I managed to crawl on top of him and grab his throat in my hands.

I squeezed and he thrashed beneath me, attempting to buck me off like a bronco.

Holding firm, I tried to apply more pressure, but our bodies were so damned wet and slippery.

Grasping hands clawed at my face, and I bit a finger that got too close to my mouth.

Balling his fist up, he began hammering it against the side of my head while the other hand pried at my slippery death grip around his throat.

Vaguely, between his gasping for air and my animalistic grunts of savagery, I began to hear a voice behind me shouting at us to stop.

But I didn't stop.

I just adjusted my grip and tried to squeeze harder.

Both of Cato's hands darted up to my face, grabbing the sides of my skull and the thumbs pressing into my eyeballs. Pain darted through my brain like a pair of needles as tears burst forth.

Roaring, I tried to pull away, but the Black Plague's arms were too blasted long.

I couldn't get away without letting go of his throat.

So, that's what I did.

Giving up on choking him to death, I jerked back to save my eyes.

Then, having enough of this bullshit, I threw myself towards my gun belt. It was time to resort to a more mannerly method of killing the bastard.

The smooth polished grip of the Colt felt good in my hand as I twirled around and found myself facing the dark muzzle of Cato's pistol.

My finger began to apply pressure to the smooth trigger.

Sometimes all you can do is hope for the best.

"STOP!" Father roared as he painfully limped between us, his crutch trembling from his effort to stand up.

I blinked through the tears of pain and slowly lowered my gun as Cato did the same. It's not like we could shoot now anyways, not with our old man standing in the way of the bullets.

"You two, knock it off!" He slammed the foot of the crutch against the wooden floor with a loud thump.

"You are ruining my house!" Doc agreed from the other room.

I touched the side of my battered face gingerly before pointing an accusing finger at the Black Plague. "He started it."

"You hit me first," Cato growled back.

"You shot our father, asshole. Threatened to shoot me, Skyla, and pretty much everyone else I care about-"

"Water under the bridge," Father chuckled as he eased himself back onto the hidden bunk with Wade's assistance.

"Water under the... what? He killed Travis! And shot you. TWICE!"

My old man waved a hand. "I never cared that much for Travis."

"He saved your life when your gang turned on you!" I shouted in disbelief while grabbing my gun belt and standing.

"Yeah, well, I saved his life once too. So, we were even."

"I reckon there ain't no such thing as honor between thieves," I snorted.

"That's how it goes, Orville. You know that."

Cato stood, slipping slightly on the floor, and slung his gun belt around his waist. We mimicked each other's movements of rearming ourselves as we watched each other suspiciously.

Ashley crunched a cracker loudly between her teeth from where she sat, a box of them in one hand and a sly grin on her face. "Well, ain't this some kind of family reunion?" She offered the box of crackers to Wade. The famed Westerner took one and bit off a corner.

I slapped my hands against my shirt and pants, disgusted at how wet and smelly they were now from the liquor and other medicinal fluids that'd spilled across the floor.

"Family reunion," I said sarcastically while probing my teeth with my tongue to make sure they were all still firmly embedded in my gums. "Yeah, and you can leave me out of it. I want nothing to do with either of you."

"Then why'd you come here, Orville?" Father asked.

"Stop calling me that! And I came to see if I needed to bury another body or not." I jerked my head at Cato who stood silently in the corner of the room looking down at the shattered bottles and jars beneath his boots. "His boss sent Pinkertons to my ranch after your failed attempt to assassinate him."

"Mr. White thought it was you," Cato said simply.

"Well, it wasn't. And now Bo and Charles are dead, and Skyla is on the verge of it." I settled my hand on my pistol. "So, I've a mind to kill you now."

Cato turned to face me, his fingers on both hands flexing slightly above his guns. "You can't."

"Hold up on the gunfire!" cried Doc from the doorway with his hands raised pleadingly.

"Yes indeed, hold up," Wade mumbled before swallowing the remains of his cracker and licking his lips. "Why are you here?" he asked the Black Plague calmly.

Cato stared silently at me for a moment before turning his dark eyes to face my father. "I recognized Eugene."

"Before or after you shot him?" I grunted in disgust.

"After."

"Well, you've been gone a long time, son," Father said with a slight grin. "And no worries, I've been shot before..." he winced, "but never twice at once."

"This is just grand." I stepped towards the door. "You two deserve each other. Crazy bastards, the both of you."

"Where are you going, Orville?"

I kicked the door jamb in frustration and small splinters flew. "It's Jed! How many times must I remind you?" Twirling around, I jabbed a finger at my childhood friend. "And that's Cato. He's the bastard that's been protecting the man who mutilated me as a child." I jabbed the same finger at him now, the anger boiling over inside me. "And you... you are the one who turned me into a murderous bastard seeking revenge for over twenty years! All I wanted was to be left alone out here. I just wanted to get away from it all. To get away from you, Father. Get away from the killing and violence and avenging the wrongs from a lost war that the rest of the country has moved past. I came to Granite Falls to start over!"

"And you couldn't. Could you?" my old man said calmly as he gently touched the bandage on his chest to make sure it hadn't worked loose.

I took a deep breath, thinking of how to respond.

With a slight smile, he continued, "That's because you're a good man, Jed. Where others see a wrong, you see a way to right it."

Wade held my hat out to me, and I realized in my anger I'd almost forgotten it. Grabbing the battered brown Stetson, I looked down at it and remembered long ago on a train ride to Cheyenne being teased by Skyla about not wearing a white hat. Glancing up at Cato, I realized there was nothing left to be gained by talking in front of him. His boss was a dead man walking and I was headed into Prehistoria to do the killing.

Without another word I stepped around Doc and walked out the door.

***

Wolverine Wade and Ashley came onto the porch as I changed shirts in the darkened street. There wasn't much I could do about my pants, but the smaller the trail of scented fluids I left behind me as I rode out of town, the less likely of anything following me.

Walking across the gravel walkway, the pair stopped at the picket fence.

I looked up and down at my friend, already having come to a decision. "I need your hat, your pistol, and your horse."

Wade choked back a laugh. "What else? My boots and underwear?"

"I'm serious."

"As am I. What do you want my things for?"

"To become someone else."

"Who?" Ashley asked, confused.

"Johnson Brown."

"And who the hell is that?" Wade stuttered, throwing his hands up in bewilderment.

"Most people have heard of me. I've been in too many damned newspaper articles now to not be known. But there's only been that one picture of me... and Skyla." The thought of my wounded love lying on a buffalo blanket without me hurt. But she would take time to heal. And time wasn't something I was going to allow Reydan to have anymore.

"You're changing your look," Ashley said with a sly smile. "So, no one will recognize you."

"Yes. I'm going to become Johnson Brown and enlist in Fredrick's Rough Raiders to get into Prehistoria."

Wade rubbed his goatee thoughtfully. "That explains why you want all my things."

"I'll take Carbine back to the Shaynee. They can keep him with Smoke until I come back."

"He won't like that."

"He's a horse and needs to do as he's told."

Sighing, Wade rubbed his mustache. "Alright, but you can't take your weapons. That means you'll have to leave the *Eighty-Six* behind, along with your Colts... you might be able to take that Bowie with you."

"No, I'll leave that with you also. My boots, jeans, and shirt are of a common enough sort. Same goes for my saddle once I strip it down and remove the *Eighty-Six* scabbard. The fancy tooling on that would certainly give me away."

"And a pistol?" He patted the Remington New Model Army revolver on his hip. "You can't have this one. Besides, do you even know how to load one of these?"

"Of course, I do. I may have been born in a house, but I grew up in barns."

Wade chuckled. "Just the same, I'm not Fredrick. I don't go travelling with a full armory and I'm not giving you my favorite and only pistol. I could ask Doc if he's got anything?"

"No," I gestured towards his house. "He's done enough shady stuff as it is. I'd rather not risk him knowing anything else. I'll get something from the Shaynee."

Ashley slapped my shoulder gently. "Just make sure it's not covered with feathers and beads."

***

We split ways.

Wade and Ashley were off to gather a few items for me while I rode towards the remains of my ranch.

Dawn was just beginning to break. It'd been a long night. Too many long nights in a row. I felt myself beginning to slumber at times and shook myself awake. Letting Carbine walk, I fought to keep my eyes open as he moved through the darkened woods. We were going in a roundabout way to the ranch, staying far from the wagon trail and away from where I assumed the Pinkerton bodies were still lying. Unless someone had noticed them missing and knew where to go looking. It was tempting to go see, but I still felt like hammered crap and not in the mood for any more brawling or shooting.

Not tonight at least.

Reaching the edge of the forest near the ranch, I slowed Carbine to a stop inside the dark shadows of the trees. There was no sign of anyone. The barn was dark inside, the horses in the corral acting typical, and it didn't look like anyone had been by since Wade and Ashley found me burying my friends.

I still waited though, with the *Eighty-Six* resting in my hands. After everything we'd been through, the rifle comforted me like an old friend that would kill for you without question.

After a half hour of waiting in the cold, with Carbine growing impatient and restless beneath me, I finally walked him out of the darkness and into the moonlight.

No one started shooting. That was a good sign.

I quickly crossed the yard and tied Carbine off at the corral. Sir Lancelot and Smoke trotted over to touch noses with my dun mustang in greeting. Reaching out, I laid a hand on the flank of Charles' beautiful Arabian horse. I wondered if the stallion knew that his master was gone.

Leaving the horses, I grabbed a lantern from a bench beside the barn and lit it with a match. The wick gave forth a burst of light that I used to navigate my way into the barn and to the Protos. The little dinosaurs milled around the fence near me, I could tell they were hungry. Not being one to let an animal starve, I hung the lantern on a post and quickly forked the little horned beasts some hay.

As they munched hungrily, I looked around the barn for what may be the last time. It was a good, solid building. I was proud of Jim and Bo's work, and I wished like hell they were here so I could tell them that.

Grabbing some saddle and tack, I began to ready Smoke and Sir Lancelot to travel.

It felt weird putting Charles' saddle on his horse. The Brit had always been peculiar about readying his own mount. But the big stallion let me strap the saddle and tack on without issue. I almost left the saddle bags where they lay but decided to throw them on anyways. There was some weight to them as I hefted them onto the back of Sir Lancelot, so they certainly weren't empty. I almost opened them to see what he'd been carrying but couldn't compel myself to go through his remaining belongings just yet.

Smoke was easy enough to get ready. The dapple gray was used to being saddled by me. She seemed worried though, and uneasy, as though she knew her master had been wounded. I gave her a pat and whispered to her that Skyla would be okay, a promise that I prayed would come true.

Wrapping their reins around the saddle pommel, I rode away from my ranch without looking back and with the pair of horses trailing behind. Wade and Ashley would take care of the Protos.

It was nearing noon by the time I reached the Shaynee village. Riding down through the tall prairie grass with the rising sun warming my back, I was watched by several pairs of braves who appeared to be loafing around. I knew there were more hidden around about me, these were just the ones who wanted to be seen. A show of force and protection of their village and its inhabitants to anyone who would consider harming them.

Otto stood by the corral as I slowed the horses and dismounted.

"How is she?" I asked the scarred brave.

He nodded curtly. "She lives. Arthur is with her."

"She awake?"

My blood brother frowned. "No. She still sleeps."

Closing my eyes, I took a moment to tell myself that she'd be okay. She was strong and healthy and would pull through this. She had to. Or I didn't know what I'd do.

I gestured towards the braves riding in tandem along the edge of the valley. "They keepin' an eye out?"

"For Pink Men."

"I worry they may come for her, or me if I stay."

"You leave?" Otto asked, his eyebrows furrowing in puzzlement.

"I go to kill Reydan and end this before more are hurt."

The Shaynee brave thumped his scarred chest with a fist. "I go with you."

"Not this time, Otto. This time I go alone."

"No! We are blood brothers!" the brave roared.

Reaching out, I put a hand on his shoulder and leaned close. "Otto, there is no Shaynee braver than you. I am honored to have you as my blood brother. But this I must do alone. If the Pink Men see you with me, they will know who I am and kill me before I kill Reydan."

"Bah!" He knocked my hand off his shoulder and turned his back, growling in frustration. "Without me, you die."

"Hell Otto, I didn't know you cared."

He kicked the toe of his moccasin against the corral post. "Don't. Besides, Skyla is my maybe-wife if you die."

I held out Carbine's reins. "Take care of him for me, will you?"

He turned back to me, his jaw dropping as he took the leather straps. "You leave Carbine?"

"Yes. He's yours until I return. Just don't sell him, and don't eat him either."

"What about others?" He raised an eyebrow suggestively.

"Don't eat any of them. Just keep them for now."

"Fine. We no eat your horses."

"Thanks." Drawing the *Eighty-Six* from its tooled leather scabbard, I grabbed my horse's big dumb face in my hand and whispered softly to him. "Hey boy, I need you to stay here. Skyla may need you and where I'm going, you can't go with me." He whinnied and shoved his head against my chest. I rubbed the light brown hair on his neck while holding back a feeling that felt an awful lot like sadness. "You'll be okay. Smoke and Sir Lancelot will be here, and Sara and Horny Devil."

"What you ride?" Otto asked as he pulled the rails in the corral apart to let Carbine in. My horse flicked his black mane angrily but let the Indian lead him in with the others.

"Wade is bringing me a horse. But I could use a pistol. Got one lying around that ain't all decorated or marked as US Government property?"

Otto thought for a moment then shrugged with a single shoulder. "Maybe?"

"If you've got one, I'll need it and a holster." I started walking in the direction of the teepee Skyla was in.

"You have two pistols!" he called after me, confused about the pair of Colts I was still wearing.

"Not after today," I muttered to myself darkly.

After today, I'd be someone else.

***

I was sitting outside of Skyla's teepee when Wade and Ashley arrived.

"Any luck with a horse?"

"Yeah, we found you a gelded mustang that's half broke."

I scoffed. "Seriously? You couldn't find me a horse I can ride?"

"He was cheap, and can't be tracked back to you. I thought that's what you were going for?"

"It is, but it's no good if he bucks me off and I break my neck."

"You'll be fine, Wade makes him sound worse than he is," Ashley chuckled as she sat down on the ground next to me. "I see you found a pistol." She pointed at the blued gun in a rough looking leather holster in my lap.

Drawing the revolver, I handed it to Ashley butt first. "Smith and Wesson Number 3, in .44-40. Courtesy of Otto. Seems he took it off a dead Pinkerton in Prehistoria."

She broke it open and dumped out the cartridges, then quickly snapped it back together and tested the action. "Kind of gritty," she said as the hammer fell on an empty chamber.

"Beggars can't be choosers."

"Charles would have approved you using that to avenge him," Wade said. The Brit's nickel-plated Schofield was a slight variation of the pistol in my hand. I'd buried the gun with him. He'd have liked that.

"Yeah…" I frowned as I wondered what the Stratten family butler would think of my plan. He'd probably think that there had to be another way. And maybe there was, but I had to act. Every day Reydan lived was another opportunity for him to kill me or someone close to me.

"How's Skyla?" Ashley asked softly as she reloaded the gun and handed it back.

"Still out. I'm worried she won't pull through," I admitted while sliding the pistol back into the holster.

"She will, Jed," Wade said. "She will. She's strong. She'll make it. Sometimes the wounded will sleep for days before they wake up, just because their body needs it. And Arthur is still keeping an eye on her, right?"

"Yeah, he's in there with her now."

Standing, I picked the *Eighty-Six* up and handed it to Wade. For Ashley, I handed her my gun belt with its matching Colt Peacemakers in their holsters and my big Bowie knife. The pistol that Otto found for me came with another belt, one that would fit me just fine.

I slid the Smith and Wesson holster onto the belt and slung it around my waist. It had an odd weight to it, as though it was off balance. Going from two guns to one made me suddenly feel very unarmed and vulnerable.

The Wolverine Slayer hefted my favorite 1886 Winchester longingly. "You don't mind if I use it, do you?"

I frowned then nodded. "I don't suppose so. Especially if I get killed. Just keep it clean or you'll have Carson Skinner and probably John Moses Browning after you."

"Don't talk like that!" Ashley said before reaching down to her own belt and sliding off the Shaynee tomahawk sheath. "And you're going to need a new edged weapon since you won't be taking your Bowie." She thrust the weapon into my hands. "Here. Split some skulls for me."

I took it reverently but hesitated. "This... this was a gift, Ashley. From Otto to you for saving his life. I'm not sure I should take it."

"Take it," she admonished, "it belongs in battle."

"And battle it shall see," I replied while slipping it on my belt. The short-handled weapon helped balance out the weight on my hips better. I practiced drawing the Smith and Wesson several times, trying to get a feel for it. I felt slow. There wouldn't be much speed drawing with it. Switching hands, I tugged Otto's tomahawk out of the sheath. Swinging it several times to get a feel for the heft, I held it up and looked through the bullet hole in the blade at the blue sky. The hole was a souvenir from the first time Ashley met Otto and he tried to wedge the blade into my noggin. I swung it again. It felt like an extension of my body. I loved it.

"Speak of the devil," Wade chuckled as Otto sauntered around the teepee.

The scarred brave stopped when he saw his tomahawk in my hand, then looked at my old gun belt and Wade holding my *Eighty-Six*. After a second, he gave me a satisfied nod. "You kill many apes and Pink Men with that. Make Shaynee proud."

"I thought the Shaynee were already proud of me."

"Maybe little bit." He smirked, kicked a dog that yapped at him, and walked off between the teepees to do whatever it was he did in his free time. Which was probably practice killing things.

"Ashley, would you do the honors?" I pointed to where she'd sat my Bowie down.

"Haircut or shave first?"

"Just hair for now, I'll shave myself."

"As you wish." She sat me down on a log and drew the nine-and-a-half-inch Bowie knife from its sheath. The blade reflected the noon sun off it as she began slicing through my hair. I was lucky, both my hair and beard had gotten shaggy over the past couple of months. I'd always been the sort to grow out my beard unless I needed to look the part of a clean-shaven good guy. It was just easier than dealing with the hassle of shaving every few days.

After a bit, she swept the last of the cut hair pieces off my back and shoulders and straightened. "That should do it."

"Do I looked soldierly?" I asked, pulling a piece of mirror out of my saddle bag to look at myself.

"Fix that beard and you might," Wade said from where he sat across the fire.

Ashley handed me the blade and I went to work on carving a mustache and goatee out of the hairy mess on my face.

"Well now, I don't recognize you at all," Wade said as he looked me over once I was finished.

"Very handsome, Skyla will love it. Of course," Ashley looped her arm in her husband's, "I'm partial to trimmed facial hair myself."

"Thanks." I glanced down at the flap on the teepee. It was time to say goodbye to Skyla. From what I'd read in the newspaper, I didn't have much time to enlist in the Raiders. Once they had enough men, they would stop taking more and they were paying with cash money and land lots in Prehistoria. That'd draw brave men like hungry flies to a cow pie.

Crawling inside the teepee, I could smell the Shaynee herbal poultices and the stark contrasting scent of whatever concoctions that Arthur had tucked away in his bags. As warm as it was with a small fire going in the center of the floor, it was almost like being in a sweat lodge.

Arthur gave me a curt nod and slid forward over the buffalo blankets until we were side by side. "She hasn't been awake since you talked to her last. We've been dripping water into her mouth to try and keep dehydration away." He glanced back at Skyla's still form. "I'll be outside if you need me. But if by some chance she wakes, get her to drink."

"Thanks, Arthur."

The Scot ducked out of the flap, and I was left alone with my wounded love. Except for the slight crackle of sticks burning, the teepee was silent. Even with all the Indians and my friends outside, it was as though we were the only two people in the world. Shaking my head free of such a notion, I shifted myself forward until I was next to Skyla and lay down on the buffalo hide floor beside her.

Her face was pale, lips cracked, and beads of sweat trickled down her forehead from the fever. She shivered slightly and a faint moan escaped her partially open mouth.

Gently grasping her blanket, I pulled it up and tucked it around her shoulders before sliding a wisp of sweat-soaked black hair away from her closed eyes. I looked for her hand and found it lying on the blanket between us. Wrapping it in mine, I squeezed tenderly.

"Skyla, can you hear me?"

Nothing. Not even a twitch. Just a continuous, low, and labored breathing. There was a canteen near her head, and a folded blue checkered handkerchief beside it. Letting go of her hand, I took the canteen and gently soaked the cloth. Holding the handkerchief up, I let the cool water drip into her mouth. She moaned weakly and her cracked lips moved slightly in response to the liquid.

"There you go." I squeezed a little more water from the cloth. It wasn't much, maybe a tablespoon of liquid in total. But it'd help. Unfolding the wet square of cloth, I laid it over her forehead to help with the fever.

"I've got to go away for a bit and take care of a few things." Removing my allosaurus claw necklace, I wrapped the leather thong around the black claw. "I'm going to leave this here with you," I looked for a place to set it, and then decided to wrap it inside her hand. "I know I promised to never take it off, but where I'm going, I can't be recognized." I chuckled dryly. "You should see me; Ashley cut my hair and I shaved a mustache and goatee out of my beard. I look like a different person... which I need to be right now. Because I'm going to track Reydan down and kill him. If I don't, we'll never have any peace." I stared at her lovely face, desperately wishing that I could see her brown eyes one more time. "And all I want is you and peace."

Leaning forward, I kissed the damp cool cloth covering her forehead and whispered, "I'll be back, I swear. No beasts or men will keep me from you."

I crawled out of the tent as a wetness found its way to my eyes that I rapidly blinked away. My friends were polite enough to look the other way as I quickly wiped the tears away before they could fall.

"Ok. Where's this junk horse you found me?" I demanded in a suitably manly way as though I hadn't just been on the verge of bawling like a little child.

"Junk horse? What about Carbine?" Arthur asked, confusion evident upon his mustached face.

"He's too recognizable."

"Ah, that explains the shave and haircut," Arthur whistled. "You're going after Reydan on the other side of the Shimmer, aren't you?"

I patted the Smith and Wesson on my hip in a reassuring manner that I didn't quite feel. "Yes."

"And how do you plan to get across?" he asked. "I'd heard they closed the Shimmer to civilians."

"I'll be enlisting with the civilian cavalry detachment that Fredrick cooked up. The Rough Raiders. That will get me across to Prehistoria. After that, I'll find a way to slit Reydan's throat."

"And Cato? What will you do about him?"

Ashley and Wade shared a look with me. We didn't know what was in the gunman's mind anymore. But I'd already decided on what to do with him.

"If he crosses me, he dies," I said simply while knowing full well what a monumental task that would probably be. Especially with an unfamiliar pistol that I couldn't draw as quick as my Colts.

The Scottish writer and trained physician stuck his hand out and we shook. "It's been an honor and a pleasure, sir. I'll keep looking after Skyla for as long as needed."

"Well, don't make it sound like I ain't coming back." I jerked my head towards the teepee. "I told her I would be and it's a promise I intend to keep."

Arthur grinned and slapped me on the back. "I'll keep an eye out for you."

"Wade, Ashley, let's go see about this horse. It got a name?"

"Bucky," Wade replied with a sly grin.

"That's a terribly ominous name for a horse," I told him with a frown. Ashley bit off a laugh.

***

The horse was an appaloosa, the sort that Reydan and Cato rode. Almost a solid white from the front, with a splash of black spots over its rear end.

"Behold, a pale horse," Wolverine Wade whispered, quoting from the Bible.

"And I intend to be death," I muttered to myself, butchering horrifically the rest of the verse from the book of Revelations.

"Give ole Bucky a try, Jed!" Ashley said while sharing a knowing grin with Wade that I didn't like.

I found out why they were smirking after he side stepped, jack knifed, then threw me on my backside moments after calmly letting me step in the saddle.

Knocking dirt and bits of grass from my shirt and pants, I painfully stood back up and watched him saunter around the corral. A dozen Shaynee were standing around the makeshift fences watching with my friends and blood brother. It was grins and smirks all around.

"Bucky's a good name for him, ain't it?" Ashley cat called while I tried to get my breath that was knocked out of me back. It was then that I decided my ribs weren't cracked after all, because if they had been they would have most likely broke when I slammed to the ground. They were just bruised. Very, very bruised. I tried very hard to not let how much pain I was in show.

"Maybe we eat this one?" Otto teased.

"Either I ride him or you," I muttered before hobbling towards the horse. He stood still and let me take the dropped reins. I ran a hand down his neck while I whispered soothingly to the gelding. "Okay, Bucky, let's try this again. Wade only brought one horse, so you're it."

"You want Shaynee pony?" Chief Toko asked with a sly grin, knowing full well that their paint ponies weren't used to a saddle and would be even worse than Bucky to break into one. And there was no way I could ride bareback without blistering my rear end and never having children.

With a shake of my head at the Indian Chief, I carefully stepped into the saddle again, my body tense as I waited for Bucky to start doing as his name implied.

But the appaloosa let me ease my rear end into the saddle and get comfortable before throwing his rear hooves up then crow hopping sideways.

I was ready this time, though.

Clamping my thighs tight, I pulled firmly on the reins and turned his head to the side, guiding him into a circle instead of allowing him to throw his head up or down to buck his rear end.

He resisted.

Snorting and fighting against the reins, he tried to take control back as I spoke to him about how we'd learn to get along or I'd let the Shaynee eat him for winter. I'd learned long ago that horses can sense fear and uncertainty, and they didn't want that anywhere near them, much less on their back. So, I kept my voice calm but firm, along with tight control of his reins and kept him turning in a circle. As for fear, I had some, but a man must learn to mask it to get by in this world.

Satisfied that he was starting to obey, I gave him a little room and turned his head in the other direction. Dutifully, he changed directions and began turning the other way.

Several of the Shaynee watchers walked away, apparently displeased with how unentertaining Bucky and I were being.

Otto, on the other hand, looked tickled and let loose a whoop. I straightened the reins out, and cautiously let Bucky walk freely forward to the edge of the corral where the scarred brave stood wearing a grin.

"Good work. He might obey," Otto said.

"I hope so," I told him as Wade and Ashley moved closer to offer their goodbyes. The Wolverine Slayer had the *Eighty-Six* slung over a shoulder and his new wife carried my old pistols and holsters in a sack. "Take care of those weapons, please. I'll be back for them, Skyla, and Carbine," I told them sincerely before adding, "Not in that particular order."

"You'd better. And don't worry about the Protos. We'll take care of them."

"Jed," Wade said. "Don't forget the shotgun."

I realized he was right. I still had the sawed-off shotgun rolled up in my bedding. Reaching behind me, I tugged the weapon free and handed it to him.

"You don't want to keep it?" Ashley asked.

"No, Detective Thompson caught both barrels of it. They'll be looking for a rider with a shotgun."

"Smart man, Jed. Good luck." Wade saluted me with its double barrels.

I tipped my hat at my friends while Chief Toko slid aside several cut poles to let me out of the corral.

Leaning down, I gripped hands with the Shaynee Chief. "Watch over Sara, please."

"I will."

"Don't let Otto ride her," I whispered. I'd seen my blood brother looking at my not so little trike and could tell the wheels were turning inside that savage brain of his.

Toko laughed. "She almost big enough. But I keep her for you. Or Skyla."

Carefully walking Bucky forward, I took one last lingering glance at Carbine. The dun mustang pawed the ground unhappily and pulled at the rope he was picketed with. Wade had the forethought to do that so he wouldn't run after me. Near him stood Sir Lancelot, the beautiful Arabian stallion watching me stoically. I hoped he knew I was going to avenge his former master. And lastly, Sara. The young trike bellowed forlornly. She was getting big and if she wanted to, could probably knock down the corral and chase after me, but for now she was with the tribe's pair of tamed trikes. Horny Devil's bitten bone shield was an ugly sight but appeared to be healing just fine while Squatting Bull worried endlessly over him. And the other triceratops, aptly named Broke Trike by Wade on account of its three legs, was awkwardly standing nearby munching on mouthfuls of grass. Sara would be just fine with them and seeing those two other trikes get ridden would help get her in the right mindset for when her time came.

Feeling woefully unarmed for the task ahead of me, I tapped my heels to Bucky's flanks and rode away from the village while praying that Skyla would be alive when I returned.

***

I rode Bucky on the quickest route to Fort York and he only tried to buck me off twice. The first time he almost succeeded, but the second time I jerked his head around and spun him in a circle so fast that he probably had whiplash. That seemed to stick the lesson home, and the appaloosa played nice the rest of the way. Which was good, because while my bruising was healing faster than usual with the help of the Indian poultice made up with ape ferns, it was still fresh and hurt like hell.

Reaching the fort, I pulled my hat a bit lower and made sure the Smith and Wesson was loose in its holster in case I needed to draw the pistol.

Backed up against the cliff face of Granite Mountains, the fort protected the entrance to the Shimmer as well as barring anything unwanted from crossing over to our side.

I was nervous, of course. I'd been through the Shimmer over a dozen times with no ill effects but a cold shiver like someone walked over my grave, but I worried someone might recognize me before I made it through this time. Yet the closer I rode across the wide-open plains before the mountain range, I realized that the odds of passing through undetected had increased in my favor.

There had to be several hundred people camping out in front of the fort. From the number of wagons, I assumed a lot of them were homesteaders waiting for the approval to cross over and stake their land. It seemed the sudden reversal of the decision to allow settlers to cross to Prehistoria had angered a lot of people. Dozens of men, women, and even children were picketing with signs and shouting at the uniformed soldiers who kept watch and tried to keep some manner of peace.

I felt a frown spread across my freshly mustachioed face. These people sure were eager to get eaten, by ape or beast. Fools, the lot of them.

I suppose that included me now, too.

Next to the wagon trail leading to the fort, a canvas tarp had been stretched over several poles to give shade from the sun, and beneath it stood two soldiers and a pair of Pinkertons stopping everyone who passed by. All of them were being turned away, but I didn't know where else to go.

Swallowing hard, I dismounted and waited in line with reins held tight in hand and kept my head on a swivel to watch the goings on. If things were going to go sideways, this was the first opportunity for it.

Once the soldiers had finished with a rough looking covered wagon in front of me driven by a scowling woman and an old man with a large unkept beard, it was my turn.

Walking Bucky forward, I forced myself to keep my hand off the Smith and Wesson's grip. "Good morning, gentlemen," I said pleasantly as I desperately searched my memory to see if I knew any of them. I didn't think I did, but the Pinkertons hadn't even looked up yet, which meant their identities were still a mystery.

"Mornin'," the first soldier muttered uncaringly.

The other, a corporal, held a sheaf of papers. "State your name and business, please."

"Johnson Brown, and I'm looking to sign up with the Rough Raiders."

The Pinkertons perked up at that and rose from where they were sitting to look me over. "Did you say Rough Raiders?"

"Yes, sir. I did."

The shorter of the two badged detectives sauntered forward, his eyes darting up and down at my appearance. I subtly tucked my chin, allowing the battered brown Stetson to conceal more of my face.

"I don't see a scabbard on that horse. How you gonna join with no rifle?"

"I figured I'd be given one."

The soldiers chuckled and the taller of the detectives barked out a laugh. "Not given, mister. Loaned. But you'll have a chance to buy it… if you live long enough."

The short Pinkerton reached out and touched the decorated tomahawk strapped to my side. "Where'd you get this?"

I bristled at the attention and closeness of the man, but I'd thought of a lie on the way to help distance myself from the Shaynee. Most white men wouldn't know the difference between tribes anyways. For them, an

Indian was an Indian, and only good if dead. But Jedidiah Huckleberry Smith was known to be a friend of the Shaynee, which meant I had to act like I wasn't.

"I bought it back in Cheyenne. Feller said it came from a Nez Perce brave he killed during the war."

The detective sucked his teeth for a moment. "Tomahawk, pistol, horse, anything else? Shotgun maybe?"

"No. That's it. Figured everything else would be provided."

He rolled his eyes but nodded to the soldier with the papers. "Looks like you got more cannon fodder for the Raiders. I doubt this one will last long." Turning his back on me in blatant disgust, he returned to his companion and settled back onto his makeshift seat. I felt my face burn and the temptation to grab the man made my hands tremble.

The Corporal smiled apologetically. "What was that name again?"

"Johnson Brown," I said blandly.

"Is that the one you want?"

"Pardon?"

The soldier wagged his eyebrows. "Some men like to make a fresh start. The Governor's Raiders is just that. You can make up a new name if you'd like. No one cares so long as you're sixteen or older." He tilted his head to get a better look at my face. "And you're certainly that old."

The taller of the two detectives spat a stream of tobacco juice and spoke over his shoulder, "They don't much care who joins, they figure ya'll are going to get killed anyways. And if you knew the sort of dandies and miscreants that'd joined, you might change your mind."

The Corporal frowned but kept silent. There were some interesting power plays going on here between the Army and the Pinkertons it seemed. But then again, I hadn't met a man yet who actually liked the so-called detectives.

"Dandies and miscreants, huh?" I repeated, curious.

"All sorts. Educated, uneducated, Injuns, cowboys, farmers, gamblers, gunmen, even a Chinaman... you name it, and they got it. Everyone wants to be a part of the big fight against the apes. Hell, probably a bunch of outlaws in there as well."

"But not the Heart Eater," the short detective spat, and I felt a shiver at the mention of my nickname that I hoped they didn't notice.

"No, not him," agreed his companion in disgust.

"Read of him in the papers," I muttered, glad that they hadn't recognized me but feeling the need to tweak the men a bit for some information. "Ain't he a hero?" I asked innocently.

Both Pinkertons jerked upright and glared. "Hell no! He's a murderous bastard!" the ruder and shorter of the two badged men exclaimed.

"And we're going to kill him when we find him!" the other bragged.

The Corporal leaned close and lowered his voice. "They're talking about Jedidiah Huckleberry Smith. I saw him once. Big guy," he looked me over again with an evaluating eye. "About your height, with a scruffy beard. Kinda ugly fellow. Rides a dun mustang named Carbine, carries a fancy prototype Winchester rifle and a pair of Peacemakers. You'd know him if you saw him. He stands out like a sore thumb."

"He a wanted man now?"

"Just for questioning. But he'd better hope the Army finds him first; the Pinkertons are out for blood after he killed a handful of them."

I wanted to pry more, but the line of folks was growing impatient behind me, and I was feeling uncomfortable talking about myself and the detectives had turned away again. It was time to get moving. "I'll stick with Johnson Brown. My ma would probably be upset if I changed my name."

He chuckled and scribbled my new name with a stub of pencil. "Got it." Raising a hand, the soldier pointed down the trail. "Once you get to the fence in front of the fort, turn right and look for the big command tent. You can't miss it. They'll get you settled in."

"Thank you, gentlemen." Tipping my hat to the soldier, I turned my scarred back to the Pinkertons and mounted Bucky.

I rode down the trail, moving between wagons and men as much as possible on my way to get vengeance. The first step had been taken and the first subterfuge made. From here on out, I was in enemy territory in more ways than one.

***

Reaching the big tent, I was relieved to not see either Governor greeting the new joins. Governor Hale, of the Wyoming State had met me a couple of times and might recognize me through my disguise. And Governor Fredrick of Prehistoria was a close friend and would certainly recognize me. Neither of them would approve of what I was here to do and would turn me over to the Army for questioning. That I could not allow to happen; if I got hemmed up in a cell, I'd be a sitting duck for Reydan to kill.

I turned Bucky loose into a corral with a couple dozen other horses at the request of a soldier standing post nearby, then entered the shade of the command tent. Out of the warming sun, the fall weather chilled me through my coat and the dragon scale vest underneath. We'd already seen snow, but there would be no use for our thick fur coats where we were going. Prehistoria was a hot, sweltering place.

Making it about three steps into the tent, I froze.

Inside a metal cage, much like a jail cell, was an ape.

At the outburst of laughter, I shook myself from my trance and saw a pair of officers sitting at a table with an enlisted soldier standing beside them. They were all chuckling at my reaction.

"That's what you'll be facing, mister," the young, fresh-faced Lieutenant said with a sly grin.

"Still want the job?" the Captain beside him asked with a raised eyebrow.

Without replying, I stepped closer to the cage. The big beast was crouched behind the bars, squatting in a mess of urine-soaked hay and feces, his mottled white and black hair was matted and dirty. My nose curdled at the stench. His brown eyes glared with an angry intelligence. Both of his massive hands were curled into fists around the iron bars before him, and from the slight bend, it looked like he was trying to subtly pull them apart.

I continued my charade of being a newcomer to the New West. "I take it that this is one of the big monkeys I've been reading about?"

"It is, sir." The higher ranking of the two officers stood and stepped around the table to stand beside me. "Don't let his caged look fool you, he's a savage beast. We captured him when they attacked this Fort several weeks ago. Took half a dozen men to subdue him, and he wounded several of them."

I didn't say anything, but I recognized this ape from that night. I had watched with Skyla as the soldiers captured him after the battle. He'd stabbed a couple men with a broken arrow before they got him down. He had a lot of fight in him then. And from the looks of the angry scowl he was giving me now, he still had a lot of fight left in him today.

"Name?" the Lieutenant asked with stub of pencil poised above a ledger.

"Johnson Brown."

He harumphed as he wrote it in the book. "A likely name. But sign here, you'll be in Charlie Troop under Lieutenant Heath. He's not here right now, but you'll meet him soon."

Ignoring the dig, I leaned forward and scratched an X on the paper beside my name at the bottom of the list. No point in appearing educated, then they might promote me to some position of importance. And that I did not need.

The Lieutenant frowned at my mark on the form, then introduced himself and the Captain with a wave of his hand. "I'm Lieutenant

Barlow and this is Captain Theo. We will be leading Alpha and Bravo Troops into Prehistoria in a few hours to begin training."

"Cutting it close, Mr. Brown, but welcome aboard," Captain Theo shook my hand. "I'm sure your first question is when you will be paid and if there are any advances. The answer to that is, no advances and you will be paid upon your return from Prehistoria in cash money and a land deed. If you don't survive, we can send your pay and property to your relatives. Do you have anyone you'd like for us to put down?"

"No."

Barlow made a mark on his sheet.

"Any other questions?" the Captain asked.

I had a lot of them but started with the most important one. "I was told I'd be given... loaned... a rifle."

"Yes, sir! A brand spanking new Winchester Model 1873 repeater. Everyone who crosses the Shimmer, even the Raiders, is issued one. And don't you worry, Mr. Brown. That rifle will work just dandy on these savage monkeys, and where we're going, you're going to want a repeater."

"Pistol?"

Theo gestured down at my sidearm. "No, sir. But we recommend everyone that has one to keep it. You can even bring that fancy tomahawk of yours if you want."

"Or you can sell it to me," Lieutenant Barlow offered.

"It's not for sale," I told him firmly, knowing that Otto would stake me over an ant hill buck naked if I did such a thing.

"Shame, it'd look good on my wall back home. If you change your mind, come find me."

"I won't." The thought of my blood brother turned sharpshooter Ashley James' weapon rusting away on an officer's wall needled me, but I kept a smile on my face.

Barlow gestured with his head behind the tent. "If you've never seen a dinosaur before, we've some trikes out back. Those are what we call the various breeds of triceratops that we've come across. Also, we've got some groups from the other side joining with us to take the fight to the apes. Shayana, they're a strange tribe of English-Indians with pterodactyls that they ride called Breehas, so if you see anyone walking around half dressed like an Indian and speaking some sort of Shakespearean tongue, and wearing an armored breastplate, that's them. They are mostly friendly."

I nodded as the junior officer continued.

"And then we have the Vikings. Or Axemen. They're fighters through and through and led by a one-armed Jarl, named Mikah." The

Lieutenant chuckled. "I don't know how useful he is, but he keeps the other Vikings in line and is some sort of big-time warrior with their people. I've never seen him smile, so I recommend keeping my distance from him. The rest of the Vikings, they're a pretty savage bunch. Some of them ride trikes just like the apes do and-"

"Long story short," Theo interrupted his underling. "Leave them alone. We've already had some misunderstandings that resulted in a couple of hurt feelings, a busted skull, and their Jarl amputated a Pinkerton's ear with his sword for disrespecting him. We don't need any more of that crap."

I looked around the room, hoping for some sort of map or something to show what exactly we were expected to be doing. Even though I just planned on assassinating the railroad tycoon, I needed to play along until I could do so.

"Speaking of Pinkertons, what are they all doing here?"

"They're on loan from the East-West Railroad to help us with peace-keeping operations on the other side."

"Peace-keeping, huh?" I couldn't keep the words from dripping out sarcastically.

Captain Theo shrugged apologetically. "They do have a reputation of sorts, but we need men, and they are for hire."

Lieutenant Barlow smirked from where he sat. "Just like you."

The thought of throttling his scrawny neck between my hands made me smile back.

"And we appreciate that," Theo said, shooting a dark look at his Lieutenant. "We expect good things out of this grand experiment of Rough Raiders cooked up by Governor Fredrick von Holsak."

I looked at the caged ape. He glared back with enough hatred that I could feel it in my bones.

Theo noticed. "You'll be killing them soon enough, Mr. Brown. The quarter master is that way," he pointed out the other open side of the tent. "He'll get you sorted away with a rifle and anything else you may need."

"Thanks." Turning to leave, I bumped into a solidly built black soldier with sergeant markings on his uniform.

"Easy there," he rumbled in his deep voice while looking past me at the pair of officers.

Tipping my hat lower, I stepped around him without a word.

It was Sergeant Gibbons.

I knew him well, having spent time in battle and visiting the Shayana with him. He'd recognize me in a heartbeat.

"Captain, any word on Jed?" Gibbons rumbled behind me. As a shiver ran down my spine, I stopped at the tent entrance and pretended to stretch and look around the fort for a moment.

"None. But we are spreading the word that we want to talk to him."

"He's gone to ground most likely," Gibbons said. "Hiding out somewhere. If he's still alive. I rode out to his ranch; it's burned to the ground and there are a couple fresh graves dug. Whatever those Pinkertons were doing at his place, they weren't behaving."

"There's no way one man killed all those detectives," the Lieutenant grumbled. "He had to have had help."

"You don't know Jed," Gibbons replied sharply.

"Sergeant, I am a Lieutenant! You will address me as 'sir'-"

"Yes, sir. You don't know Jed, sir," he rumbled as he cut off Barlow sarcastically.

Having heard enough, I stepped around the Private standing guard and went to find the Quartermaster. My legend appeared to be growing. It wasn't something that I cared about normally, as I was a wanted man in hiding, but in a situation like this I liked the notion that my reputation put fear into men who were against me. And I hoped it kept Reydan up at night.

***

"Here is your new Winchester Model 1873 in .44-40. Sign here, Mr. Brown."

Scribbling a quick little X next to where he pointed, I took the rifle from the Quartermaster and worked the lever. With a snick, the chamber opened, and I looked inside to make sure the weapon was empty.

Satisfied it was, I worked the lever, then jerked the stock to my shoulder and pointed the iron sights at a fluffy cloud peeking over the edge of the Granite Mountain range. The weapon pointed nice enough. I tested the trigger out and felt the clean break as the hammer fell on an empty chamber.

"Seems like you know what yer doin'," the portly Corporal said. It was just the two of us standing in the open amongst the bustle of the camp. Empty rifle crates were stacked behind him, giving him somewhere to sit out of the cold wind blowing as he waited to issue out weapons. There were two more crates of rifles in the back of a parked wagon nearby. One was nailed shut still, and the other, the crate he pulled my rifle from, appeared to be about half full. They'd been passing out a lot of guns today.

"I've seen them used a time or two before," I told him with a grin.

"Well, you'll be getting some use of that one soon enough on the barbarian apes. There's a range about a mile thatta way if you want to make sure the sights are aligned. Most folks don't, but I've come across some who care."

I ran a hand down the smooth walnut stock; this rifle would do just fine. It wasn't anywhere as nice as my *Eighty-Six*, nor as hard hitting of a caliber, but it'd have to do. It was the only option I had without standing out or being recognized.

"I reckon you saw that ape when you signed up. It's something, ain't it? I was here when they captured him, ya'know. When the fort was attacked." He spat a stream of tobacco that splattered against the packed dirt between us. "The apes were worse than the damned Injuns, riding in on them trikes, burning everything, and cutting everyone down. I got lucky. I was inside one of the buildings that wasn't burned when they hit us. I used a '73 rifle just like yours to fend the hairy bastards off. I bet I got five or six of them, and dropped at least one trike," he bragged.

"Thanks for the gun," I said, not believing a word the man said.

"Don't thank me; if you lose it or break it, it comes out of your pay. But if you survive, you'll have the opportunity to buy it if you want for a nice discount. And are you sure you don't need anything else? Blankets? Bedding? Boots?"

"I could use some more .44-40 ammunition for my pistol if you've got it."

"Hmmm... You're in luck having a pistol in the same caliber as your rifle," he scratched his face, then passed me a couple more boxes of cartridges. "We can spare them, especially since there aren't likely going to be more folks signing up."

I looked down at my gear. I sorely needed a blade of some sort; the tomahawk wouldn't do for daily knife work. "Got a blade?" I asked, sheepishly.

He laughed and rummaged around in the back of the wagon. Finally, he drew a rough looking leather scabbard with an antler handled blade shoved into it. "It's junk, but it's sharp," he said, almost apologetically as he handed it over. "I already issued all the good blades."

"Thank you, it'll do." I glanced at the Corporal while sliding the sheath onto my belt. He was certainly the talkative type. I decided to nudge him a bit in the right direction. "So, the apes... they as bad as they look?"

"Worse! They carry these great big stone axes and clubs, plus spears and bows and large arrows that'll go straight through a man!"

"Sounds like you did a good job then, fending them off."

The Corporal stood straighter. "Yes, I did. One of them I killed face to face. Shot her as she reached through the window for me. Put the bullet right through her painted monkey face!"

Now I knew he was a liar. The apes that night hadn't been painted like usual. There were no colorful swirls and markings on their face and torsos, just a bunch of cold monkeys trying to get home to Prehistoria. The man disgusted me, but I still hoped he could give me some information I could use.

"I heard that railroad tycoon was here when it happened."

"Sure was. Thankfully, too! That gunman of his, the Black Plague, and Jedidiah 'Heart Eater' Smith, they saved the day by using the Maxim machine gun on top of his armored car to stop the attack."

At the mention of my name, I shrugged deeper into my thick coat. Danged the luck, it's like everyone around these parts had heard of me.

"That tycoon still around?"

"Why?" The Quartermaster peered at me suspiciously. "What you want with him?"

I shrugged my shoulders and tried to act as innocent as possible. "I'd just like to get a peek of this machine gun of his. Sounds like something we need with the Raiders."

"It's a neat lookin' thing. But he's in Prehistoria right now, waiting on the big attack."

"Waiting on the big attack?" That was a curious thing for the Quartermaster to say.

"Yup! Colonel Carver and the others are adamant that they'll face the apes in an open battle soon. They're going to use you Raiders to try and draw them out first. But he's pledged that if the Army meets the apes on the field of battle, he'll be right there with them."

**

That was an interesting development, I thought, as I carried the rifle away. It was just the bit of news I was hoping for, some sort of word on his plans or his whereabouts. And it seemed like his involvement in the attack might just give me an outstanding opportunity for his long-awaited demise.

"Hey! Hey you!" It was Lieutenant Barlow's voice, coming from behind me.

Moving my hand near my pistol, I glanced over my shoulder cautiously. I had been heading to find Charlie Troop and Lieutenant Heath, but instead the annoying young officer gestured towards a large gathering of men past a couple of buildings and near the trike pens. "Head over there, Brown." He smirked. "Got a speech to attend."

Without saying a word, I took off at a brisk walk towards the crowd. It'd been a while since my stint in the Army, but the adherence to orders that'd been instilled in me kept me from dallying. And there was no point in standing out.

The group of men looked to number over a hundred. I assumed they were the other Rough Raiders as they were all in civilian clothing, most of them carrying matching Winchesters, and looked to be a ragtag bunch of individuals. I pushed a bit, moving into the group so I could hear whatever was about to be said. Surrounding me were many whispers, laughter, and the coarse talk of a disorganized bunch of men wondering what the hell we'd just signed up for.

At the front of the group, Governor Fredrick von Holsak climbed aboard a wagon and waved at everyone to settle down. As always, he was impeccably dressed. A dark suit coat this time, with a dark tie and black hat resting at an angle on his head. His mustache moved as he gave a broad grin towards the crowd. Governor Hale followed him into the back of the wagon, wearing a heavy coat over his brown suit. Beside the wagon stood a member of the Shayana tribe and a scowling Viking. I didn't recognize the tribesman, but the Viking was Asger. The stout, bearded man was one of the few who spoke decent English that I'd met when we crossed paths with the Axemen. He and his trike mount, Sleipnir, helped us kill the Tyrannosaurus that ate Oscar.

"Okay! That's enough. Listen up," Hale warned with a shout.

The noise abated a bit, but not enough to suit Fredrick. Drawing a pistol, he fired it into the air.

"He said shuddup!"

Shocked, the crowd grew quiet while several trikes bellowed angrily behind the governors in the pens.

The famed Westerner holstered the pistol beneath his suit coat and nodded at Hale.

"Thank you, Fredrick. But a warning next time would be appreciated," he shouted with an easy laugh. Hale was a nice fellow and a tough bird. His office was located in Cheyenne and I'd met the man before the Battle of the Apes at the town of Granite Falls. He'd sent a platoon of soldiers and a cannon to support us. He and Fredrick also went way back, having had some previous adventures of a sort.

"I'll be quick. I'm Governor Hale and this is Governor Fredrick. I run the State of Wyoming and he runs the Prehistoria Territory. He's got some words that you need to listen to. But first, I'd like to personally thank you all for answering the call and signing up. I wish the best of luck to you on the other side and will be here to see you when you return victorious."

"You ain't comin' with us?" shouted a laughing voice from behind me.

Hale smirked. "If I went, there'd be no need for you."

The crowd guffawed but appeared to enjoy the brag.

Giving a slight wave, Hale climbed down from the wagon, leaving Fredrick standing alone.

The Western hunter turned politician ran a hand over his mustache while looking out over the gathering as though mustering his thoughts. Seemingly satisfied, he nodded to himself and began talking loudly.

"Gentlemen. The Rough Raiders is an experiment of the fortitude of the American man. You all have exhibited extraordinary bravery by enlisting in this civilian attachment to fight against the unknowns of Prehistoria. On the other side, there are all manner of magnificently deadly beasts we may encounter, many of which are yet unknown to our own scholars and scientists. And perhaps most dangerous of all is the savage ape." He paused theatrically. "You all saw the one in the cage when you enlisted. I beg you not to underestimate their abilities. They are powerful foes. With their axes and clubs, they will crush you. With their spears and arrows, they will pierce you. And if you find yourself within their grip, they will break you. Make sure to keep your distance."

Raising his own rifle, Fredrick spoke firmly. "Gunpowder, gents. It is our only edge over their abnormal savagery, brute strength, and callousness to human existence. If you are taken alive, they will sacrifice you on an altar of evil with your beating heart ripped from your chest and eaten to please some dark ape god.

"This will not happen under my command! No man is to be taken alive by these damned heathen monkeys. You will fight until your last breath! Be it with pistol, blade, or teeth." He lowered his Winchester and glared at the silent group of men. "The Raiders will not suffer from an affliction of cowardice. You will fight! And make no mistake, we are going to take the fight to the apes."

"Holy shit… what'd we sign up for?" I heard muttered behind me in disbelief.

"War," someone else whispered back.

"The apes control fearsome beasts, as some of you may know," Governor Fredrick continued. "Trikes, raptors, and even dragons. But with our allies by our side…" he gestured a hand at the Viking and Shayana standing stoically before us, "…we will even the odds."

The famed Westerner turned Governor stepped forward in the wagon, bracing a foot on the siding and introducing the trio of officers who'd made their way to the front during his speech. "Now, to my right are Captain Theo of Alpha Troop, Lieutenant Barlow of Bravo Troop, and

Lieutenant Heath of Charlie Troop. Check in with your commander, then ready your horses, load your rifles, and prepare to cross the Shimmer. We've no time to waste."

The group broke apart with much murmuring and talk of dragons, war, and bombastic brags of what they would do when they met the apes on the field of battle. I kept silent, slowly moving through the crowd towards where Lieutenant Heath stood with a piece of paper in hand.

"Hey there, stranger," came a familiar voice that I couldn't quite place.

Stopping abruptly, another man bumped into me from behind, swore, and glared. After a long second, where I glared back, he finally moved on. Standing firm against the flow of Raiders, I peered through the crowd, trying to figure out whose voice I heard.

I swore under my breath when I saw him shouldering his way towards me. "Wesley Clemmons," I muttered.

The notorious outlaw held up a hand to hush me. "Name is Wesley Simmons... for now."

Chuckling, I shook his hand and looked him over. He'd ditched his gambler appearance and the brace of pistols he kept tucked in his vest for a common looking cowboy attire with a single Colt Lightning strapped to his side. The newly issued rifle was slung over his shoulder like mine. "Those two names sound awfully alike."

"It helps me not get confused when I hear it." He lowered his voice to a whisper, "And who are you... Orville?"

"Johnson Brown."

"Terrible name."

"It'll work for now."

"It's two last names strung together."

I sighed.

He jerked his head towards the front of the line that was beginning to form. "Charlie Troop?"

"Yes, sir. Looks like we'll be together."

We kept our voices low in the loud crowd as we caught up on past events since we last saw each other at the Battle of the Apes. Apparently, the reward for his arrest and hanging had risen substantially, and he decided to lay low for a bit. And he figured what better way to lay low than to cross over to a wild and lawless territory?

"Shame to hear that about your lady. I hope she pulls through," he said after I briefly told him of why I was here.

I swallowed a lump in my throat that'd suddenly appeared. "Me too."

The outlaw pointed at my belt. "You any good with that Smith and Wesson? You're going to need to be to take on the Black Plague."

At the sound of my childhood friend's name, I snorted. "No need. I plan on shooting him in the back."

"How noble of you," Wesley chided sarcastically.

"You once killed a man for snoring," I snarked back.

"I shot him through a wall in a hotel. A bit different than through a man's back."

"Well, if I had my Colts and was good enough, I might try bracing him from the front."

"I've seen him. He's extraordinary. You'd certainly die."

"This is why how I kill folks is none of your damned business."

He chuckled and lit a cigarillo with a match. "Johnson, I tease. We both know that fairness is for suckers. Just do what needs to be done however you can." He took a deep drag and blew the smoke out.

"Aren't you worried about what you're about to do?"

"You mean riding across this mysterious Shimmer thing, into an unknown prehistoric time, against a monstrous enemy, with a misguided bunch of outlaws, cutthroats, farmers, and cowboys? Yes. Very much so." His eyes cut slanted at me. "And don't you mean what *we* are about to do?"

"Yeah. That's what I meant," I lied.

He stared at me for a few long seconds, as though trying to see my thoughts. I stared back, expressionless.

"Un-huh," he finally said before looking away with an eye roll. "I figure you and I, we've got some more talking to do."

"If we survive," I was sure to emphasize we.

"Yes, if."

It was my turn to stand before Lieutenant Heath. He was a bright, and young looking fellow with a blonde mustache and an immaculate uniform. I hoped he wasn't a shitbag who was going to get us all killed.

"Sir, Johnson Brown reporting for duty."

With a stub of pencil, he made a check mark on the piece of paper. "Nice to meet you, Johnson. I'll be quick with a couple questions. Can you ride, shoot, and speak the truth?"

"Yes, sir."

"Excellent, otherwise we'd have no use for you. What about prior military experience?"

There was no point in lying as it'd be hard to hide my knowledge and with everyone using fake names, there shouldn't be any concern over what I said. "I fought in the Nez Perce wars."

The officer raised an eyebrow and made another mark. "Impressive. What was your rank?"

"I was just a trigger pulling private."

He looked skeptical. "Hmmm. Well, it's good to have experience in our midst. I see your new Winchester, have you received everything else you need from the Quartermaster?"

"Yes, sir."

"Good." He stuck his hand out and I shook it. "Welcome to C Troop. Fetch your horse and ready your gear. We depart within the hour."

"Where to?" Wesley asked from behind me.

"Prehistoria. That's where we'll be training and raiding, gents."

***

It'd been years since I'd been enlisted, but the old habits came back quickly. Once Wesley and I rode through the Shimmer with the rest of Charlie Troop, we were immediately assigned a tent and guard duty.

Then we began training.

During the long and sweltering hot days, I managed to avoid anyone who knew me and painfully heal the bruises and cracked ribs from being shot by a bunch of sadistic chickenshit Pinkertons. And the entire time, I hoped and prayed that Skyla was healing well. Thinking about her was driving me insane, so I threw myself into the training we were receiving.

Wesley and I were lucky to have Lieutenant Heath. He cared for his men, knew his job, and was adamant that we knew ours.

From what I observed of the other Raiders' training, Captain Theo seemed like a decent enough leader, but Lieutenant Barlow was a piece of work. I fully expected him to be shot in the back during their first meeting with an ape.

We were taking our turn standing guard over the Prehistoria valley this side of the Shimmer when George walked down with a sack full of mail.

George was a Chinaman. When he signed up, it seemed Lieutenant Barlow couldn't figure out how to pronounce his Chinese name properly, so he told the short statured fellow that his name was George now. He spoke some pretty good English, threw himself into training with everything he had, and was generally a nice fellow. From a distance he'd even pass as a really tan white man by the way he dressed, except for his hat. He stuck to his big China hat. One of those large, cone-shaped woven hats. Considering how hot the sun was over here, after a few days of observing how much easier he had it, I was tempted to turn my Stetson in for one.

"Brown, Simmons..." he read our names from a pair of envelopes and handed them over.

The pair of us looked at each other for a moment before hesitantly taking the letters. The Chinaman shifted the sack of mail and rifle slung over his shoulders and left us to our reading.

"You expectin' a letter?" I asked Wesley.

"Sort of," he stared at the envelope in his hand. "What about you?"

"Yeah… I told my friends what name I'd be using so they could write if anything changed with Skyla."

"You worried?"

"Been worried."

"I never noticed," Wesley teased.

I slit the top of the envelope open with the antlered hunting blade as Wesley carefully pried his open using his fingers.

Pulling the folded letter out, I quietly read the neat script.

"Sir,

Your father and sister are recovering from their illnesses and being well taken care of by your brother. They worry for your safety and expect you to return successfully without being maimed or eaten. As for your family horse, dog, and garden tools, they eagerly await your appearance on the horizon."

Chuckling, I waited for Wesley to finish reading his before handing mine over to him.

"Everything ok?" I asked as he folded his with a frown and stuffed it deep into a pocket.

"It seems some people are rather anxious that they find me. But all will be well with time." He smoothed my letter out with his hand and read quickly. Pursing his lips, he took a guess, "I take it your father is your father, your sister is Skyla, your brother is Otto, and family horse is Carbine… but dog and garden tools?"

"I never told you, we adopted a baby triceratops. Named her Sara, she follows us around like a big dog. And the garden tools would be my lovely matching Peacemakers and *Eighty-Six*," I sighed wistfully. "I do miss them."

"I understand the feeling," Wesley said as he patted the Colt Lightning holstered at his hip. "Going from two pistols to one makes a man feel terribly underpowered and borderline defenseless."

"Agreed!"

***

"Gentlemen," Lieutenant Heath stalked in front of our squad. He'd had us sit and get comfortable instead of standing at ease while he spoke. One of the perks of being a civilian attachment is that we didn't have to entirely adhere to the strictness of the regular military. I shifted my rear end, trying to find a better position on the uncomfortable sawed log seat. He continued after a slight pause, "Charlie Troop is being honored with our first task of getting to punch the apes in their ugly faces."

George let out a rebel yell that sounded like a cat being strangled.

We broke into a chuckle at that while another Raider pounded him on the back in approval.

So far, none of the troops had gone on any missions yet. And the training was becoming tedious for those of us who joined up already knowing what we were doing. But after one of the Bravo Troop Raiders turned out to not know how to ride, we'd been forced to prove ourselves in all sorts of silly ways.

"Well put, George. I agree with the enthusiasm." Heath propped a booted foot on an empty log seat. "We will be traveling with a bunch of Shayanas. They've spied some of the big monkeys from the air, and we'll be hitting them from the ground. We leave at dawn to do as our name suggests, to raid. Simple and sweet. You see an ape, you kill it."

Wesley raised his hand slowly.

Heath looked annoyed as his blue eyes stared at the disguised outlaw in hiding. "Yes, Simmons, what is it?"

"How do we know they'll still be there when we arrive?" Wesley asked softly.

"They've moved into one of the villages that the Pinkertons torched a few weeks back. They appear to be rebuilding the huts and improving the defenses."

"How many of them? And any raptors?" a man asked from behind me.

"Two dozen, give or take a few. No raptors or trikes spotted. Anything else?"

"Will the Shayanas be flying on their Breehas?" another Raider asked excitedly.

"No. They'll be on foot. We are trying to keep the mounted pterodactyl riders in reserve for the big offensive. We don't want to risk them for anything but keeping watch for ape movements. What else?"

Silence.

Lieutenant Heath appeared to nod to himself as though satisfied with his short briefing. "Alright. Have your gear packed, your weapons ready, and your horse saddled before daybreak. We ain't got time to spare, it's a long ride there and back. Good evening, gentlemen."

While the officer sauntered away, C Troop broke into smaller groups of two or three men as we all talked amongst ourselves. Wesley and I walked back to our tent, silent in our own thoughts.

Reaching the tent first, the outlaw ducked his head beneath the canvas and stepped inside. I looked around us for a moment to make sure we were out of anyone else's hearing before following him.

"You going tomorrow?" Wesley asked as he opened the cylinder on his pistol and dumped the loaded bullets onto his blanket.

"You say that like I got a choice," I muttered back as he picked up each round, inspected it carefully, then loaded it back into the pistol's cylinder. He did this every morning and every evening, regardless of how tired or exhausted we may be. A cautious and paranoid man lives longer than most.

"You could ride off to Whitesberg tonight. Take care of your business."

My business being Reydan's death.

"Maybe. But it'd be hard to get in by myself. A lone Raider would be met with suspicion. I can't have that." I sat on my blanket and pulled off my boots. "Guess I'll be riding with you."

"Good." He snapped the loading gate shut on his pistol and slowly rotated the cylinder, listening to the gentle clicks as each bullet lined up in the barrel. "Because they'd probably ask me where you are." He grinned mischievously. "And I'm a terrible liar."

I snorted and looked out the open flap, watching more Raiders trickle back to their tents to prepare for tomorrow. "We've a pretty good group, and the Shayana are fearsome fighters. We'll be fine tomorrow."

"You say that like you're trying to convince yourself."

"A little. Most of these men have never killed anything that could kill them back."

"That's why I'm glad you're coming with us," Wesley said as he carefully wiped his Colt down with an oiled cloth. "You're a killer and they're going to need you."

"Coming from you? I suppose that's a compliment."

He smirked.

***

Lieutenant Heath lied. We left before dawn. I didn't mind that so much, I couldn't sleep. It seemed to be a problem that most Raiders had considering how few had to be roused awake. George was one of them; the Chinaman slept like the dead and I thought I was going to have to fire my freshly cleaned Smith and Wesson next to his ear to wake him.

Other than those men who were standing post around the circular defenses of the Shimmer, there were very few soldiers or Pinkertons to watch the first civilian Rough Raider detachment ride out on the attack.

We rode into the forest, walking our horses as we moved along the beaten path. A lot of men had ridden out this way, I tried to think that most of them came back. But the memory of Fort Jipson falling was still fresh in my mind, we lost hundreds of men that day. I almost bought the farm myself, and a good friend of mine had.

Thinking of Captain Brandthorn's death led me to think about Lieutenant Daniels. I'd cautiously asked around about the young officer and learned that he'd been posted as part of the command for Whitesberg's military attachment. Sergeant Gibbons was with him, so I figured he was safe enough. I'd dodged a pair of bullets there. Had those men been given over to help train or lead the Raiders, I'd have had a hard time avoiding them and not being recognized.

Somewhere in the darkness ahead of us a pterodactyl screeched. Instinctively, I flinched and looked up at the sky that was just beginning to glow with light from the morning sun.

Wesley chuckled as if amused but shifted his grip on the Winchester repeater he carried in his hands.

I'd told him of the Merhas I'd encountered over here before. The giant pterodactyls would occasionally attack the Shayana's Breehas in their mountain fortress. The leathery birds were so large they could skewer right through a fellow or rip a man in half with their beaks.

Frightening things.

But they weren't the only thing in the sky that could kill us.

The apes had dragons as well. Ugly beasts.

They appeared rare but facing one of them was like facing a forest fire with your manhood in hand.

It was a fight that was hard to win. Yet, it entertained me to no end to hear the repeated story of how Otto defeated one single handedly when we retook Fort Jipson from the apes. I was proud of my blood brother, and as the story grew and changed, taking on a life of its own, I just grinned and nodded with each retelling. The ugly, scarred Shaynee brave would be a legend someday.

I shifted in the saddle carefully lest I get Bucky to try and throw me again and shifted my loaned rifle across my pommel. Jedidiah Huckleberry Smith on the other hand, was already legendary around these parts. I heard a lot of talk of my exploits, and a good bit about things I hadn't done but sounded impressive. When I got back to Skyla and the Shaynee, I'd make sure to tell Otto I was more well-known than he was. That'd tickle his jealous bone.

The line of riders slowed, and I shifted Bucky to the right side of the trail to get a better look ahead. It was still dark inside the forest with faint trickles of morning light making their way to the ground. But from what I could recall of this area of the forest, there was a clearing ahead littered with many burrows of the small brown furry rodents of this side.

A murmured whisper made its way back to me, and dutifully I turned and passed it on to those behind me.

Shayana.

The Old World settlers mixed with Indian tribe would lead the way on foot. But it wouldn't be slow going. The tribesmen could really move it on the ground considering how much weight they carried in armor and weapons.

"Why didn't they just meet us at the Shimmer?" Wesley whispered in a hushed tone.

"The Shimmer is watched by the apes. Just a guess, but the Shayana probably don't want them to know who all is on the move right now."

"So long as we hit the village before they see us coming, I'm fine."

"Agreed."

If the apes were warned, we'd be hitting a hardened defensive position. Even with the Shayana, we'd have a rough time cracking that nut. As it was, we hoped to hit them unaware and unprepared.

"Here we go," whispered George as the line of mounted Raiders began moving again through the darkened shadows of the prehistoric forest.

I gently nudged Bucky with my heels to goad him forward. He went, but I could tell he wasn't happy about it. The more I rode this troublesome appaloosa, the more I missed my troublesome Carbine. If you're going to have an asshole for a horse, it might as well be a well-known asshole.

Something roared terribly. It was loud and close enough to send most of our horses sidestepping or shifting in fright. I worried about that too as I fought Bucky to keep moving forward.

I felt like we weren't fully ready for this with only a few weeks of training. But the Governors were anxious for us to prove our worth.

And that's just what we were about to do.

***

Grasping a low hanging branch, I pushed it aside and slowly let it go to keep from smacking the rider behind me with any force.

From the muffled swear, I could tell without turning he hadn't been paying attention and got thumped with the leafy limb.

He wasn't the only one; we were all keeping one eye on the river beside us as we rode towards the crossing the Shayana had led us to. The lithe tribesmen were still leading the way, but that didn't prevent Lieutenant Heath from consulting the map from time to time. I reckoned that meant either he didn't fully trust the natives from this side of the Shimmer, or he wanted to know where we were in case we had to skedaddle. Either way, I approved. Trust no one, verify everything.

The river beside us was deep and wide. And on the far side a herd of long necked gray and brown dinosaurs were feasting on leaves from the trees that leaned over the water. The dinosaurs were massive. Towering high above us, the animals gracefully pulled mouthfuls off the branches and crunched them. Bits and pieces of partially chewed leaves fell around them, dropped from the sides of their mouths, and the smaller beasts... calves I suppose... playfully snatched the bits out of the air hungrily.

"Never thought I would witness such things," Wesley said in awe.

"You ain't seen nothing yet," I warned him while turning away from the peaceful dinosaurs and keeping a wary eye on the thick brush around us. There was no threat from the long necks unless they stampeded, but there was no telling what sort of beasts might be lying in wait, hidden, and prepared to munch on us.

Knowing what I did of this side was a problem. I had to keep my mouth shut to complete my goal of killing Reydan. If I spoke out too often, or too knowingly, the other men would wise up and question how I'd known such things if I'd never been across the Shimmer like them. Playing dumb meant I was playing with their lives.

Not much I could do about that, except tell Wesley what I knew to help keep my lone ally on this side alive.

But looking at George's toothy grin and that damned Chinaman hat he was determined to wear, I knew that I was growing close to some of these men. Our training did what it was supposed to. It bonded us to one another. Unified us. Better enabled us to kill the enemy. All of that.

Which meant that keeping quiet about what could kill them all caused a helluva lot of convictions of my dubious morals.

My internal turmoil left me with a monstrous splash and a short-lived scream as a Raider and horse disappeared into the river.

I caught a glimpse of something massive with a muddy, uneven shell move back under water.

"Did you see that?" a Raider shouted while twirling his mount around. "It grabbed Jethro!"

"Jethro? Noo!" another Raider yelled as he raced his horse to the edge of the riverbank. The mount's hooves were dangerously close to slipping into the water, but the man didn't seem to care. His wild eyes stared at the thrashing beneath the reddening water. Kicking his feet free of the stirrups, he dove into the water with knife in hand.

"What was it? What the hell was it?" Lieutenant Heath screamed as his horse came barreling down between confused Raiders. "And get that man out of the water!"

"It was a…. giant turtle, sir," one of the Raiders said hesitantly as he started to move towards the water, then stopped.

"A turtle? A TURTLE took a man and his horse? Bart! Get out of the damned water, you fool!"

Splashing in the reddish-brown water, Bart kicked his booted feet up and went underwater.

At the same moment, the mangled remains of a horse floated to the top. The saddle was missing, and a large piece of the beast's neck and flank was ripped away. Bloodied flesh and torn sinews floated in the water beside the gaping wounds.

A large wave sloshed against the shore, as something colossal in the water moved. The muddy water was too churned to get a good look, but a dark shadow glided away.

"I think it's leaving!" someone shouted.

Bart broke the surface, splashing with one free hand as he moved towards the riverbank. The other dragged something large still hidden in the murky water. On the opposite side of the river, the long necks were moving away from us almost frantically and sending large waves of muddy brown water slamming against the Raider and whatever he pulled behind him.

Slipping from my saddle, I thrust my rifle into Wesley's hand and drew my pistol.

"Cover me," I told the gunman.

This is a foolish thing to do, I thought, while sliding down the mud and grass into knee deep water while keeping my gun above the water and ready to fire a round at anything that looked prehistoric.

Bart slipped, fell to a knee, then staggered up and grabbed my outstretched hand.

Pulling him, I saw what he had in his other hand.

A saddle with deep gouges along the sides of the leather and a pommel missing.

There was also a severed leg and booted foot still in the stirrup.

"Dammit Bart, leave it behind," I told the man.

"He's my brother!" the Raider cried out desperately.

"He's dead!"

"I gotta bury him!" Tears were rolling down the man's face and disappearing into his water-soaked clothes as several pairs of hands reached down and helped pull us out of the water.

Along the bank, most of the men in our unit along with the Shayana tribesmen had rifles pointed at the river in case the monstrous water beast should appear again. I appreciated the notion, but suspected if it was a prehistoric turtle, we'd never penetrate the shell with what we were carrying.

Back on slightly dry ground, I realized that one of the Raiders who helped pull us out was Lieutenant Heath. I gave him a quick, respectful nod when our eyes met. An officer who was willing to get his boots muddy to help his men was a good thing to have.

Heath stepped back into the water and grabbed a torn edge of the saddle and helped pull it and Jethro's remaining leg onto the bank. Bart was shaking, his hands trembling hard from the shock and loss of his brother. He sat, hid his face in his hands, and wept.

"It's coming back!" someone further up the line shouted hoarsely.

Sure enough, there was a V-shaped wave coming towards us. It appeared the turtle was coming back for seconds.

A scattering of shots rang out, the bullets making small splashes as they impacted against the water's surface.

"Piss on this, our rifles won't penetrate that shell anyways," Heath rushed over to his saddle bags and pulled out a bundle of dynamite. Quickly unwrapping the cord from the boom sticks, he freed one and struck a match to it.

"It's getting close!" someone warned.

Moving away from the river's edge, we all backed up as we kept one eye on the dangling detonation cord sparkle as it burned shorter and shorter and the other on the submerged reptile moving closer.

Wesley appeared beside me, the gunman moving noiselessly and handing over my rifle.

"Lieutenant, that det cord is getting short," the outlaw-turned-Raider warned softly.

"Tell me when I've an inch left," our commander said calmly as he watched the approaching crest of water.

"About.... Now."

With an easy overhanded toss, the Lieutenant chucked the stick into the river where it landed slightly behind the V wave and to the right. Almost immediately it exploded.

BOOM!

Water rained down on us.

Then pieces of shell began pelting us and our horses.

Bucky didn't like that one bit and began bucking as I dropped my rifle to hold onto his reins and get him to calm down.

Wesley shook drops of water and shell off his hat and placed it back on his head. He pointed a finger. "That didn't do the beast in." The V turned and was moving away quicker than it came. We could see the top of the scarred shell now, there were cracks and pieces missing that'd scattered all over the river and embankment from the blast.

"No, but it taught it a lesson," Heath said wryly as he checked his saddle bag. Pulling the loose bundle out, he rewrapped the cord around it before sliding it back into place and closing the leather flap.

"Where'd you learn to handle dynamite like that?" I asked.

"Mining coal, started when I was twelve years old." He frowned. "Lost a lot of friends in that place. It's not for the faint of heart."

I tipped my hat to the man and turned back to Wesley.

"He won't be the last we lose on this side of the Shimmer," he said softly as to not be overheard.

Ignoring the outlaw, I slung the weapon and walked back to one of the pack mules. It was best that we get the remains buried before any other dinosaurs were lured in by the scent of blood and death. Already, armor plated fish were nipping and tearing at the dead horse floating slowly down the river and small pterodactyls were landing in the trees around us like buzzards. The wildlife here knew death well and our party of Raiders was learning still.

George beat me to the mule and had already grabbed a shovel. We walked together back to Bart. The Raider had gotten ahold of himself and was wiping tears away as he talked to our commanding officer.

"Lieutenant, I can't tell my mama he was ate!"

"I know, son. We'll tell her it was an accident and that we did right by him. See? Johnson and George have a shovel, and we'll bury Jethro's remains right over there." Heath pointed at a small, raised place near where we stood. A single white prehistoric flower bloomed among a stand of purple and green ferns. "It's a pretty place."

George walked towards the flower, leaving me to carefully pull the severed leg from the stirrup. It was tangled but using the antler-handled knife, I sliced through the wet straps and freed the booted stump.

Trying to be as solemn as I could with the limb, I carried it to where the Chinaman had begun to dig and carefully set it down on a bed of tall grass.

Wesley, a couple of Shayana tribesmen, and several other Raiders followed us and stood guard as George quickly shoveled a hole in the ground.

"Damn man, you didn't have to dig an L-shaped hole," one of the Raiders guffawed. "The foot we could just leave sticking up a little."

Resting on the shovel, he shrugged and squinted at the man who'd spoken. "Respect the dead. Or what is left of him."

Shaking my head, I gently laid the mangled limb to rest, making sure to turn the boot to the side to fit in the hole that George had so carefully dug.

Bart was walking our way, and any softly spoken talk ceased as the grieving man reached the edge of the small hole. "So long, Jethro," he said to the leg with a sniff. "I'll let mama know that you died bravely and not to worry. And I'll come back and kill that sonuva bitch turtle after we beat the apes."

Wesley patted the man on the back gently. "I'll wager it will make a mighty fine soup."

Wiping the back of a hand under his nose, Bart sniffed. "Damn right."

George began gently shoveling dirt into the small hole. No one else spoke. I was willing to bet every man of us was thinking of how it could have been anyone that got snagged by the turtle. Out of nowhere, no warning, no chance to fight back, just a large chomp and you're gone.

Being eaten was a terrible way to go.

***

The leader of our little Shayana attachment looked every bit like a Shaynee from our side except for his blue eyes. He carried a traditional bow and quiver full of arrows instead of a rifle. The armor he wore was well used but functional, and there were gouges from claws scratched into the front plate.

His name was Afton, and he wore a necklace of ape ears.

"Nice accessory," Wesley commented as we rode away from the sight of Jethro's demise and burial. Now the Shayana were scattered throughout our column to help the newcomers to Prehistoria keep an eye out. There were a lot of things over here that we'd never seen before, but they'd not only survived, but thrived in this deadly world.

"A bit barbaric if you ask me."

"Where's your necklace? I recall you wearing one with a claw."

I thought of Skyla and swallowed the sudden catch in my throat. I missed the girl something awful and without the necklace, I had nothing to remind me of her. "I left it behind."

The outlaw leaned in the saddle and lowered his voice. "You recognize any of these Shayanas?"

"A couple. But they haven't recognized me back."

"Let's hope it stays that way."

Afton held up a hand as we came to a wide spot in the river. Here the water was calmer than normal and from the bits of rock jutting up and tree branches stuck amongst them, it appeared shallow as well.

"Thy will cross here." Drawing his sword, the blade sparkled in the sun as the Shayana leader waved us forward.

There was a moment of hesitation, then Lieutenant Heath led the way into the water. The Shayana tribesmen around us drew their swords and began to walk into the water with blades held high and rifles strapped to their backs.

Drawing my Smith and Wesson pistol, I urged Bucky forward in the column as the other Raiders were taking their time getting wet.

"What's your hurry?" Wesley asked with a sly grin as I impatiently pulled back on my horse's reins to slow him back down. The Raiders were all bunched up now, moving at different speeds, and looking in every direction except the one in which they should be going. And Bart, bless his sorrow-filled soul, looked terrified.

"If the Shayana got swords out, they got a reason. So, I'm going to have my pistol out and get across before something bad happens."

After a split-second of thought, the outlaw slid his Winchester rifle back into its scabbard and pulled out his pistol. Cocking the Colt Lightning's hammer back, he gave me an uneasy grin as our horses entered the water.

Splashing through, the river was about knee deep on the Shayana walking through with swords out and eyes on the water around their feet. I saw things swimming, but nothing that looked nearly as dangerous as the turtle from before.

One of the mounts got nipped by something.

Startled, it raced through the water, bucking his rider off.

A few men laughed, but the fellow closest to him helped him onto the back of his horse and carried him across riding double. Once on the other side, he got his horse back and found a small bite had been taken out of one of its rear legs.

Then we were across and wondering what the fuss had been about.

As if knowing our thoughts, Afton waded back into the murky water with his sword drawn and the tip slightly submerged. We all watched, curious as to what the tribesman leader was going to do. After a minute or two of watching him stand still, he finally thrust the blade forward, pinning something down to the floor of the river.

With a savage twist of the blade, Afton reached into the water, pulled his blade back, and raised one of the armored plated fishes we'd seen earlier. At about two feet long, they were frightfully nasty looking things with sharp teeth, thick overlapping shimmering scales, and beady little eyes. The Shayana tribesman quickly climbed out of the water and tossed the dead fish onto the grassy bank where it lay still, a large gash through its back from the sword.

"This bite thou mount." Kneeling, he pulled out a small blade that'd been tucked into his leather boot and slipped it between the fish's teeth to show us how jagged they were. "They swim by dozens, feasting on flesh." With visible disgust, he wiped the blade on his leggings and slipped it back into the sheath.

Lieutenant Heath looked annoyed. "Why didn't you mention these creatures *before* we crossed?" he growled.

"Then thy wouldn't cross," the Shayana leader grinned back broadly as though having enjoyed pulling one over on the officer.

"I don't like being tricked. Don't do that again."

"Certainly... Lieutenant," Afton replied, his grin replaced with a disgusted frown.

Wesley walked his horse beside mine as we continued north away from the river. Glancing over his back to make sure we could speak without being overheard, he leaned a bit towards me. "How much do you trust these Shayana people?"

"Not a whole lot. To be honest, I've always found them a bit suspicious."

"Well, I'm going to keep an eye on that Afton fellow. I got the feeling he may try to shit us after the Lieutenant calling him out like that."

"Not a bad idea." I stretched a bit, feeling the familiar tugging of the scarred skin across my back and shoulders as I nonchalantly looked around us. The Shayana were still staggered around us, and I noticed more than a few lustful looks from them towards our weapons and mounts. The Army had armed them with outdated single shot Springfield rifles. A better weapon than their homemade black powder muzzle loaders, but nothing as good as the repeating Winchesters we all carried.

"I'm betting if any of us get killed on this little excursion, the Shayana get to loot our dead."

I chuckled at Wesley's optimism.

I didn't know what to make of the Shayana. I know I didn't care for them that much, and they seemed to have their own agenda. It seemed like they were on the verge of becoming an enemy to us, especially if they decided they could use our weapons and equipment better than we could.

***

As we had been told, there were noticeable fresh improvements in the ape village compared to the last one I'd seen. And this one had the beginnings of being rebuilt to defend against another attack by mankind.

The Pinkertons were ruthless in their destruction, burning everything, and leaving scatterings of corpses in their wake.

Just like when they hit my home, I thought grimly as I peered out between the brush that hid the Raiders and our mounts.

And it was bothering me to no end that I hadn't managed to find the opportunity to kill Reydan yet.

I hadn't even seen him yet. He'd been holed up in Whitesberg the entire time, plotting the demise of the apes and hopefully fretting over my abrupt disappearance.

Good. Let the Yankee Raider sweat. I hoped he lay awake at night fearing my blade thrusting into his throat.

George's horse stamped its hooves, snapping a small twig and pulling me out of my grim daydream and back to the task at hand.

The village.

It had a large rock wall built around it; even from here you could see the scorch marks on the old rocks from where the village and crops surrounding it had been burned. It looked like rocks had been shifted and moved, giving an uneven appearance to the top of the wall. From behind the wall, I could see fresh fern thatching over the huts being worked on by apes, and there were dozens of two wheeled carts strewn about outside the wall and near the entrances. It appeared that the apes were not only beginning to rebuild the village, but also beginning to replant the fields.

Several apes were in sight, one pulling a cart, while the others worked with sticks to plant seeds in rows.

And one ape, a large fellow, thus probably the leader, stood nearby with a spear in hand and I could hear his guttural voice in the distance shouting at others.

Behind him, on the other side of the wall, I could see apes moving around.

"How many do you reckon?"

One of the Shayana near me shrugged.

"You didn't get a count?"

He shrugged again and pointed at Afton.

The Shayana leader was conferring with Lieutenant Heath, pointing at things below us in the village. I wondered if Afton knew, or if we were going blind against an unknown sized enemy force.

Which was pretty much stupid, all things considered.

I was glad we had Lieutenant Heath. I was certain that B Troop under Lieutenant Barlow wouldn't give a flip about information like that, and just go charging in... but our commander? He knew his stuff and I was willing to bet if he got a bad feeling about this attack, he'd back us off rather than risk sending his Raiders in to a certain death.

Our young officer gave a quick nod of his head to Afton and moved into position near the center of our line that stretched through the shadows of the trees that towered overhead. Looking up and down the line, he drew his sword from its scabbard.

It looked like the raid was on.

I checked the chamber on my loaned Winchester, a movement that had gone from habitual to almost obsessive since I'd left behind my beloved *Eighty-Six*. As there was last time I checked, there was still a cartridge in the chamber, ready to fire.

Wesley shifted the holster slightly on his waist. Seemingly content, he then pulled the pistol out slightly before letting it drop back in to make sure it was loose and available if needed.

He'd fought at the Battle of the Apes with me, using his pistols to great effect defending the Bucket O' Blood... until the end when he used those same guns to rob it.

But there was nothing to rob here.

Just some killing that needed to be done.

I knew I could count on Wesley for that.

Lieutenant Heath slashed his sword downward, chopping through a large fern in front of him as he led the charge into the scenic valley.

I kicked my heels against Bucky, and with a lunge the horse was off. We'd done a fair amount of shooting off horse back during our training, and while my borrowed mount seemed to handle it well enough, I wondered how he would do in a fight.

I supposed that I was about to find out.

With the thundering sound of hoof beats, we raced down through the tall grasses towards the reinforced village. Behind us came the Shayana on foot, running in a vain attempt to keep up and falling behind just the same.

Ahead of us the village came alive with guttural shouts from the apes who saw us first.

Grabbing weapons, they moved to their reinforced rock walls, or shifted behind the large two wheeled carts or circular village huts. The one pulling the cart dropped it and ran with long loping strides back behind the others as they all moved back to a defensive position in the village.

Within seconds, arrows began to rain down amongst us from the apes' powerful bows.

Several Raiders fired rifles, but at this distance and at this speed, I doubted they hit anything.

Still, even as arrows zipped past us and thudded into the ground, our horses ran forward.

Nearing the small stream, Bucky leapt across as I pulled the '73 Winchester into my shoulder. Gripping the rifle tightly to keep from dropping it, I waited until the iron sights fell on the closest ape and I squeezed the trigger.

Missed.

The bullet impacted against a large rock a foot to the right of the ape drawing back her bow. It made the hairy monkey duck back though, spoiling the shot and causing her to release the arrow into the ground a dozen feet in front of me.

Racking the lever under the rifle, I tried again, this time at another ape further back but more exposed from their position pressed against the rock wall.

Hit.

Spinning, the brown mottled ape dropped to a knee, clutching his chest.

Boom!

The ape collapsed as Wesley racked another round into his rifle.

"Good shot!"

"Quite right!" he replied happily.

Along the line of rushing Raiders, rifle fire crackled and boomed. Splinters of rock exploded from the walls, apes fell, and more arrows were unleashed in our direction.

Screaming, a horse to my right fell with a pair of arrows jutting from it. Bart was thrown to the ground with an ugly crash of horse and man flesh. But there was no stopping the skirmish line of racing horses; the Shayana would have to tend to him if he was still alive.

Wesley slammed the rifle into its scabbard and drew his pistol as we closed our distance to the village wall.

Turning Bucky's head, I rode him towards an open point in the rock piles encircling the village.

Out of the corner of my eye, I saw Wesley leap his horse over the wall while firing his pistol.

Show off.

An ape loomed before me in the opening. Stone axe raised high, yellowed canines bared in a throaty roar, the beast took my bullet at point blank range into the chest.

Before the monkey could drop, Bucky had slammed his white shoulder into the ape, squishing the barbaric ape between hundreds of pounds of horse flesh and large unforgiving rocks. If he wasn't quite dead from my bullet, I'd wager Bucky just polished him off.

Raiders raced around me, firing guns into the apes who were doing their dangedest to keep us from killing them.

I reared Bucky with a yank on the reins, slowing his gallop down and turning him to find Wesley.

We made it a dozen steps before an ape lunged out of a hut, jabbing with a spear that narrowly missed poking me in the face.

Swatting the weapon away with my rifle barrel, I drew the Smith and Wesson pistol with my right hand and fired downward into the ape.

The bullet went somewhere important in his shoulder. The monkey's left arm dropped the spear uselessly, but then he grabbed me by the leg with his good hand and tried to drag me from the saddle.

Kicking my free heel against Bucky, I tried to get the appaloosa to get me away, but the ape's grip was like iron, and I felt like my britches were about to split and my leg was about to be ripped off.

Giving up on trying to get away, I changed direction in the saddle and leaned towards the ape, jammed the muzzle of the pistol against his big sloping forehead and squeezed the trigger.

With a look of horrid surprise frozen on its face, the dead monkey let go of my leg and fell aside.

Slipping my boot back into the stirrup, I took a moment to shove the Smith and Wesson pistol back into its holster and rack another cartridge into the rifle. Then we rode forward, towards where Wesley leapt the wall.

A shrill screech I recognized all too well echoed through the village, followed by another.

Raptors.

Damn the luck.

A Shayana tribesman climbed over the wall to my left followed by another. They made it several steps before one of the little feathered bastards leapt on top of the first man.

Its rear claws scratched at the metal breast plate while the man fought to hold the snapping maw away from his face.

The other tribesman fired his Sharps into the raptor. It shrieked in pain as the bullet pierced through the dinosaur's body but continued to scrape its large toe claw against the metal plate, digging furrows in the forged metal.

I aimed my Winchester, but there was no shot. Even if I hit the thrashing, twisting birdlike dinosaur, the bullet could easily pass through its lithe body and into the man I was trying to save.

Dropping the empty single shot rifle in disgust, the free Shayana drew his sword and thrust it through the beast's body, twisted the blade savagely, and jerked it back with a spray of blood and feathers.

Satisfied there was one less raptor to worry about, I kicked my heels to Bucky and rode past.

By the time I found Wesley, he lay on his back with his horse nowhere to be seen and dodging a spear thrust by a monstrous black ape. I was out of ammunition in my rifle and my horse was bearing down on the pair locked in mortal combat at a speed too fast to stop.

Without thinking, I whipped Otto's tomahawk from my belt and dove off the charging appaloosa towards the big monkey.

The monster ape twisted and swung the spear sideways, hitting me across the chest and knocking my body into a rock hut. Bits of fresh thatching fell from the roof, making me sneeze painfully, while the ape turned back towards Wesley.

The outlaw-turned-Raider was still sprawled on his back, frantically dropping cartridges out of his pistol.

"Hey!" I shouted and threw a kick at the monkey's hairy leg. It was all I could reach and thumped uselessly against the back of his knee.

With what seemed like an annoyed growl, the ape turned and swatted me into the stream with a free hand.

Rolling in the cold water brought a crazed moment of refreshment that was immediately taken away by the pain across my face and chest.

Grabbing a rock, I hurled it at the back of the beast where it thumped against where I assumed a kidney would be. It bounced off harmlessly. But that's what happens when your strong hand has a Shaynee tomahawk in it and your left is not used to throwing anything.

The ape roared in angry frustration, turned back towards me, and pounded the spear against its chest.

"Oh, I'm sorry. Did I make you angry?" I shouted while climbing to my feet. I was hurt, wet, and now just plain mad. By his size I could tell he was of the ape's dangerous leader caste, but I didn't much care at that point; killing him was all I could think of.

"C'mon!" I screamed before raising the tomahawk overhead and charging the ape that stood a good two feet taller than me.

The hairy monkey swung the spear sideways again. The wooden shaft went over my head as I ducked and closed the distance between us.

Slamming my shoulder into his stomach, the monkey barely budged, until I swung the bullet holed tomahawk blade into its knee.

With a disgusting thud and crunch, I could tell I'd ruined the beast's knee cap.

Roaring in pain, the ape dropped.

I raised the tomahawk to try and decapitate him.

Jerking back the spear, the ape thrust it forward before I could move away.

With a fierce burst of pain, I felt the obsidian tip hit my black vest and shatter into tiny black bits of stone against the dragon scales.

Falling backwards, I lost Otto's tomahawk.

Thrashing desperately, I tried to get the Smith and Wesson free of its holster. Even wet, the weapon would still fire. God bless metallic cartridges.

Assuming I could get the gun out quickly enough. It was hung up underneath me.

Bam-Bam-Bam!

Like rolling thunder, bullets burst forth from Wesley's pistol and into the back of the ape.

Pitching forward, the black-haired ape fell onto his face. Then, with a final shudder, the monkey twitched violently and lay still.

Standing, Wesley put another round into the corpse to make sure.

With his free hand, he helped me up. "How many times must I save your life?" he said with a sly grin before dumping out cartridges and beginning to reload his gun.

Picking up Otto's tomahawk, I slipped it back into my belt. Around us, the gunfire was tapering off to a few occasional booms. "Pretty sure I saved yours just before you saved mine," I told him.

"Beginner's luck."

Ignoring him, I nudged the ape leader's corpse with the wet toe of my boot. "That's a good kill."

Afton ran between us, bloodied sword held low as he looked for more apes to slay. Behind him came two more of the Shayana tribesmen, one limping slightly but both alert as they moved through the village.

Drawing my pistol, I broke the pistol open and dumped the empty cartridges onto the ground. Smith and Wesson Number 3s like mine were quick to reload with their break open and eject design. If I hadn't been so attached to my matching Colt Peacemakers, I'd have gone to these a long time ago.

Snapping the pistol shut, I followed Wesley's lead as we began carefully stalking through the village on foot.

We came across several dead apes and a single wounded Raider who was trying to coax his horse to stop moving long enough to mount.

Grabbing the reins, Wesley held the horse in place as I helped the man climb back into the saddle.

"You haven't seen my appaloosa, have you?" I asked him.

"No, but thanks for the hand, Johnson." He looked at my companion, then nodded towards a dead she-ape, "Wesley, I saw your mount. It trampled that one as it ran by."

"Now comes the fun part, rounding all the damned horses up," I grumbled to myself.

The outlaw-turned-Raider patted the horse on its reddish colored flank, "Thanks, Talon."

He nodded and rode away.

"Talon," I said as we walked towards where we assumed the center of the village was. "That can't be his real name."

"It's not, he picked it when he signed up. He told me Talon sounded a lot better than his real one. Which must have been bad as he wouldn't tell me what it was."

I knew all too well about being branded with a bad name. I stepped over an ape corpse lying in the fire. The scent of burning hair and flesh stung my nostrils as the wind shifted the smoke in a swirl around me.

Wesley had spent a lot more time with the other Raiders, learning their names and such.

But not me.

No. I was too intent on my true purpose in Prehistoria to sit around fires and joke.

So, I stayed the loner. Going to bed early as the others stayed up and talked. Keeping an eye out for anyone who may recognize me. Trying to stay unseen as much as possible. It meant I didn't bond as deeply as Wesley with any of the other Raiders, but that was fine with me.

Because, at some point, I was going to betray them all when I snuck off to kill the railroad tycoon.

I just needed an opportunity.

Small pterodactyls were beginning to land around us to feast on the dead. The long beaked prehistoric buzzards chirped and screeched at each other as they hopped on the rock walls and thatched huts.

Spying a growing group of Raiders, mounts, and Shayanas near the center of the village, I holstered my pistol.

"Looks like we win," Wesley said softly.

"Appears so. Let's see who we lost. I saw Bart go down earlier when his horse took a couple arrows."

Wesley gestured with his free hand while his other stayed glued to the pistol grip. He wasn't taking any chances. "He seems alright."

Sure enough, there was Bart in the back of the group. His hat was held in hand, and there was a large knot forming on his forehead with a trickle of blood that ran down around his nose and into his stubbled beard.

Walking through the growing crowd, I found someone holding Bucky's reins and took them. "Thanks," I said sincerely.

"Un-huh," the Raider said indifferently. I noticed a splash of blood across his chest and arm. It looked like ape blood since he didn't appear wounded.

Afton approached with his Shayana tribesmen in tow. Most of them looked satisfied. I figured the ones who were frowning were the ones who didn't get to kill anything. The tribal leader had something in his hand that he was fooling with. Squinting, I saw several freshly cut ears in his red smeared hands.

He noticed me looking and grinned toothily.

Lieutenant Heath moved to the center of the group and propped his boot on a large flat rock that looked like it'd been used to grind grain.

"Gentlemen," he said loudly. Then, nodding at Afton, he added, "And our Shayana brethren... You did good. A few wounds that will heal, but no deaths on our side. We caught the apes with their hairy butts out and spanked them good."

The Raiders cheered and a few fired shots into the sky as the Shayana raised bloodied swords.

"Stop shooting in the air, you jackasses," Heath chuckled while waving his hands at everyone to lower their weapons. "Those bullets are going to come down somewhere. Collect your mounts, ready your weapons, and we move in twenty minutes. Except you, Bart, since your horse is dead, you'll ride double with George. Heaven knows that Chinaman can't weigh more than half of a white man."

George grinned from under his wide brimmed hat and nodded.

I was glad we'd all survived, but especially George. He'd turned into something of a mascot for our unit.

"And I see our silent friend, Johnson Brown, managed to take a bath while our honorable allies were taking ears." The Lieutenant chuckled with the others as he stepped down from the rock and moved among us, slapping backs and congratulating everyone on a well performed raid.

A commotion arose behind us. Turning, we watched a pair of Shayana tribesmen walk a couple of small apes into sight. The young apes' hands were bound, and their feet restricted with short lengths of rope to keep them from running away. Around their necks were nooses, tied to tighten if they tried to pull away from the men walking them into the group at gun point.

The one in front, a female about five feet tall, bared her canines and growled in defiance. The second, a male youngster, stared at the ground, defeated. I didn't know how old they were, but they looked little.

"Shit," I thought to myself.

Slaves.

"What's this?" Lieutenant Heath asked in surprise.

"Workers," Afton grumbled as he stepped forward and grabbed the female by the ear with one hand and drew a small blade with the other.

"Whoa there," I said as I pushed through the crowd. "No need for that."

The leader of the tribesman ignored me and sliced off the ape's right ear.

She roared and twisted, the noose tightening around her hairy neck as she raised her hands to grab at the Shayana man holding her ear triumphantly overhead for everyone to see.

"What a bastard," I heard Wesley uncharacteristically swear from the crowd.

"Let's kill them apes!" a Raider shouted.

"Yeah!" another cried as he pushed through the crowd eagerly. This one was a large sized fellow, big on brawn but shy on brains and named 'Fred'. "The Pinkertons had it right. Kill them all! Teach them not to mess with the white man!" He stopped for a moment, looking chagrined. "Sorry, George," Fred mumbled to the Chinese Raider.

"No sorry. Kill ape!" the little fellow repeated excitedly.

"Yeah! Even George wants to execute them!" Fred shouted, shaking his Winchester rifle overhead.

The bloodlust was strong with this crowd.

Heath put a stop to it.

Holding his arms in the air, he stepped between the apes and the Raiders. "No. If the Shayana want them alive, we'll honor our allies' wishes."

The Raiders mumbled dejectedly.

"Oh shut up. You'll get to kill more of them," the Lieutenant pulled a gold watch from his pocket and flipped it open.

He made a show of checking the time. "You got fifteen minutes left! Get to saddlin' up!"

We got moving while a thin trickle of blood ran down the side of the she-ape's black face.

***

Traveling to and from the raid took longer than expected. And as such, we had to make camp in the woods as Lieutenant Heath didn't want to go riding the last few hours in the dark.

Having traveled through Prehistoria at night after the fall of Fort Jipson, I couldn't blame him.

This was a scary damn place in the sunlight. At night it was just plain terrifying.

None of us had much for the way of gear, certainly not canvas tarps to make tents. Instead, we just rolled out our slickers and lay down with weapons at hand beside some big fires at fifty percent watch. Meaning half of us were awake and standing post while the other half cradled our rifles and tried to get some shut eye without being eaten.

But not me; I couldn't sleep.

Prehistoria is hot and humid, making for terrible sleeping conditions. And then you have all the terrifying sounds out there in the darkness that made your imagination run wild.

Laying on my slicker, one side backed up against a large-sized rock to give me some manner of shelter from an attack, all I could think about were those two stupid ape youngsters that'd gotten caught.

I'd learned from one of the Shayana tribesmen that they'd been hidden in one of the huts. One, or more, of the big apes had cared enough to rip thatching down from the roof and cover them up during the brief battle.

They were lucky we weren't Pinkertons, or we'd have fired the huts along with everything else in the village and burned them alive.

Unfortunately for them, they were still unlucky enough that they were captured by the Shayana.

Now they'd spend the rest of their short lives as slaves for the tribesmen, being whipped and worked to death on the top of their mountain retreat. Until they grew too large. Then they'd be thrown over the side to their death before they could become a threat to their masters.

I gently eased my Winchester rifle around slightly; the stock was digging into my shoulder from where it lay within quick reach. As I shifted the weapon, I tried to fight against the growing urge inside of me to do something about it.

But the longer I lay there, staring at the twisting pillars of smoke that rose from flickering flame towards the towering trees overheard, the more the urge grew.

Annoyed with myself, I rolled onto my side and pressed my back against the rock while closing my eyes. I knew I needed to catch what little sleep I could while I could. In a few hours it'd be my turn to stand post.

One of the little brown rat-like creatures that were everywhere over here ran across the rock, chittering unhappily. Or maybe it was happily. The hell if I knew.

I closed my eyes and steadied my breathing.

Skyla.

I wondered how she was doing. If she was getting around well, if she needed anything. Strangely, I trusted Otto now that we were blood brothers. The Indian would take care of her.

And as long as she stayed with the Shaynee, she should be safe from Reydan. I doubted the Pinkertons would dare attack the Indians, at least outright. Not now while they were basically a national treasure and talked about in every newspaper across the country in awe of their red skinned achievements. Otto's fame from killing a dragon single-handedly probably saved his entire tribe from being forced onto some horrid reservation somewhere.

Skyla.

My thoughts kept going back to her.

I missed my lovely paleontologist something fierce.

And then my thoughts turned to Reydan.

What a bastard.

I wondered what sort of chaos Skyla's father had raised after he found out about his daughter being shot and their family butler-turned-guardian being murdered. He'd probably be out for blood as well. The legal kind of blood.

And that sort of trouble could be even worse than the trickle out of your veins and onto the ground kind of blood.

Smiling to myself, I thought of what might have happened when Morgan Stratten and Otto met. That'd have been a meeting worth watching.

I blinked.

Damn it all.

Skyla would never forgive me if I didn't do something about those apes.

Sitting up slowly, I leaned against the rock and began pulling my boots off.

Luckily for me, I'd hunkered down near the outside of the camp. It was a matter of trading safety for protection. I felt like having the big rock against me was more important than being in the center of the camp near a fire.

That meant that I was in relative darkness as I prepared to possibly start a war.

Socked feet sprawled out before me as I quietly shuffled some things around. My rifle went out of sight, tucked under my slicker towards the rock.

I'd be going Indian on this little attempt. Which meant going lightly armed and stealthy.

There wasn't much I could do if someone noticed an empty sleeping spot. Hopefully they'd think I went for a quick bathroom trip. But if they saw I'd left a rifle behind, someone might get concerned and the whole jig could be up.

My boots, I stuffed under my saddle that I'd been using as a makeshift pillow. From the saddle bags, I pulled out my secret weapon and slipped it into a pocket.

Making sure the Shaynee tomahawk and Smith and Wesson pistol were loose on my belt and ready to grab should the need arrive, I slowly slinked into the darkness in a crouch.

Several steps into the darkness, I saw the red tipped flow of a cigarillo flare from someone taking a drag.

"Where you headed?" Wesley whispered.

Sighing at being caught, I stood and moved closer to the little glow.

"Lose your rifle?" He paused and I saw his hat tip down slightly as he looked me over. The thin cigarillo was shifted to point at my feet. "And your boots as well? If I didn't know better, I'd say you were up to no good tonight."

"That's right."

He took another drag as he mulled over the possibilities.

"Need a hand?" he finally asked.

"Not tonight."

"Good luck then." He dropped the cigarette and ground it out with the toe of his boot before rising and stretching slightly. Without another word or glance, he casually walked back towards the center of the camp where I knew he'd set up his sleeping spot.

I waited, smelling the scent of his smoke in the air while my eyes adjusted to the darkness. I shouldn't have been surprised by Wesley. I was getting careless.

That would get me killed if I didn't pay attention.

After several minutes my eyes adjusted, and I carefully made my way towards the Shayana camp with a newfound sense of carefulness. My steps were light, and the socks helped me navigate through the darkness without breaking any twigs or rolling stones.

I was helped by the fact that two of the Raiders posted for guard duty were whispering back and forth and chuckling at whatever was being said while watching away from our camp. They didn't care what was going on in the camp behind them, just that nothing broke through and ate us.

Still, I had to get past them because unfortunately, they had the best place to cross undetected.

Crouching behind several ferns, I waited for my opportunity while slowly sliding the tomahawk out of my belt.

I didn't have to wait long.

One of the Raiders, I recognized him as Talon when he turned his head to spit, declared that he had to take a leak. The pair laughed one more time, then split apart and went their own ways.

Still crouching, I quickly made my way through the ferns, brushing aside the leaves with the handle of Ashley's tomahawk.

Without any ceremony, I left our camp and moved towards the Shayana's.

Theirs was close to ours but separated by about fifty yards.

I don't know why they set their camp apart from us. Lieutenant Heath hadn't bothered telling any of us, but secretly I wondered if it was because of the horses.

The tribesmen had disdain for our domesticated mounts, feeling that the animals were not sturdy enough to survive long enough on this side to bother using and that they'd draw unwanted attention from predators.

Smoke from the Shayana's single large fire drifted into my face, and I stifled a cough while dropping to a knee to get below it.

They were cooking something though.

Something… meaty.

The scent made my stomach rumble after the cold meal of hard tack, jerked meat, and lukewarm water I had enjoyed earlier.

Military rations are never anything to write home about. Unless it's to write home about how they are terrible. That's a fact that has and will always stand the test of time.

I moved slightly, tilting my head to look through a screen of brush for any guards.

There weren't any that I could see.

But, after counting heads, I realized they were all around the fire except for two.

Which meant somewhere in the darkness around me, there were two lethal tribesmen armed with rifles and swords that they were not afraid to use.

That wasn't good.

Shifting my crouch slightly, I started to circle the camp looking for guards or the young apes.

A twig snapped beneath my socked foot, and I froze while mentally swearing at the muffled sound.

To my right I heard the soft scraping of leather against branches.

I was deep in the shadows and doubted that anyone could see me, but still didn't dare move anything except to rotate the tomahawk around in my hand so the forged blade was pointed upwards.

There.

A glint of firelight on a steel breastplate as the man moved closer to me.

He still hadn't seen me, and I waited while my heart pounded in my ears.

The tribesman slowly stepped in front of me, unaware that I was behind him.

I swung and hit him over the head with the back end of the Shaynee weapon.

He crumpled, falling against my leg, and sliding to the ground with only a small ding of his sheathed sword and his armor colliding.

Moving only my eyes, I looked at the campfire. No one seemed to notice that I'd possibly just killed one of theirs.

Lowering myself to a squatting position, I used my free hand to find the man's face. Touching his lips, I could faintly feel breath blowing out on my hand. That was good. I'd gotten lucky with that swing and knocked him out.

Because I certainly wasn't willing to commit murder to save a pair of apes.

Stepping over the tribesman, I stalked around the edge of the fire, watching for the other missing man and the apes.

And the apes I found.

Moving as stealthily as possible, I slid up beside them.

They'd been tied with their backs to a thick tree. Coils of rope were wrapped around them, and their hands were tied separately behind them.

The female ape had been gagged with a piece of rope and cloth. She glared at me with a look that could kill. The male, he appeared defeated still and stared at the ground as though awaiting an execution.

From my pocket I produced a chipped obsidian spear point. I'd hacked it off the thick shaft back at the village after the raid, hoping to give it to Skyla's father when I saw him.

But this use would work.

Ignoring the subdued boy ape, I slipped the spear tip into the female's hand. She still had some fight left in her.

Her eyes were black in the darkness of the forest, but I thought I saw her large brow move downwards in puzzlement.

Not knowing what else to do, I gave her a pat on the shoulder.

It was up to her now.

I just hoped she would make the decision to flee instead of killing all the tribesmen.

Or the Raiders.

Or me.

Her hand moved slightly as she began working the sharpened edge against the ropes.

It would take her a while to cut through them, giving me plenty of time to return to my spot before she broke free.

Turning away, I quietly began making my way through the brush back towards the Raider camp.

***

I was standing post when they found the body.

Afton came rushing to our camp, shouting angrily, and firing his rifle into the air to wake us.

He raced right by me, his ape ear necklace bouncing against his armor.

Our camp came alive at the shot.

There was lots of confusion and shouting and even a couple of guns were fired off into the darkness before things simmered down.

Lieutenant Heath spoke with the Shayana leader for some time. Word spread quickly that they'd found a dead tribesman lying in the brush, with several compys gnawing on the corpse.

I did my best to keep the surprise off my face when Talon told me the news.

Damn it all. I'd killed the man, after all.

Or the scavenger compys had while he was knocked out.

Either way, his blood was on my hands.

The thought reminded me, and I quickly looked down at the tomahawk in my belt. There was a smudge of dried blood on the backside of the weapon. As nonchalantly as possible, I rubbed it clean with spit on my fingers.

The apes were gone too. Both of them.

Afton wanted to go after them, believing that they had killed the Shayana standing guard to escape and that they couldn't have gotten far.

Thankfully, Lieutenant Heath refused and stated that the risk was too great and that their escaped slaves were none of our business.

Afton stormed away, took half of his men, and darted off into the darkness towards the ape village we'd attacked as our camp settled back down. I hoped the young apes had a good enough lead time and weren't stupid enough to head back to where they'd been captured.

By the time dawn broke, I was exhausted. Stretching the scarred flesh on my back, I yawned, then flicked a little green bug off my rifle's stock. When I wasn't getting scared half to death by random noises in the forest, I was thinking repeatedly about how I killed a man to save a pair of apes.

What had I been thinking?

Was that Shayana tribesman's life worth a couple of hairy youngsters' lives that we may face in battle one day?

I wasn't sure.

And it bothered me that I seemed okay with how last night worked out.

But I'd never been a big fan of the Shayana.

Wesley moved over to my position. I hadn't seen or talked to him since he caught me last night.

"Ready to move out?" he asked casually with the Winchester rifle cradled in his arms.

"Yeah."

Our eyes met and I wondered what he was thinking.

"Good morning, fellow Raiders!" Talon said, pushing through some thick ferns to where we stood and interrupting any possible discussion between myself and the gunman in hiding.

"Mornin'," Wesley replied.

"This has been quite the trip, hasn't it?" The stocky Raider munched on a piece of hardtack, bits of the hardened biscuit spewing from his mouth as he talked. "I got two kills yesterday." He raised his rifle to show us the fresh grooves that had been carved into the stock.

I tried not to frown.

"That's a fine start, Talon," Wesley said, but I could tell the counting of kills bothered him as well.

If only Talon knew who he was bragging to. Between the outlaw and I, we'd have filled two types of graveyards. One of men and another full of apes.

"I heard you guys got the leader."

"Yup."

"Should have taken his thumbs." He patted his pocket. "I took the ones from mine."

"I don't think they're paying bounty for dead apes on this side, just the other. And I think most of them got wiped out when they attacked Fort York a few months back."

Talon sighed, pulled the pair of thumb stumps out and tossed them into the brush in disgust. "Well damn. I was gonna use the money to help buy this rifle. Growing up, we never had anything so nice as this." He looked down at the rifle in his hand. "All we had was a rusted-out scatter gun held together with wire and cuss words."

"Show the Quartermaster the carved kills," I teased with a smirk. "Maybe he'll cut you a discount."

Shaking his head, the Raider didn't reply but walked away looking dejected.

"You need to bond with these men," Wesley warned.

"No. I don't."

"You'll need them to help keep you alive until you get your chance. Try it. They aren't so bad."

Lieutenant Heath shouted from behind us for the guards to come in.

"Wesley. I'm going to betray these men when I leave to kill Reydan. I'd rather not get close to any of them."

"Just me then, huh?"

"You're the only ally and confidant I've got right now. That's why I'm trying so hard to keep you alive."

He chuckled as we headed back.

The Lieutenant was standing with his back leaning against a tree and the Raiders spread out in a semi-circle in front of him. Next to him stood Afton and another Shayana. They must have just returned.

I felt a knot of dread fill my stomach.

Wesley and I were the last ones to arrive, and we stood in the back of the group. I glanced over at the horses, wondering how quickly I could get to Bucky. Immediately I knew that was a foolish thought, my appaloosa was unsaddled, and I was no Indian when it came to riding without one. That blasted cantankerous horse would throw me in a split-second if I tried to mount him without a saddle.

No, whatever happened was going to happen. I realized my hand had settled on the butt of the Smith and Wesson pistol and I moved it away. There'd be no shooting. No more men would die because of those apes.

"Gents, as you all know, we lost a Shayana tribesman last night," Heath started, and I held my breath.

Wesley took a couple of casual steps away from me, nonchalantly acting as though he was trying to get a better view through the crowd. But I knew that he was just trying to put distance between us.

"Because a pair of apes got free."

I let the air out of my lungs slowly, daring to believe that they still thought the death of the tribesman was from them.

"It looks like they cut the rope with something. From the frayed edges, probably a sharp rock. As they escaped, they knocked..." he looked at Afton.

"Amos," Afton said angrily.

"Amos," the Lieutenant repeated the name before continuing, "over the head, killing him. Then the damn compys got to him and chewed him up pretty good before he was found. Gents," he stepped away from the tree, his expression serious, "we must be more careful out here. With the exception of Bart's brother, we had a successful raid that culminated in the killing of twenty-six apes and a couple of raptors with only a dead horse to show for it... then we lose our second man on the return trip. We need to tighten it up, pay attention, and shoot first. No questions asked. You see something go bump in the night, if it's hairy or fanged or even remotely dangerous looking, you kill it!"

He clasped Afton on the shoulder, "We are sorry for the loss of your man. But grateful for his sacrifice in helping us to defeat the bloodthirsty apes. He will be long remembered."

I swallowed hard, feeling extremely uncomfortable during the entire speech.

Wesley shifted back beside me, shrugging at the dirty look I gave him.

***

We left the Shayana at the campsite. As we rode away, they gathered wood for a funeral pyre for the man I'd killed.

Guilt gnawed at me, and it took a lot of effort to pay attention to the dangerous surroundings without becoming lost in my thoughts.

We reached the river crossing, and that bastard turtle was washed up in the shallow water against the muddy embankment.

The large prehistoric beast appeared to have died from the dynamite and half a dozen pterodactyls of varying sizes from small dogs to one the size of a horse was pecking at the open wounds on its back from the blast. Others wrenched off pieces of flesh from the exposed fins and head.

"Looks like the Lieutenant beat the monster after all," Talon said wryly.

Bart let out an angry growl from the back of George's horse and slipped down. Drawing his pistol, he marched to the edge of the riverbank and emptied the gun into the partially devoured head of the massive snapping turtle. Bullets puckered small holes in the side of its large greenish-black face, blowing out one glazed over eyeball and chipping a chunk off its hooked beak.

The small leathery birds flew away with angry screeches. The big pterodactyl carried a ragged strip of turtle meat the length of my leg hanging from its mouth as it flapped its enormous wings and moved to the far side of the riverbank to eat in peace.

Lowering his pistol, Bart dumped out the empty cartridges from the cylinder.

Lieutenant Heath swore. "You finished?" he called out to the avenging Raider.

"Yeah! I am!" Bart shouted back.

"Then get back on George's horse, we've got to find another place to cross. If you hadn't noticed, that turtle is being chewed up under the water by those ghastly flesh-eating fish. We ride in there, we'll lose men and mounts. I'm not risking that." He looked downstream thoughtfully. "Since we've already ridden the other way coming here, and without the Shayana to tell us where to cross, we're on our own." He turned his horse's head and began walking it downstream along the grassy bank. "Let's go!"

Tapping my heels against Bucky, Wesley and I rode after him. We were at the front of the column this morning with the rest of the Raiders behind us.

After a long hour of riding through the sweltering heat and humidity, getting tormented by river bugs that attacked us in thick swarms to suck our blood, the Lieutenant finally found a place that looked good to cross. The water was slow, but the river wide. And while we could see the bottom, it still looked significantly deeper than the previous crossing place.

Slowing his horse to a stop, Heath turned around to face us.

"Johnson, Wesley, you're up."

"Is this a bad time to tell you I can't swim?" Wesley quipped.

"Are you serious?" the Lieutenant said with a frown.

"Sort of." Wesley chewed on his lower lip. "I can kind of doggy paddle if need be."

"For crying out loud, Wesley," I said. "Just ride upstream of me and if you fall off, grab onto Bucky."

Shaking his head in disgust, the outlaw tapped heels to his mount and walked him down the riverbank and into the water. "I'd rather die wet, than live embarrassed," he called over his shoulder.

Chuckling, Bucky and I followed him while keeping one eye on anything in the water and one eye on the opposite bank.

The water was warm, and as Wesley said, wet. It sloshed against my appaloosa and soaked my boots and pant legs. I held tight to the reins, worried that Bucky's hooves might slip on an algae-covered rock beneath the water and send us for a dip. But the horse walked gamely through the water.

The outlaw-turned-Raider stayed slightly ahead of me and upstream. I didn't have a rope on my saddle, but I figured we might be able to grab him should he fall off.

He didn't though.

Instead, he got to the other side, shook his legs to get some of the water off, and grinned at me happily as we rode around a handful of large rocks and into the forested river edge.

I didn't see anything ape-like or hungry and waved my hat back at the Lieutenant that it was safe to send everyone else over.

"Hey Jed, you see these tracks?" Wesley asked to my left. There was a pair of large trees between us, and I could only make out the back half of his horse.

Riding over, I dismounted and studied the imprints in the ground.

Big.

Really big.

Three toed and pressed deep.

Not for the first time I wished that Skyla was with me. At times, I'd have even take Oscar back from the dead for his knowledge. They'd know what type of dinosaur might have made these. But they weren't here. One was wounded and one was dead.

"I would say we should be worried, but I'm always worried," I admitted.

Wesley looked back into the river, watching the column of Raiders moving towards us slowly. "You want to talk about last night?" he asked softly while pulling a cigarillo from his pocket and lighting it with a match.

"I thought we were talking about these tracks," I ran a finger around the edge. They were fresh, probably within ten to twenty minutes ago.

"I was thinking maybe you'd like to talk about that dead tribesman?"

"He was breathing when I left him."

"Don't matter to me. I don't care for slavers." He fixed me with a glare that reminded me very much of a similar look I'd seen on Wolverine Wade's face before. "I just want to make certain your head is screwed on straight. I don't need you moping about and getting us killed over that fella."

"You're all heart, but I'm fine." I wiped the dirt off my hands and stared at the tracks. "We need to tell the Lieutenant when he gets here. This thing might still be nearby."

Our commanding officer reached the bank as I mounted Bucky and dealt with his horseshit of trying to throw me to the ground. He'd gotten better, a lot better, but he still had his moments. Twisting his head about, I stopped him when we were facing the Lieutenant.

He had a wry grin. "You know, Johnson, we could try to find you a better horse."

"This is all I can afford until we get paid," I told him the half-truth easily. The real truth was, Jedidiah Huckleberry Smith was a fairly well-off fellow, but Johnson Brown? Broke and down on his luck. That's why he was here. And that's the story I was sticking too. I changed subjects. "Wesley found some tracks," I pointed at them. "Big ones."

While the other Raiders crossed, Heath looked over the tracks.

"Whatever it is, I don't want to face it without a solid defensive position and some Gatlings. We'll get moving in a minute. Keep your eyes open. If we cross it and it's hungry, we'll have to run."

"Yes, sir," Wesley and I both said together.

A ferocious roar echoed through the trees, coming from somewhere deeper in the forest.

"That's a bit ominous," Heath said before twisting in his saddle and waving his hat at the last couple of riders in the water to get moving.

In a few minutes we were back in a column, riding upstream and soon we were headed back along our old path towards the Shimmer.

***

We returned to no fanfare. Just a slow ride into the heavily guarded encampment that encircled the Shimmer.

The only people that seemed to care we were back, were the other Raiders. They watched us, knowing that we were the first of our experiment to be battle tested. And with Lieutenant Heath at the front of our column, we rode back victorious.

Governor Fredrick von Holsak sat on his horse watching us ride in. I was too far away to be recognized in my disguise, but his spectacles twinkled in the sunlight as he looked over our column.

I figured my friend would be pleased. We did as our name said, we raided. Successfully.

After watering, brushing, and turning our mounts loose in the corral, we sat under the shade and cleaned our weapons. Most men removed their hats and wiped sweat from their brows. I left mine on. Wesley was sitting beside me, and he did the same.

I was starting to think that every man who left their hat on had a wanted poster and every man who took their hat off didn't. If that was the case, I'd say about twenty-five percent of us were bad men.

A young fellow walked in front of our group. He was dressed like an Easterner with white shirt and black trousers. There was a bag strapped over his shoulder with a canteen and a pistol in a flap holster. The gun he wore awkwardly as though it didn't suit him, or he hadn't grown used to it being there yet.

Wesley nudged me with his elbow. "I heard about this kid. He tried to sign up as a Raider. Almost made it too, until Lieutenant Barlow tricked him into admitting he wasn't sixteen yet."

"Pretty gutsy."

"Smart as a whip too. You should hear him talk about dinosaurs."

I eyeballed the kid, trying to figure him out. "Is that why they let him stay?"

"Yes. But the Captain would only let him cross the Shimmer if he was armed."

"Does he know how to use it?" I asked skeptically.

"I hope so."

Tipping his hat at the group of tired and sweaty men, he perched on a convenient log stump that'd been rolled in front of us. After taking a sip of water from his canteen, he pulled out a leather-bound notebook and a piece of pencil from the bag.

"Good afternoon. My name is Irving, and I was told that you encountered several beasts on your attack, and I'd like to hear about them. Lieutenant Heath has stated that they were a prehistoric turtle and an unseen creature that left a large footprint."

He looked up, peering at us with brown eyes from beneath the brim of his hat. "Can any of you draw?"

No one said anything.

He waited a moment longer, tapping the pencil against his leg as though he had all day. "No one?"

I looked around; everyone was tired and worn out from riding. Nobody was going to offer any help when there was weapon and gear cleaning to do, but I was finished with mine and just rubbing oil on the blued steel barrel to add a little rust preventative for this damned Prehistoria weather.

Slowly, I raised my hand. "I can draw, a little."

Irving looked at me skeptically. "And you saw both the tracks and the turtle?"

"Yes."

With a smile, he held out the book and stub of pencil. "Please draw them to the best of your recollection."

Placing the Winchester rifle down on the rolled out blanket Wesley and I were using to clean on, I rose and walked over to the kid.

He handed me the pencil and then the book.

Walking back to my place, I sat down, balanced the leatherbound book on my lap and began to sketch quickly. I'd never been the best at drawing, I was lucky I had the ability to draw stick figures. But the three toed footprint was pretty easy to draw from memory and since I'd been the one to dismount and look at it, I was able to give rough measurements on the length, width, and depth of the track.

That damn turtle was another story. I'd never gotten a good look at it during the attack, but I could recall seeing it dead and washed up a handful of hours ago. The problem was trying to make it look right.

I sketched, smudged some lead around, then drew some more.

Finally, giving up, I got up and passed the book back over.

He smiled as he took it. "Thank you."

"You're welcome, kid." I stood there, looking back at our group. Most of them had finished their weapons and had wandered off to find food. Even Wesley had abandoned me to my poorly attempted drawings. I wasn't hungry and didn't really know what to do with myself.

Irving had put the book away and was looking at me as though wondering why I was still standing there.

An idea struck me.

"Hey, you know how to use that thing?" I gestured at the pistol on his side.

He shrugged with one shoulder. "No. They just told me I had to wear it."

"Okay." I offered Irving a hand to help him up. "What do you say I show you?"

"Sure, mister!"

"Name's Johnson, Johnson Brown."

***

It took some effort, but I was able to get Irving and myself permission to go back through the Shimmer to use the range that'd been built by idle soldier hands at Fort York.

Once we crossed, I almost immediately regretted it. It was freezing cold compared to the hot, sweltering climate of Prehistoria. But I'd made the kid a promise and was going to see it through.

Luckily, Lieutenant Heath loaned me a coat and Irving had his own. I could have gotten mine back from the Quartermaster who was holding on to all of our things from the other side, but that would have taken too long and the talkative, portly fellow would have wanted to hear all about our raid.

No thanks.

But the coat still didn't help my cold hands as much as the fur lined gloves I owned would have.

Winter had arrived while we'd been training, and I immediately wished that I was curled up in a warm teepee with Skyla and a bunch of buffalo hides instead of out here trying to avenge her and Charles.

And as soon as that thought crossed my mind, I hardened my resolve. Charles would have done the same for me had I been killed instead of him; I was certain of it. *Reydan needed to die.* That was my mantra until he stopped breathing.

Some pistol practice would be a nice help. I'd gotten slack during the exhausting training of being a Raider the last few weeks and a refresher would be useful.

We spent a couple hours shooting together. And like most range trips with people, you either learn to like them or dislike them quickly. And Irving, I liked. He was like Wesley said, smart as a whip. A good solid learner that soaked up knowledge of firearm safety and use like a handkerchief dipped into spring water. Before long he was hitting the targets with passable regularity. Then we moved on to practice drawing.

A flap holster is absolute garbage for drawing quickly. But it's what Irving had, so it's what we practiced with.

Right off the bat he struggled with getting it out.

"Best thing I can tell you, kid, is to keep that flap uncinched. That way, whenever you need to draw, you just fling that flap back and there's the grip of the gun waiting for you. Here, uncinch it and give it a try."

He freed the flap and straightened his shoulders, looking at the makeshift targets at the end of the range.

"And…. Draw!"

He drew and fired, much quicker and smoother than before, then half-turned to me with a grin. "How was that?"

"Well, you won't be a gun slinger anytime soon, but you'll be able to defend yourself, given a chance."

The kid looked pleased.

"Tell me, Irving. Why are you here?" I asked while breaking the top open on the Smith and Wesson pistol and dumping out the empty cartridges onto the cold ground.

His pleased look turned to one of confusion. "Because you asked me to come."

"Not here, here. I meant over there," I jerked my head towards the fortified tunnel entrance to the Shimmer, "in Prehistoria."

Behind us, I heard the train blow a sharp whistle as it approached the fort. We'd become so used to hearing the trains on the other side serving raw materials to Whitesberg that we ignored them. But here, on this side, I was a bit more on edge from the risk I was taking.

"I like dinosaurs."

I stopped putting fresh cartridges into the revolver's cylinder and looked at him.

"What do you mean, you 'like' dinosaurs?"

"When I was a kid, I found one. A fossilized skull, I mean. Not an actual dinosaur."

"You found a skull? Of what kind?"

"Spinosauridae. It was mostly intact and massive. About as long as you are tall."

"Good grief. What sort of dinosaur is that?"

Irving thought for a moment. "Big meat eater, one of the largest ever found. At the time, my family was in Africa as missionaries to bring Christ to the jungle people. But once we brought it home, I wanted to learn as much as I could about them. I came from a," he glanced around and lowered his voice, "rather wealthy family who were understanding of my devotion to creatures from the past. And once I read about Jedidiah Huckleberry Smith's discovery in the New York Times, I knew I had to come out here and meet him and see the other side for myself. I ran away from home with my savings, waited in town for a few weeks, then heard the bad news. After that, I decided to do what he'd have done: sign up for the Raiders and see Prehistoria for myself."

"You said you heard 'the bad news' about this Jedidiah fellow…" I stared at him. "What bad news?"

"That his farm had been put to the torch and he was missing." He shrugged with one shoulder. "Most people seem to think he's dead, but I think he's alive."

I slipped the final cartridge into the cylinder and closed the top of the pistol awkwardly. Inwardly I cursed. I needed more practice with these fancy break-top revolvers. I focused back on the discussion at hand.

"Why do you think he's alive?"

"Because he's too tough to die. He's a hero. Well. Sort of. Most civilians think so, and the Army seems to like him, but not the Pinkertons. They hate him. But those detectives are rather unpleasant people, so I decided their opinion doesn't really matter. Especially if they are the ones who attacked his farm."

I smiled. This kid was alright.

"Let's shoot a few more rounds, then head back to Prehistoria. I'm freezing," I told him while raising the pistol and aligning the sights on the target.

"Yes, sir!"

***

Once we crossed through the Shimmer and back into Prehistoria, I left Irving and went to return the borrowed coat to Lieutenant Heath.

Walking through the encampment, I wondered if it should have been given a name. I supposed by association, it was sort of the backside of Fort York. But this place was really its own living and breathing monster of men, steel, and guns. The beautiful valley that had greeted me so many months ago was gone. In its place was row after row of palisades and defenses cut into the sloping side leading to the cliff face with the Shimmer. Gatlings, cannons, and lots of armed men sleeping unsoundly in tents.

We had etched out a small chunk of civilization, if that's what you wanted to call it, in Prehistoria. And it seemed humankind was damned if they'd give it up without a fight.

Personally, I didn't like it.

I liked civilization well enough, but only in small doses.

Reaching the Charlie Troop portion of the encampment, I walked to the Lieutenant's tent. There was no real signature or anything denoting that it was an officer's, except that it was the first one you came to in our area.

Heath was relaxing in a small folding chair outside his tent, a lit pipe in one hand and an open book in the other.

"Sir," I said, holding his coat out to him. "Thank you."

"Not a problem, Mr. Brown." He took a puff of his pipe then gestured with it towards the chair across from him while blowing the smoke out of his lungs. "Have a moment?"

"I do." I settled uneasily in the chair and wondered what this was all about.

On the cliff face behind me came a pair of screeches from nesting pterodactyls. The leathery birds didn't seem to care that we'd moved into their valley, they still had nests in the cliff face of the mountain that towered over us.

"Stinking birds," Heath said while closing his book. "It's hard for a man to get any sleep around here, or some reading done with those things squawking constantly." He fixed me with a squinted look.

"I'd like you to take over as second in command for C Troop. No title, as the Governor hasn't settled on them yet," he rolled his eyes, "but it'd be a decent pay increase with the promise that I'll work you like a rented mule."

I hesitated a moment before answering, "No thanks, sir. I'd rather just be your average Raider, doing as I'm told."

He smirked at me. "First off, you're not an 'average' Raider. Most Raiders wouldn't even know that word unless they were well educated. And you are educated, no matter how much you try to hide it."

I held my hands up defensively. "Caught me. I went to school for a few more years than most." It was the best lie I could come up with.

"I won't call you a liar, because out here that's inviting a fight. So, I'll just call you a… misdirectioner of the truth." He chewed on the end of his pipe thoughtfully before speaking again. "You're also a loner. Except for that Wesley gentleman. I would offer him the job, except he strikes me as a gambler, and I do not gamble with my men's lives. But being a loner has helped you form a buffer of sorts between yourself and all the other Raiders. I believe that will behoove you in your new duties."

"I haven't accepted yet-"

"You don't have a choice, Mr. Brown. You will be my number two."

Somewhere, another damned pterodactyl screeched.

"Yes, sir," I finally admitted. If anything, taking the position would give me more flexibility on my movements in Prehistoria. That was something I could use to my advantage to get to Reydan.

"Good. Now go get some chow and sleep. You'll need it tomorrow."

Standing, I nodded and walked away.

This was an unexpected development. I couldn't wait to tell Wesley.

***

The next morning, a patrol of Pinkertons were ambushed by apes. Wesley and I had guard duty, standing near the edge of the encampment behind a short palisade and keeping an eye out for anything hungry or angry that might come into the valley looking for humans.

The riders burst through the forest edge, whipping their horses, and riding like the devil was after them.

They raced through our lines, their mounts blowing foam and streaked with sweat from being ridden hard. One of the badged men had an ape arrow through his back and was bent over the neck of his mount.

"Down three men," Wesley noted calmly as he shifted his rifle and took a kneeling position behind the sharpened palisade in case something was following them.

"Bad day to be a Pinkerton," I agreed while settling down beside him and resting my rifle carefully between a pair of posts. The iron sights I pointed at the forest and my finger I rested beside the trigger, ready to squeeze off a round at a moment's notice.

Nothing moved. The ferns and low hanging branches settled back in place, but still we stayed in place.

Wesley started to stand, and I grabbed his sleeve, pulling him back down behind the safety of the makeshift wall.

"What?" he asked.

"Well, it certainly wouldn't do for us to stand up and take an ape arrow through the chest if the big monkeys were waiting for us to relax."

"They can hit us from this distance?"

"Yes. The accuracy may be a bit loose, but they can sling them out here."

Wesley shifted, getting comfortable. The palisade across from us to our right, also facing the wall, had Talon and George. The two morons never even took cover, they just watched the Pinkertons ride through and turned their backs on the forest to see them race up the valley.

I shouted at them to watch the forest and they complied, although begrudgingly from the looks of their body language. They were talking amongst themselves now, most likely annoyed at me for getting after them.

I tried to not push the second in command part hard on anyone, but if a man was bound to get himself killed, the least I could do was give him a fair warning first.

From up the valley, I heard the shouting of Lieutenant Barlow. At this distance it was hard to make out what he was saying, but during training we'd all learned his obnoxious voice and leadership style well. It was loud and hateful.

"I bet Talon a dollar that he gets killed by his own men first time out," Wesley said as the shouting echoed down around us.

I chuckled. "That might be now, it sounds like he's getting Bravo Troop ready."

Twenty minutes later they came thundering down the trail, weaving between palisades, cannons, and Gatling defenses of the Shimmer and past us.

Talon whooped while George removed his big hat and waved it over his head excitedly.

"Looks like they're about to get theirs," Wesley said. "One way or another."

"Best of luck to them. I reckon we'll find out if they are as horrible as Barlow says when they return."

Wesley pulled out his pocket watch and glanced at the time. "Few more minutes and we'll be relieved."

I stared at the tree line, half expecting to hear a barrage of firing as the troop was ambushed. But it was only the pounding of hooves followed by silence.

"Good luck out there, boys," I whispered to myself. They would need it, especially with a blow hard hot head like Lieutenant Barlow leading the way.

***

The US Marshals must have arrived during our guard duty because everyone was talking about them when we got our chow and settled down to eat.

"I heard one of them is a lady Marshal," Talon whistled. "Ain't that something? I bet she's beautiful."

Wesley grunted a wordless reply and shoveled another forkful into his mouth.

I'd stopped with my fork halfway to my mouth. "A lady Marshal, huh?"

"Yup!"

Shit.

It couldn't be.

But what are the chances there was more than one female Marshal?

This wasn't any good.

"I wonder who they're looking for," George muttered.

"Probably that Heart Eater of Granite Falls feller," Bart replied. "You heard about him?"

Wesley's eyes met mine as the Chinaman nodded. "I've heard a bit... Army wants to speak to him and Pinkertons want to kill him. What's the story?"

"Depends on who you ask," Talon answered. "Detectives say that he went loco from everything he'd been through. Killed his girl, his friends, and a dozen Pinkertons before torching his own house."

Wesley snorted then coughed as he choked on a mouthful of beans. "That sounds like some blatant bullshit."

"Yeah, most people agree. The Army says they just want to talk to him. Apparently, he's got some friends in high places that are vouching for him. But no one has seen him since the Pinkerton killings. Most folks think he's holed up in the Granite Mountains somewhere, or maybe slipped over here to Prehistoria and gone to live with the Shayana or Vikings."

"I bet he'd stand out like a sore thumb around either of those groups," I chuckled uneasily as I crammed the last piece of bacon into my mouth.

A shout came from the edge of the encampment. Setting my empty tin plate aside, I stood and looked down at the valley below.

B Troop was returning.

Even from here, I could tell from the way the Raiders slumped in their saddles as they rode between rows of palisades that they were worn out. Only Lieutenant Barlow at the front looked perky, and I was willing to bet he was just putting on a show.

"Looks like you owe someone a dollar," I reminded Wesley of his bet.

"I'll win it back playing cards later."

Lieutenant Heath sauntered over. "Mr. Brown, with me. The rest of you gentlemen, eat up. You'll be heading out shortly."

"After some more apes, sir?" Talon asked with a grin. The man seemed eager to put some more notches on his rifle stock.

Our commanding officer shook his head with a frown. "No, not today. Today we're doing something else."

Turning my plate in to the cook, I walked alongside Heath and out of earshot of the Raiders of Charlie Troop. "What is it, sir?"

"Hopefully an easy day. You'll be taking C Troop and riding escort." He squinted his eyes at me. "Will that be a problem?"

"No, sir. But you said I'm taking C Troop? Where will you be?"

"The Governor of Prehistoria has called a meeting of the Pinkertons, Army, and troop leaders. I'm not sure what it's about, but I'd assume he wants to escalate things with the apes and lure them into a big decisive battle."

"I take it the homesteaders are getting anxious to cross the Shimmer and get eaten?"

"They are, Johnson. And they are raising ever-loving hell on the other side." He snickered. "From what I hear, even Reydan White's father, the Senator, is trying to get his son to open the railroad up. But he won't; Reydan would rather sacrifice some wealth to have his day of glory in defeating the apes."

I ground my teeth at the mention of my enemy's name. Then I had a glimmer of hope. "You said escorting, sir? Would we be escorting Mr. White?"

"No. He's got the Black Plague and Pinkertons for that, plus his armored passenger rail car. He's safe as safe can be over here. You'll be escorting the Marshals to Whitesberg."

"Shit." The word fell from my lips before I could choke it back.

Heath looked at me funny. "You don't like that idea? You were alright with riding escort a minute ago."

"I'm alright with it, sir. It's just that... we're Raiders, not escorts. And I'd rather we be doing something useful. Can't we have the Pinkertons escort them? Or regular army?"

The Lieutenant stopped walking and looked me straight in the eyes. "Cut the crap, you and I both know we've wanted men in the Raiders. Is that it?"

"Sir, I don't know what you're talking-"

He threw his hands up. "Hell, Johnson. Don't play dumb with me. I'd bet a gold eagle that Wesley friend of yours is a wanted man. You can't hide that smooth, polished personality of his. He probably slept with someone's wife back East and is on the run for it."

"Yeah," I chuckled, my mind racing furiously. "You're right. He told me he had."

Heath clapped his hands victoriously. "I knew it! Barlow wanted to bet me he killed someone, but I knew better. That Wesley ain't the killing type."

I laughed then choked it off before it turned hysterical. Our leading officer had no idea of the caliber of men under his command.

Still chuckling, he continued as we walked together. "You'll be fine. But there is one caveat; instead of escorting the Marshals on the train, you'll be taking them the scenic route in a stagecoach."

"What the hell, sir? The scenic route? In a stagecoach?"

"It won't be so hard. The old construction trail alongside the railroad bed is still there, just lead them along that until you get to Whitesberg."

"Just us and the Marshals?"

"And some Axemen."

We stopped at a large tent. From the shadowed interior came a trio of people in single file. Their badges glinted off their chests in the sun, the star circled by a ring telling everyone within sight that these people were of a higher law and order than most.

"Johnson," Heath began, "this is Marshal Hintos Carlos, Marshal Michael McGibbons, and Marshal Pearl Landry."

Marshal Carlos was a short, Hispanic looking fellow with a face that I was willing to bet never smiled. McGibbons was the opposite, an older and clean-shaven black man, he had deep laugh lines and wore two pistols.

And Marshal Pearl Landry... well...

When our eyes met, she gave me a subtle wink.

I frowned back.

"Marshals, this is my second in command, Johnson Brown. He'll be escorting you with Charlie Troop to Whitesberg today."

"I understand there will be some Vikings as well?" Marshal Carlos asked while picking a rifle up from the cot inside the tent.

"Yes, sir," Heath said. "There'll be a pair of them traveling with you. You'll be well guarded."

"Shouldn't you Marshals just take the train and look out the window?" I asked while refusing to look at Landry again. "It'd be a lot safer."

"We are not here for safety, Mr. Brown," Marshal McGibbons said. "We're here to assist Governor Fredrick von Holsack with peace keeping once the settlers are allowed to cross."

"There aren't any settlers yet, not until the apes are dealt with," I told him.

Lieutenant Heath patted me on the back and laughed hesitantly. "Mr. Brown is blunt and to the point. But he is a fine man and will get you where you're going, regardless of the method you've requested."

I tipped my hat at the trio of Marshals. "You ask and we'll do." I looked at Heath, "I'll go ready the Raiders."

"The Vikings are already waiting at the rail."

"Are they mounted?"

"Yep."

"Good." I turned to leave.

"Mr. Brown, would you mind if I tagged along? I'd like to see more of this encampment," Marshal Landry asked with a slight smile.

"Sure, go ahead. Johnson will take care of you," Heath told her before I could voice an objection.

Without waiting, I turned my back on the group and stalked off while chewing on my lower lip angrily.

"Johnson," Landry said as she quickly caught up with a slight jog. "Long time, no see."

"What are you doing here?" I growled back as we stepped around several cooks cleaning tin plates in buckets of steaming water over a fire.

"That's an abrupt way to say hello. How long has it been? Ten years?"

"Not long enough," I spat back.

"Father sent me."

I stopped and felt my jaw clenching and unclenching angrily as I thought of what to say. "No shit! If he hadn't ratted out who I was and what I was doing, you'd have never seen me again."

She grabbed my arm and pulled me aside between tents while a mounted rider rode past. "He's worried about you."

"Me? I'm fine."

"He doesn't like you doing this alone."

"It's got nothing to do with him… or you."

She slapped me across the face, hard.

Shocked, I tripped backwards and fell against a tent. Someone inside shouted a string of swear words as I steadied myself.

"Of course, it's got something to do with me. You're my little brother! What Reydan White did to you affected all of us!" she hissed. "You think you lost something that day? What? Some skin off your back and our home?" She laughed as a lone tear trickled down her face. "I lost two brothers and a father that day. Cato was gone, and you and Father were never the same! And then you two left! You left me and Mother... alone. And I had to watch her die! Alone! All because you two were off murdering someone!"

Enraged at everything from our past that she'd thrown in my face, I shoved her. "And then what'd you do? Go law and order on us? You betrayed us!"

She punched the dragon scale vest on my chest. "I tried to save what was left of you and Father from your madness of revenge!"

"By turning us in?" I almost shouted but managed to choke it back to a loud whisper.

"I had a deal already worked out with a judge. All you had to do was ride into town and he'd have given you leniency. A few years of time behind bars and you'd have been free."

I spat on the ground. "Hell with that. We weren't done yet. But I'm about to be." I gestured at my back. "There's only one man left from those who did this to me. And he dies as soon as I get the shot lined up."

"And what about Cato? You going to kill our little brother?"

"He's not our brother anymore and he dies if he gets in my way. Same goes for you."

Brushing past her, I could faintly hear her still speaking as I stormed off, but the throbbing rage in my body filled my ears with a pounding. I just wanted to feel Reydan's throat in my hands and watch the light leave his eyes as I squeezed.

***

"Are you serious? You have a sister?" Wesley asked quietly as I filled him in.

"Yeah."

"I never knew that."

"Well, I went on one side of the law while she tried the other. We didn't mix well after that."

He whistled and slipped his rifle into its scabbard behind his saddle. "So, Talon was right... A lady Marshal, and your sister. Man, I bet she's a tough hombre."

"She is." Holding Bucky steady, I pulled myself into the saddle and eased myself down, waiting for him to start bucking.

He didn't disappoint.

His rear end flew in the air, his legs kicked back, and I stayed right where I was in the saddle until he stopped.

"You know, you could always go into a rodeo after this Raider business is over." He chuckled. "Or as a rodeo clown?"

I laughed; it felt good on my face after all the scowling I'd been doing. "No thanks, but I do miss Carbine. Something awful. And that's saying a lot considering what a pain in the butt he was."

"He was a beautiful horse."

"Yes, he was," I said wistfully as I remembered the stupid dun mustang and all his tricks. He was such a pest, but loyal at the same time. I patted Bucky's neck while thinking about how this horse wasn't too bad. He just wasn't what I was used to. I chuckled. I bet Carbine was driving the Shaynee nuts on the other side of the Shimmer trying to get to me.

"George, Bart! Let's go!" I called out to the line as the pair of them stood talking to each other instead of saddling up.

Once they were mounted, I led the column through the encampment to the western side. From there the freshly built steel railroad ran to Whitesberg. A locomotive puffed smoke and steam as it sat idle on the tracks. Most of the cars behind the coal car carried lumber for the new town that was positioned on the edge of Prehistoria against an ocean filled with prehistoric monstrosities.

And beside the locomotive stood an impatient team of horses attached to a brown stagecoach, and a pair of Vikings mounted on trikes that were bellowing softly to each other and anything else in ear shot.

"Those don't look like ape trikes," Wesley whistled in appreciation.

One of the triceratopses was mottled brown and yellow, and only had a single large horn coming from the center of its face, above the beak. The other looked like a normal three horned trike like my Sara, except it was a third larger than any I'd ever seen before and there was a pair of egg-shaped holes in its bone shield. "They're not. The Axemen were getting all sorts of different trikes from traders catching them somewhere else and bringing them here. They're... diversified in their mounts, just like us."

Reaching the stagecoach, I pulled back on the reins and slowed Bucky and the rest of the column behind me to a stop. Leaning over, I looked through the window of the stagecoach. Inside were the three Marshals and Irving.

"What are you doing here?" I asked the youngster in surprise.

"Governor Fredrick... I mean, Governor von Holsak asked me to come. Said he wanted to talk dinosaurs."

"And you couldn't ride the train?"

"Oh, c'mon Johnson, I never get out of the encampment. I wanted to see Prehistoria up close."

Taking my hat off, I raked a hand through my short hair while considering the risks he was taking. "Alright, fine. Just stay in the coach and shoot anything or anyone that doesn't look friendly."

"For God's sake man, he's in the company of three US Marshals, an entire troop of Raiders, and a pair of Vikings riding horned dinosaurs… I do believe he'll be fine," Marshal McGibbons chuckled.

I met eyes with Wesley and the outlaw shook his head slightly as if to say there was no point in arguing.

Gravel crunched as the Vikings turned their trikes around to face us and the coach. "You two got names?" I asked them. The Axemen looked at each other, back at me, then one, a mighty fellow with a streak of green ink tattooed across the bridge of his nose and cheeks shrugged.

"Okay, you speak English?"

Silence. Then one of them drew a long-handled axe and waved it at me with a look on his face as though I asked him a dumb question, like were they armed.

I pointed a finger at myself, "Johnson." Then pointed a finger at Wesley, "Wesley."

The tattooed one nodded in understanding and pointed at himself, "Knud." Then he jabbed a thumb towards the other Viking on the single horned trike beside him, "Ulf."

"You boys ready?" Talon shouted from behind me.

Ulf lowered his axe and shouted, "Ja!" back at him.

"Well good, they understand some it seems." I jerked my chin up at the Pinkerton driving the stagecoach from the top. "How about you? You ready?" The detective pulled a double-barreled shotgun from beneath the seat, broke it open, and seemingly satisfied that it was loaded, gave me a thumbs up.

"You ride in the middle of the column; the Raiders will split up around you."

"What about the Axemen?" the Pinkerton driver asked back.

"I dunno what they've been told, and it'll take too long to draw them a picture, so we'll just let them do their thing." Looking through the window of the coach, my eyes went from Irving to Marshal Landry. My sister gave me a slight smile that she was ready.

That was good enough for me.

"Let's ride!" I shouted and waved my hand forward.

***

The noise of the stagecoach's steel-clad wheels was annoyingly loud behind me as it bumped over the gravel trail left from the railroad's construction. The trail had never been meant to be maintained, it was only hastily built to move material along the front of the rail's placement. It was only through the constant abuse that it resembled anything useable for passage. There were large dips and humps, with lots of puddles filled with water and mud. Bucky stepped around them, but the stagecoach rolled through them, and I was sure the riders inside weren't comfortable bouncing around so much.

But then, glancing back at the coach and seeing the heads of the Marshals and Irving sticking out of the windows, I reckoned they weren't really caring about their comfort. Not when there was so much to see.

We'd already passed a few dinosaurs. Nothing spectacular, a half dozen armor backed ankylosauruses with their clubbed tails eating grass between the railroad ties. They wandered off as we approached, swinging their bone knotted tails casually, as though it wouldn't absolutely pulverize one of our horses with a single swipe.

Inside the brown painted coach, Irving was spouting off all sorts of information about them to the Marshals, and from what I could tell, they were eating out of the palm of his hand.

At the front of our column rode the two Axemen, then myself and Wesley, half of the Raiders, the stagecoach with my sister and her law officer friends, and behind it, the other half of the men of Charlie Troop. All said, we were a decently imposing force should we chance upon any dinosaur short of a Tyrannosaurus, or Toothed One, as the Vikings called them.

To our left was the steel tracks and steep mountainside covered in trees and large slabs of stone, while to our right was an open field about a hundred and fifty yards across. We were in the open, riding down the trail, keeping an eye out, and so far just babysitting the Marshals.

"This railroad is quite the engineering marvel," Wesley was saying.

I hadn't been paying attention, as I was lost deep in thoughts about my sister being back and the ramifications of that. "What's that?" I asked, shifting slightly in my saddle to ease the numbing in my left butt cheek.

"Well, maybe engineering is the wrong word for it. But it's quite the marvel that they were able to run a train through a prehistoric world filled with dinosaurs and APES!" he shouted while lifting his rifle and firing upwards into the steep forested mountainside to our left.

Wesley must have set the ambush off with his shout and quick rifle fire, because within a second, arrows zipped from between the trees as other apes flung themselves off the mountain and amongst us.

The first ape landed with a heavy thud in front of Bucky. Heavily painted, with swirls of red and yellow across his face and chest, the hairy ape reached for my appaloosa.

I jabbed my boot heels into my mount's flanks and yanked back on the reins.

Bucky did what he did best, he reared up and kicked with his front hooves. A steel horseshoe crushed the ape's painted face before my horse dropped and continued bucking like a mad horse.

"You-" I began to swear at Bucky.

His rear end raised and I bit my tongue trying to lean back in the saddle.

"Stupi-"

He jack-knifed, and my face collided with his broad head in a shower of bright twinkling stars across my vision.

"Sonbitch!"

Savagely, I twisted the reins, jerking Bucky's head to the side and putting him into a spin. He trampled the dead ape under his hooves as gunfire and shouts of battle echoed around me.

"JED! Get a hold of that damn horse!" Wesley shouted between shots as he rapidly fired his rifle at the mountain to our left.

An arrow thwapped into my saddle, burying itself in my bedroll and narrowly missing pinning me to Bucky.

My horse slowed, and I twisted my head around to survey the fight.

Several Raiders were down, obviously dead, but we'd killed most of the apes who'd leapt amongst us. Arrows were still coming from the mountainside, and the men were keeping up a steady stream of fire at the apes hiding behind the giant trees.

"Come get some, cowards!" George shouted as he fired his Winchester empty behind me. Swearing, he began fumbling for cartridges from his bandoleer across his chest to reload.

Loud bellowing came from our right flank.

Twisting back around, my blood went cold.

Over a dozen trikes were charging across the open field towards us. Their riders were standing tall on the backs of their horned mounts, firing arrows ahead of themselves as they bore down on my unsuspecting men.

"Ride!" I shouted while jerking my rifle up and putting a bullet into the bone shield of the trike closest to me. There was no other course of action, it was either move forward and try to outrun them or die here when the trikes impaled us against the towering rock and shrub-filled mountainside. Our horses would never be able to stand against such a charge of heavy horned cavalry that outweighed them by three to four times as much.

"Ride!" "Ride!" "RIDE!" was shouted up and down the column as men and beasts began to race past me along the trail.

Ahead of me, Ulf slammed his axe into the collarbone of a female ape and began moving his trike forward. Beside him, Knud's trike flicked his horns and knocked another ape to the ground who was immediately trampled under a fleeing Raider's horse.

"Go! GO!" I shouted at the Axemen while waving my rifle forward.

They caught on and got their horned dinosaurs moving as they shouted what sounded like Viking cheers to each other.

Glancing over my shoulder at those behind me, I saw one of the stagecoach's horses was down with an arrow through its side. The dying beast flailed about, hopelessly tangled in the harness. Above the coach, the Pinkerton driver was lying on his back grappling with an ape trying to spear him.

My sister pushed the door open, grabbed the top of the coach, and hoisted herself up high enough to fire her pistol into the ape's side. Snarling, the gray monkey let go of the driver and turned his attention to the female Marshal only to receive another bullet, this time through his open and roaring mouth.

The monkey fell on the driver, who frantically struggled to get free from the dead weight holding him down.

Swearing, I slipped off Bucky, slapped his rear end with my hand and ran towards the downed horse. Arrows rained down and I prayed none would skewer me to the ground.

The horse still had some life in him when I skidded to my knees, drew the hunting knife, and began cutting through the harness. When the Quartermaster had given it to me, I'd expected it to be rusted and dull and was pleasantly surprised to see that it had a fine edge and wore a thin coat of oil. Whoever it had been before me, they'd taken care of it. I put the blade to work. Slicing through leather straps, the horse kicked itself upright and staggered a few steps away.

The last of the Raiders were passing us now, a few slowing hesitantly as if unsure about leaving the coach and myself behind.

"Go!" I shouted at them while throwing my rifle under the seat of the stagecoach and climbing aboard.

The coach wouldn't be left behind.

Well, it might have been if it hadn't had my sister in it.

There was no time to fool with the dead ape weighing down the Pinkerton. Grabbing up the reins from where they'd been dropped, I slapped them down and the coach lurched forward.

The charging trikes had begun to turn, most of them moving with the running column but a few stayed straight, coming at us with horns down and apes slouching behind the bone shields.

Gun blasts came from the windows of the coach, and in such a rapid succession I was sure that most, if not all of them, were still alive inside.

"Irving!" I shouted to the youngster, "Keep your head down!"

A trike slammed into the wounded horse I'd cut free.

The black horns impaled the mount, lifting it screaming off the ground for a moment before throwing it down.

We rode past the intertwined modern and prehistoric beasts as the trike struggled to twist its horns free and an ape rider chucked a spear at us.

The obsidian-tipped weapon slammed into the stagecoach behind me. I didn't hear any screams so I assumed it was a miss of any people.

The horses were beginning to pick up speed along the dirt and graveled trail as the mounted trikes charged alongside. I cracked the reins over the beasts' backs to urge them to pull harder and run faster.

I didn't feel bad about abusing them; they either got us all to safety, or they got eaten by the apes.

An arrow thumped into the dead ape sprawled over the Pinkerton and he yelped in surprise while still struggling to free himself.

"C'mon, dammit!" I shouted at the useless detective. "I could really use some help up here!"

Screaming obscenities at me, he shoved the body a final time and it rolled off the coach top and under a rear wheel. The stagecoach bumped hard as the back end lurched up, then slammed down. I almost lost my seating.

The Pinkerton slid into the seat beside me.

He had the typical handlebar mustache that a lot of the detectives wore; I suspected it was to hide their wimpy upper lips.

Reaching beneath the seat, he pulled out the sawed-off shotgun.

I snatched it from his surprised hands and passed him the reins. "You drive!"

Cocking back the first hammer, I crawled onto the top of the coach. I'd be danged if I was going to drive when there was shooting to be done.

A trike was mere feet away, his rider already removed from this world judging by the bloody smear across the back of the green and yellow striped beast and the dropped reins. The dinosaur was blocking the other mounted riders from getting to us, but it was also making it hard for the Marshals inside the coach to get any shots off with the big bodied beast in the way.

I tried to recall where we were.

I'd only ridden the train a couple of times to Whitesberg, but if I remembered right, the train moved away from this damnable mountainside and into the open ahead somewhere. That would give us more maneuverability, but it'd also let the apes get after us from both sides.

I sneaked a peek ahead of the coach.

There.

The track turned to the right into the open clearing between the cliff face and forest. That lasted a couple miles. If we could make it past that, we'd be back into the forest and the trikes wouldn't be able to ride alongside us and we'd be much better off.

Or we'd be dead by then.

It was a coin toss.

I fired the first barrel into the trike beside us.

With the bloom of smoke and peppering of buck shot, the beast bellowed in pain and turned abruptly.

It ran into another trike, squishing a rider's leg between them and causing a scream of pain that was quickly silenced by a well-placed shot from one of the Marshals.

The coach was thrust forward suddenly. Losing my balance, I fell to all fours and caught myself at the cost of the shotgun that slid out of my reach against a luggage rail.

Behind us, an evil-looking ape with white streaks of paint below his eyes flashed his canines as he rammed his trike into the back of the coach again. The black horns of the trike impaled and tore the back end, ripping free luggage cases tied to the back. Screaming something in ape speak, the big monkey shook a spear in the air.

"You little shit," I growled as the coach was picked up then dropped again by the trike.

My head bounced off the top of the coach from the hard drop.

"Grrrr," I grunted.

Drawing my Smith and Wesson while still lying prone, the ape ducked behind the bone shield as I fired.

The bullet clipped the shield, knocking a small piece off but leaving the ape and his mount unharmed.

Holding the pistol in both hands, I sprawled my legs flat on the coach's top and tried to line the sights up. The jostling of the trike horns poking the rear, coupled with the bumps and ruts of the trail, was making it near impossible to get a clean shot at such a small target.

I wished Ashley James was with us right now. She'd be slaying the apes left and right with that *One of a Thousand* rifle of hers.

Giving up, I fired anyways and wasted another bullet into the bone shield of the trike. The beast bellowed and shook its horns, tearing free one of the Marshal's luggage boxes. Falling beneath the feet of the trike, it was trampled flat, and someone's nice white shirts were ruined in the mud.

A painful shout came from inside the carriage. Glancing over the rail, I saw the right side of the stagecoach below me was practically a pin cushion from ape arrows and thrown spears.

My sister's arm thrust out the window with a revolver blooming fire at the muzzle. She'd always been a good shot, and she was making the most of her bullets now.

The rear end bumped again, thrashed from behind by that damnable ape and trike.

Without thinking, I slammed the half empty revolver back into its holster, jerked out the Shaynee tomahawk and hurled myself off the back of the stagecoach.

***

The ape didn't look so big and bad when he saw me flying towards him.

His jaw dropped open, fully exposing yellowed canines in shock. A split-second later, I was sprawled across the trike's bone shield and slamming the edge of the tomahawk into the ugly monkey's painted forehead.

Blood sprayed, streaming down the white face paint as the fresh corpse slid off the dinosaur, nearly wrenching the tomahawk from my hand.

One less ambusher and I had absolutely no idea what I was going to do with myself now.

The trike tossed its big head, unhappy about me lying across his face.

Grabbing the bone shield, I braced a boot against an upper horn and pushed myself over and onto the back of the galloping beast.

The Pinkerton driver glanced back, and his jaw dropped lower than the ape's had a moment ago.

Grabbing the trike's reins seemed like the most natural thing to do now, so I scooped them up from where they'd been dropped with my tomahawk still in one hand.

I'd only seen them used by attacking apes before and hadn't paid much attention at the time since I was trying to stay alive but, now with the leather straps in hand, I wished I had.

It seemed obvious that pulling in one direction or the other would get the trike to turn, and maybe pulling back would make it stop. But I'd no idea what to do to make it go forward.

A trike slammed into the side of mine, almost crushing my leg between the pair. An obsidian-tipped spear was thrust at my face with the point coming fearfully close to jabbing flesh.

Swatting the weapon aside with the tomahawk, I dropped the reins, drew the Smith and Wesson and fired it into the she-ape's torso.

She pulled the reins while falling off the dinosaur and the trike ran away minus its rider.

A pair of arrows slammed into my trike.

One drove deep into the rear end and the other glanced off the bone shield, ricocheting away in splinters. Bellowing in pain, my mighty beast shook its horns and moved to hit the coach in front of us again.

Tugging the reins, I managed to get the trike to move to the right and by thumping my boots against its side as though riding a horse, the wounded dinosaur bounded forward alongside the arrow and spear-riddled stagecoach.

The look on Irving and the Marshals' faces was worth every rear end busting bound the wide-bodied dinosaur made with each running step.

We raced around the final thicket of trees, getting some respite from our attacking mounted apes, and into the large open clearing.

It was absolute pandemonium.

The tall grass was being trampled down by horse and trike alike as the Raiders and apes circled each other, exchanging arrows and bullets. Dust swirled in the air filled with shouts and bellows of pain and rage and I was pretty certain I heard George rebel yelling in the midst of it all.

"Keep going!" I screamed at the Pinkerton driver.

Not that it looked like he was about to stop. He was cracking the reins on the back of the coach's team as fast as he could flick them.

Ahead of me, Ulf and an ape's trikes collided face first in a horned charge that probably shook the ground beneath us. The pair of dinosaurs thrust horns back and forth while the Viking shot an arrow at the ape across from him jabbing with a broken tipped spear.

Desperate to avoid hitting them with my own dinosaur, I yanked HARD on my trike's reins.

The wounded beast responded, but more sluggishly than before.

Glancing at the arrow impaling it behind me, I saw the stream of blood running down the animal's side. My mount was losing steam.

Looking forward again, I had only a moment to brace myself before the trike trampled an ape rider who'd been dismounted. The ape was leaning back with a spear in hand, aiming to throw. The accidental timing of my trike charge was perfect as it raised its head and horns and stomped the ape into the ground.

"Nice mount!" Wesley shouted as he raced through the swirling dust on his horse.

With a snapshot of the Smith and Wesson, I managed to wing the ape chasing after the outlaw gunman. He slumped slightly, losing his grip on the stone axe he was wielding.

I was either empty or down to a single round in the pistol, I hadn't kept count very well. But drawing a bead on the closest ape, I squeezed the trigger anyways and received an unsatisfying click in return.

Angrily, I slid it back in the holster and noticed for the first time that there was a spear still strapped on the trike.

Perfect.

I was down to a tomahawk and a spear.

Stone age weaponry.

I'd have really preferred a Gatling or a Maxim right now.

You know, gentleman's weapons.

Tugging the spear free, I twisted the trike beneath me around and we raced through the grass and dust looking for something to impale.

Unsure of what else to do with the spear, I held it like a jousting knight. Tucking the thick shaft beneath my armpit, I struggled to keep the chipped obsidian tip of the heavy eight-foot-long spear up.

A trike and rider appeared in front of us. It looked like the ape had lost control of the mount, and it was standing in place stamping its feet as the monkey screamed and jerked at the leather reins.

Slamming my heels against my wounded mount, I urged the dinosaur forward.

The tip of the spear hit the ape at the same time the horns of my mount pierced the sides of his.

The impact of the dinosaurs threw me forward as the spear slid free beneath my arm. I was flung against the bone shield, the bare bone protrusions along the top digging painfully into my upper chest. Giving an unmanly grunt, I let go of the spear and pushed myself upright.

Blood.

There was blood everywhere.

The spear was sticking halfway through the ape. The dying monkey gurgled thick, red blood from between her teeth then fell over as my trike struggled to pull its horns out of the other dinosaur.

My mount shook its head mightily back and forth with a muffled bellow. The flesh on the dead trike in front of us was rendered and torn open as the wounds stretched and ripped from the thick black horns.

An arrow sprouted from my beast's head; it'd thunked hard into the skull but didn't appear to penetrate. Angrily, the trike shook its head harder, flinging dead dinosaur blood and flesh and goo several feet.

Another arrow clipped the bone shield in front of me before I could react, showering me with splinters as it exploded into hundreds of shards and bits of tiny broken obsidian from the tip.

I swiped my eyes and tried to blink out the debris.

Realizing I was still sitting on the trike in the open, I hurled myself to the opposite side of the bow and arrow shooter, just as another arrow zipped through the air where I'd been a moment before.

Kneeling, I patted myself to confirm the harsh truth...

I was down to jack shit, and Otto's tomahawk.

Jerking the smooth-handled weapon from my belt, I gave as mighty of a roar cry as I could and ran around my struggling trike with the tomahawk held overhead.

The ape that'd been flinging arrows at me had become confident.

As I dashed around the collided trikes, I saw the brown and red mottled ape had slung his bow and was stalking forward with stone axe in hand to polish me off.

His snarl turned to surprise as my tomahawk slammed down.

My aim was off.

Instead of hitting the hairy beast at the intersection of neck and collarbone where I intended, it smashed into the bow slung over the ape's shoulder. Splitting wood, severing bow string, and hacking half a blade deep into the shoulder joint, I threw my entire body weight behind the attack.

Tumbling together, we fell to the ground with myself on top.

The stone axe dropped to the ground, forgotten in the mad scramble as the ape snapped his large canines at my face. Shoving backwards, I sat up, straddling the ape and wrenched the tomahawk free with a spray of blood.

Raising it high, I smashed it down and drove the small axe into the hairy monkey's face. The wedged blade split his skull like a melon, and bits of yellowish-white brain oozed out around the blade.

"Ugh," I stepped on the corpse and yanked the blade free.

The apes were either dead or retreating and the chaos of the battlefield was calming. My trike was still struggling to free itself but appeared to be rapidly succumbing to its own wounds. Its front legs were splayed out, and the rear legs bent over under its weight. It bellowed pitifully.

Slipping the gore-covered tomahawk back into my belt, I drew my Smith and Wesson and broke it open, spilling empty shells onto the trampled grass underfoot. Reloading with one cartridge at a time from the loops along my belt, I stopped at the trike that'd served me so faithfully as a temporary mount. Looking into the dark eye that shined with intelligence, I silently asked it for forgiveness while placing my pistol barrel between the two large top horns and pulling the trigger to end its suffering.

I walked to the far side of the clearing, dodging dead mounts, apes, and the occasional Raider to where the stagecoach lay overturned on its side. Along the way, I found Talon with an ape arrow through his thigh. Helping him up, the Raider leaned against me and swore with every painful step.

Reaching the stagecoach, I found Irving, and two US Marshals.

"I think I winged one!" Irving said excitedly as he stepped out from where he'd been kneeling behind the coach for cover and reloading his pistol.

I gave the kid a grin; he was handling his first brush with death and danger quite well. "You did great, kid."

"They took Detective Hathbert and Marshal McGibbons," my sister told me with a frown. The other one, Marshal Carlos, I reminded myself, already had a sling tied around his arm and neck and looked like he'd eaten a good bit of pain when the coach flipped. There was a good-sized lump forming on his bald head also.

Wesley pranced his horse to the coach, tugging a pair of ropes attached to Bucky and another horse. Except for his hat missing and hair blown astray, the outlaw-in-hiding seemed to be his typical calm self.

"Irving, stick with the Marshals," I told the kid while taking my appaloosa's reins from Wesley. "And you," I told the gunman. "You're in charge. Get the men and horses rounded up and moving to Whitesberg. Bring back any dead Raiders."

Irving walked to a downed trike nearby while I talked. With his free hand, he gently caressed the wounded dinosaur's pebbled hide as it bellowed softly. The beast looked like it had collided with the stagecoach and its entire side was practically flayed open from the impact.

"Magnificent," I heard Irving whisper to himself.

I remembered that feeling from the first time I'd touched one.

"I don't want to be in charge," Wesley told me abruptly, his voice soft and low.

"Too bad. I ain't got time to argue. If they don't listen to you, shoot them. And you, what the hell are you doing?" I asked my sister.

She responded by taking the other set of reins from Wesley and climbing into the saddle. "You aren't going after them alone."

Wesley grinned at her, then me. I rolled my eyes.

Stepping over to the overturned stagecoach, I looked under the seat and found my rifle lying half under the coach with a busted stock. I pulled it out and shook my head at the damage. "That's gonna cost me, I bet."

"Here," Wesley pulled his Winchester out of its scabbard and handed it to me. "I just reloaded it."

"Thanks." I slid into the saddle and for once, Bucky didn't appear eager to fight me. I hoped it was the taste of the fight we just had taking out some of his piss and vinegar.

"Let's go," Pearl said before whipping her horse around and galloping away.

Shaking my head at Wesley and Irving, I pulled my appaloosa's head around and rode after her.

***

After following the mounted trikes' tracks for about a mile, we found Detective Hathbert.

The Pinkerton's neck had been snapped and the body dumped next to the trail of trike tracks we'd been following.

"Shit," Pearl said as she eyeballed the dead detective's corpse. His head was spun at an awkward angle from his shoulders and his face frozen in a grimace of pain.

"You know you aren't supposed to swear, right? Being a lady and all," I reminded her as I kept an eye on the surrounding trees and ferns for any ape hiding spots. Unfortunately, there were a lot of potential ones. I adjusted my tight grip on Wesley's rifle.

She dismounted and looked at the body. "I didn't get to be a Marshal by being a lady. And besides, I only do it around you."

I didn't say anything. I didn't get to be who I was by being a soft-spoken gentleman, so who was I to nitpick.

Bending over, she scooped up a small silver derringer from the grass several feet away. "Looks like he went for a hideout gun." She snapped it open and pried out the fired cartridge.

"He got one shot off." She looked around and pointed suddenly at something I couldn't see. "Drops of blood, right there. He made that one shot count."

"And it cost him his life," I told her.

"Yup. They snapped his neck for it."

I nodded in agreement.

When we'd played Indian as kids, my sister was always better at it than Cato or me. She had a knack for picking up trails and signs that would leave a Shaynee brave confounded. I often figured the only reason she never caught Father or I was because she didn't really want to.

Sighing, I looked at the trail we'd been following. "Let's get going. Before they kill or sacrifice McGibbons."

Pearl climbed into the saddle, adjusted her holster slightly so she could draw faster, and thumped her heels against the horse. "No time to waste, Orville."

"Don't call me that," I said as I rode after her.

A couple miles further, we came across an ape. Not stopping, we rode by, giving the body a wide berth in case he was playing possum. But he didn't jump up, didn't attack us, and just lay there, sprawled out and dead.

"I'd say that's the one your Pinkerton friend got," I told Marshal Landry.

"He wasn't a friend, but yes. I'd tend to agree." She leaned over in her saddle to get a little better look. "I see a singed chest wound, bit of curled burnt hair from getting shot at close range."

"One less to kill."

She sat back up in the saddle. "Let's get McGibbons, he's a good man and a good Marshal... and he'll fight to the end. I'd rather not lose him the same way."

"There." I pointed. There was a thin tendril of smoke in the distance that wafted above the trees.

"I see it. Probably a mile away. You think that's them?"

"Might be some Axemen, we're getting near to their territory. But I'm willing to bet it's the apes."

"We'll ride a little closer, and finish the way on foot," my sister said. It wasn't a suggestion or a question. She'd always been a bit bossy.

"No."

She spun around and glared at me. "Orville! This is my man, my fellow Marshal. We will not leave him to die."

"I don't recommend we do, but I do say we do something a bit different."

"And what's that? Ride in? Guns blazing?"

"Yeah. We ain't got time to waste sneaking around on foot. He may be dead by then."

Her brow furrowed as she scowled at me. Then she glanced at the smoke in the distance, thinking it over. After a minute, she turned back and pursed her lips.

"Okay."

***

We hit the apes' campsite with a pair of rebel yells and guns in hand.

McGibbons was already tied to a nearby tree. His hands were stretched out overhead, his booted feet barely touching the ground below him. The dark coat and white shirt he wore had been ripped or cut open, exposing his belly and chest.

And boy, did he look angry.

There were five apes and only three trikes. The trikes we rode around at full speed, and the moment the first ape stood up beside the fire, my bullet hit him in the throat. Then Bucky's shoulder knocked the dying ape sprawling into the fire. Flames and sparks shot into the air as pandemonium and chaos set in.

Pearl twirled her horse around, firing her pistol left and right into the cluster of unsuspecting apes.

Bucky trampled an ape on the way to McGibbons. Reaching him, I hacked the taut leather rope apart with the tomahawk. He jerked his hands down and I passed him my pistol. He could fire that with his hands still tied together.

A second later, he was firing at the final ape jabbing a spear towards Pearl and her mount.

A couple seconds after that, it was all over.

Pearl slipped out of the saddle and stepped over an ape corpse to get to McGibbons. The Marshal had taken a knee and was silently praying. She rested a hand on his shoulder as he finished.

"Carlos is good, as is Irving."

"Thank God," McGibbons said as he crossed himself and stood. "What about the Raiders? How many did you lose?" he asked me as I drew my knife and began cutting the braided leather rope away from his wrists.

"Not sure yet, I didn't have time to take attendance before we came after you." I knew we'd lost men. Or rather, I'd lost men. But I didn't know how many and wouldn't until we returned to Whitesberg.

"Thank you for coming for me, Mr. Brown."

I stared at him for a second as my brain caught up to the fact that Johnson Brown was my name now. My sister appearing and calling me Orville repeatedly had put a crack in my fake identity. That meant I needed to get my head screwed on straight. I was Johnson Brown, Raider of Charlie Troop, nothing else.

"Yeah, you're welcome." I looked around. "It's getting late, and I don't recommend riding when we can't see."

"You want to make camp here?" McGibbons asked in shock, pointing at the dead apes with the barrel of my Smith and Wesson.

"No. The corpses will draw scavengers and predators. We don't want to be here when they come calling. There was a place about a mile back, near where we first saw the smoke. That'd be a good place to hole up for the night."

"Let's go, Mr. Brown. Lead the way," Pearl said as she stepped into her saddle and offered her hand to McGibbons. He climbed behind her, shifting awkwardly as he adjusted himself to ride double on their mount.

It was dusk when we reached the place I'd picked out.

A trike followed us and after killing the one I rode earlier I didn't have the heart to chase this one away. He ended up bedding down beside our pair of horses for company, and I figured that he'd be a good warning sign for anything coming near us. Except apes, of course. He may welcome them with open horns. Which meant we'd have to keep an eye out for them. But other dinosaurs? Those should rile him up a bit.

After getting a small fire going, McGibbons turned in and began snoring shortly. I'd traded guns with the man, and my borrowed Winchester was tucked under his arms while my pistol was back in my holster where it belonged.

I had a feeling the Marshal wouldn't be taken alive again.

My sister dusted off her pants, and carrying a pair of saddle bags, sat beside me.

From one of her bags, she pulled out a small flask and a plug of tobacco. With her knife she cut off a chunk of chew and stuffed it into her mouth. The flask she offered to me, and I accepted.

"Don't let Father know you're chewing again," I told her before taking a swig.

The unknown liquor inside burned my mouth and throat on the way down. But it also gave me a warm feeling in my stomach that was pleasant.

"That's the good stuff," she said as she took the flask back. "And no, don't you tell him I'm chewing."

I nudged the end of a stick into the fire, chuckling as I remembered. "Yeah, I remember that time Mr. Turbin caught you and told Father."

She took a swig and twirled the cap back on. "He made me cut my own switch. I went through about three of them before I picked one he was happy with."

I looked at the ground between my feet, suddenly overwhelmed with memories of Mr. Turbin's body hanging from the same oak tree I was tied to and whipped. "He was a good man," I said softly. "Mr. Turbin, I mean... although really, him and Father were both good men back then."

Pearl stared at me for a moment then looked away, her jaw flexing as it worked on that chunk of tobacco.

"I met Skyla," she finally said, after a long minute of quiet. "And Otto, and Wolverine Wade and Ashley..."

"What? How? When?"

"Someone sent a telegram to Skyla's father, telling him to request me to escort her back East," she spat a stream of tobacco juice into the fire. "I found out later that was Father's doing when I arrived at the Shaynee village to get her."

"Our father was there?" I said in shock.

"Yup. Living with the noble savages... at least that's what he said, but you know how he is. He laughed when he said it."

"I've only had one letter," I admitted. "I didn't know about all this."

"You know how mail is, slow and behind the times, always. Even when you ain't that far away."

"Skyla is back East... good. She'll be safe there, I think."

"She will. I've seen to that. Although you may want to start worrying about her mother; that lady does not like you one bit."

"Feeling is mutual," I grumbled. "She hit me once after finding out who I was; she'd probably shoot me now after getting her daughter almost murdered."

"Speaking of that, after I got her settled, I found out Fredrick had requested some Marshals to investigate the rumor of a dozen dead Pinkertons feuding with some famous Heart Eater. Reydan has managed to keep it out of the papers, but word has gotten around. And once I knew it was you involved, I had to come."

"Yeah. I killed them," I admitted.

"No shit." She spat another glob of stinking tobacco juice at the flames lapping the chopped sticks in the fire. "What's the story, Orv... Johnson?"

"I guess Father told you most of it by now."

"He did, but I want to hear it from you."

"It was Reydan White that burned our home, stole Cato, and had me whipped. When I told Father that, he went after him, and got shot up some. Best I can figure, Reydan thought it was me, so he got tired of playing and sent the Pinkertons to wipe me out in return. And they almost did." I gently touched my black vest. "If it wasn't for this, I'd be dead. They ambushed me getting the horses ready. Killed two of my friends and almost killed Skyla. Would have, if it hadn't been for Otto."

"Yeah, about that Otto. He's a good-looking fellow. Especially with all that scarring across his chest."

"Oh, Lord…"

"He was pretty talkative. He seems to be proud of his blood brother, Huck Berry." She smiled. Dark bits of tobacco were stuck in her white teeth.

"Ha! Just the same, you'd better watch out," I teased her. "Sounds like he may try trading Father some horses for you."

"A gal could do worse." She opened the cap of the flask again, took a swig, then thrust it against my chest. "Drink."

I took another sip. It didn't burn as harshly this time.

We were quiet as the minutes passed to the tune of McGibbons' snoring and the crackle of flames. I thought of our childhood, and everything that'd been taken from us. My sister and I had turned out vastly different from each other, but in some ways, we were still alike.

"I didn't know Mother was sick," I finally spoke with something stuck in my throat. "I didn't get the letter until it was too late, and I was too far away. I came back though, found where you'd buried her, and read the note you'd left me. But by then, you were long gone."

"We've run into each other three or four times since then," she sighed. "Why are you just now telling me this?"

"Because it's been long enough that I can speak of it." I swallowed back the pain. I missed our mother something awful and the note that my sister had left, accusing me of everything I was guilty of, had hurt.

"Is that why you didn't tell Skyla about me?" Pearl asked softly.

"I told her, in a way. When we first met, I mentioned that I had a sister. But never spoke of you again. To be fair, for a long time, she didn't know who I was or what I'd done."

I took another sip, then held the flask out for her. She closed her hand around it, but I held it firm as she tried to pull it away.

"I'm going to kill him. For everything he's done to us and those we don't know about."

"I know," she said, carefully prying the flask loose of my grip.

"Don't get in my way."

"I won't. But I also won't help you. I swore an oath to uphold the law, and I'm going to do that."

"You going to come after me afterwards?"

"Maybe."

Looking away, I smiled at the darkness surrounding us. "Good luck."

***

The next morning, the Pinkerton's body was gone from where we'd left it.

Mostly.

There were still bits and pieces of tattered and shredded cloth scattered around the trampled down and blood-smeared area where the corpse had lain. *Somethings* had eaten it. I wasn't sure what, the tracks pressed into the ground weren't that large, but there were a lot of them. It looked like an entire pack of prehistoric creatures had completely devoured the man.

"It appears we will not be bringing his body back with us," Marshal McGibbons said dryly from where he sat behind my sister. I caught myself there. It wasn't safe to think of her as my sister, but as Marshal Landry. If I slipped up, there'd be hell to pay, and my cover would be blown.

Without a word, I tapped Bucky's black spotted flanks and urged him on. We were still a good way from Whitesberg, and as little armed as I was with just a pistol and tomahawk, I didn't want to spend a minute longer outside those towering walls than needed.

As we rode, we circled wide around yesterday's battlefield. I was curious as to what sort of dinosaurs would be out there feasting on the slain apes and mounts, and a small part of me wanted to see if I could find a discarded rifle. But the risk wasn't worth the reward, so we kept moving. From the distance we were at, I could hear the occasional roar and an almost constant screeching of pterodactyls. The leathery birds were certainly picking the bones clean.

McGibbons tried several times to make small talk with me. After a couple failed attempts that were met with my blunt and short replies, he gave up.

That was fine with me. I wasn't in a talkative mood, and I wanted to keep my attention on our surroundings so we wouldn't get eaten or sacrificed.

A few hours later, we reached Whitesberg.

The town was like a medieval fortress. Pointed logs placed into the ground and stood upright formed a protective wall around the buildings and people. As we rode closer, the Pinkertons who stood watch on top of the wall with several Gatlings and cannon emplacements shouted to those inside of our approach.

McGibbons waved his rifle from behind Landry, and the large metal portcullis that allowed the railroad and train to run inside the town was raised by wheels and levers inside.

"Impressive," Marshal Landry said.

"That's just for the train. They keep it closed and raise it just when the train is arriving or leaving. Mainly people use the side gates to come and go. There's one on each wall."

"Oh, have you been here before?" McGibbons asked. Landry shot me a questioning look with an arched eyebrow.

I could have kicked myself if I hadn't been riding in a saddle.

"No, I've just heard a bit about the place," I lied to them both. "There's not much for us Raiders to do other than raid, train, eat, and talk."

Wesley met us once we rode through the iron reinforced and banded gate and stopped our horses inside. The town had grown in the weeks since I'd been here last. For one thing, the wall appeared to have been finished on the far side of town that bordered the ocean shore. For another, more buildings had been completed and there was even gravel spread on the roads between them. And what I thought were Gatlings mounted on the walls, I realized now were the newfangled Maxim machine guns from Europe.

"Good morning, lady and gentlemen," the outlaw said with a slight smile and a partial bow.

"Now you're just putting on airs," I said while dismounting and trying to look around nonchalantly. Somewhere in this town was Reydan and Cato. And probably Fredrick. Plus, a couple other savvy characters who would deduce my identity at a glance.

I tugged my hat brim lower over my eyes.

"Sorry it's just me, Johnson. The rest of the Raiders are resting or being tended to. And ah," he stared hard at me as if to make a point, "no one else, of any particular stature in this town, cares about your arrival. At least enough to present themselves. And Governor Fredrick is back at the Shimmer."

"That's off putting," Marshal Landry said as McGibbons climbed down from behind her. When he wasn't looking, she glanced at me as though to see my reaction to the news that Reydan wouldn't be walking up to us to take my bullet this fine morning.

I tried to keep the frown and frustration from my face.

It was probably a good thing. I couldn't simply gun the man down in the streets, as much as he deserved it. I needed a plan. And so far, no opportunities had presented themselves short of my arrival to the same town Reydan was in.

"Think I'll go look around," I said abruptly.

"The men are in the stables," Wesley said quickly, pointing towards where I knew the building and corral was located. "They'll be pleased to see you're alive."

I gave a grunt but said nothing. Of course, I would be expected to check on the other Raiders first, they were supposed to be my top priority.

"Johnson... my rifle?" Wesley asked bluntly with his hand held out.

"Marshal McGibbons has it," I said as the black lawman passed the Winchester to the outlaw with thanks.

Pulling Bucky's reins, I led the appaloosa in the direction he'd pointed.

"Where's Marshal Carlos?" I heard Landry ask behind me.

"Walking the wall," Wesley replied.

When I reached the stable, I found Talon lying on a slab bench outside, with his hat covering his face and apparently trying to get some sleep. His leg was propped up, a white dressing wrapped around the wound in his thigh. George was sitting beside him, and when he noticed my approach, he jumped upright and gave a shrill whistle to alert the others.

Talon flipped his hat off and gave me a wave as the others came out. The Raiders looked pleased at my reappearance, and I was bombarded with questions.

Raising my hands, I quieted them down to a low murmur while looking over the crowd. We'd lost a few men for sure, but it wasn't as bad as I originally thought.

"First things first. Anyone got a spare rifle? Mine was crushed under the stagecoach."

"I got one!" someone shouted.

"Thanks. And second, we were able to get Marshal McGibbons back, but not the Pinkerton." Try as I might, I couldn't recall what his name was. I think it began with a H... It wasn't my fault, if they wanted to be remembered then they shouldn't all look the same.

There was some muttering at that, but nothing bad. The Pinkertons had managed to anger pretty much everyone they came across with their arrogance and the authority from the East-West railroad that they lorded over everyone with.

A Winchester was passed to me. Snicking the lever down, I opened the chamber and observed it was empty.

"What? No cartridges?" I chuckled.

George passed me a bandoleer as Wesley walked up beside me.

"Thanks." I looked at the other Raiders; it was like they expected more of me.

Swallowing, I tried to think of something rousing to tell them.

"You all did a fine job. We were ambushed and took a licking, but we fought through it, and beat them on the field of battle. Lieutenant Heath will be pleased, as will Governor Fredrick. But for now, get some rest, we'll be heading back soon."

The men went back into the darkened interior of the stable, and Talon lay back down with his hat over his face again.

"Soon, huh? How soon?" Wesley asked.

"I'm going to poke around a bit first."

He pulled a cigarillo from his pocket and lit it with a match, "Need some company?"

"No." I watched the last of the men enter the stables. "How many did we lose?"

"What do you mean *we*?" He pulled a piece of paper from another pocket and handed it to me, still folded. "Four dead. Six wounded. Three of those wounded will need to stay here until they can move them with a train."

"Horses?"

"We got enough for everyone who can ride."

"What about the Vikings? Where are they?"

Wesley blew a puff of smoke and smirked. "When we arrived, they just turned around and went back towards the Shimmer. Just as nonchalantly as could be, without a care in the world."

I shook my head. "The Axemen are some mighty hard people. I'm glad they're on our side."

"Me too." He took another drag of the thin cigarette. "You sure you don't want company?"

I opened the piece of paper and read the list of names quietly to myself before pocketing it.

"Yeah. I appreciate the offer though."

"Well, don't go getting yourself into any trouble you can't ride away from. And just so you know, every gate is closed and guarded, and the portcullis is down. No one is riding away from here quickly."

"You're all subtlety and rainbows, you know that?"

"Just trying to keep you alive. Otherwise, they may put me in charge." He blew smoke as I turned away.

"Oh, one more thing, Johnson."

I looked over my shoulder and he grinned slyly at me like he knew a secret before uttering words I never thought I'd hear.

"The Shaynee are here."

***

Wesley said he'd overheard from a couple of Pinkerton detectives that the Indians were mainly staying to themselves in the southwest corner of the town. That was opposite of where the stables were, and I hoped that meant my chances of running into them was slim. Even one of them would recognize the distinctive bullet-holed tomahawk of Otto's that I carried. All I could do was hope that my blood brother had warned them all to keep quiet about what I was doing.

And if there was a group of Shaynee here, Otto was certainly with them.

I needed information about Whitesberg from someone I could trust, and there was only one person that I knew was bound to be on this side. And I was fairly certain he wouldn't mind my goal of assassinating the town's founder. Grabbing a small bundle out of one of my saddle bags on the back of Bucky and stuffing it most of the way into a pocket, I went for a walk.

The brand new carved wooden sign that hung over the boardwalk was a beauty.

At the top, in white scripted font was 'Liberty Arms'.

Below that, it read 'Purveyors of Fine Arms and Ammunitions'.

It was my favorite store in the world.

It was also built like a fortress. Even for Prehistoria, the building stood out compared to the others along the street. The glass windows were caged over with wrought iron bars. The siding was thick and overlapped, and it gave off the appearance of a Sheriff's jail more than a fancy gun store.

The small bell attached to the thick slab door tinkled as I pushed it open, giving warning to anyone inside that someone was entering.

I stopped abruptly and my hand dropped onto my pistol grip.

Greeting me, front and center, was a raptor.

A big one.

About four feet tall and six feet long. A light tan colored, furry in the body but colorfully feathered along the outstretched arms equipped with black claws and tail that balanced the mount. Red feathers were slicked back from the top of the sloping head, the snout blunt and reptilian. This one was mounted with its mouth open and teeth showing.

A chuckle came from the back of the store followed by a southern aristocrat accent, "Don't mind the raptor, it's harmless."

Reaching out, I gently touched the feathers on the stuffed raptor's head. The Shaynee used them to decorate their weapons, much like eagle feathers from our side. If it was true and there was power from the feathers of such ferocious beasts, I might end up tying some to my guns before this adventure was over.

Moving past the mounted dinosaur, I looked around while walking down the center aisle towards the back of the store. Shelves and racks lined the walls, filled with various sizes and types of leather holsters, belts, empty bandoleers, even saddle bags. Tables filled the floor space, piled high with various odds and ends. Shirts, vests, pants, things like that. Items to add to the income of a store that mainly sold firearms and firearms-related merchandise.

I slowed as I neared the back of the store.

Here were several tables covered with ape weapons for sale. One was covered with mainly obsidian chipped knives, bundles of ape arrows, and a couple of spears. The other, a more sturdily built table, held a couple of heavier examples of stone clubs and axes.

I picked up one of the knives. It reminded me of the sacrificial ape knife that Skyla carried. Same general shape, made of chipped glossy black obsidian, but the handle was different. Where my paleontologist's handle was made of trike horn, this one appeared to be of bone.

I hoped it wasn't human.

Setting the knife back down on the elk hide that draped over the table, I walked past.

A tall, almost gaunt looking gentleman stood behind the counter that ran the length of the back of the room. Behind him was a stairwell leading to what was likely his living quarters above the store.

His high cheekbones shifted as he gave a ghost of a smile. "Well, well... Jedidiah Huckleberry Smith. Still alive..."

"Still alive," I repeated before taking off my hat and setting it down on the counter beside a partially disassembled Sharps rifle.

"Good. Can't have my favorite customer getting murdered by a dozen Pinkertons."

I rapped my knuckles against the leather vest with its hidden dragon scales inside. "If it wasn't for this, I would have been." Opening my fist, I tapped a spot near the center of my chest where I'd put a couple of stitches in the leather to cover the bullet hole. "This one almost got me."

Carson Skinner gave a rare grin. "I knew that vest would come in handy."

"I owe it to you and Skyla."

"And how is she?"

"She's back East, recovering. Other than that, I don't know."

He gestured with a finger towards my goateed face, then swirled it into a circle indicating the rest of my outfit. "Good disguise. I take it you left the guns and Carbine somewhere safe?"

"I did."

"And what name are you going by?"

"Johnson Brown."

"Noted." He ran a hand over his goatee and mustache. "Now. What brings you to my store?"

"Information."

He chuckled dryly and slightly shifted the pistol holstered to the front of his pants. He wore it in a cavalry draw, butt forward on the weak hand side, so it wouldn't interfere with riding a horse. "About Reydan White, I'd hazard a guess."

"You guess right. I want him and I want him dead."

He leaned forward on the counter, his face suddenly hard. "This ain't killing no Yankee carpet bagger or typical Union degenerate raider abusing the South. This man is a king in his own kingdom here. He's got the Black Plague, an army of Pinkertons, Maxim machine guns, and enough friends in the Army like Captain Hawney to have you hanged or shot for trying to escape before you go to trial." He straightened and spread his arms wide. "This is his castle, his fiefdom... his territory. And you are deep in it, my friend. Tread carefully."

Setting my elbows beside my hat, I leaned close to him. "I don't care if he sits on a golden throne surrounded by an army of Pinkertons in white robes. He shot my girl, and he killed my friends. He dies."

"So, it's not about just you and your ruined back anymore?"

"No," I admitted to both Carson and myself for the first time. "Our feud has gone far past that."

"I just wanted to make sure you realized that."

"I do," I growled.

He nodded curtly. "Well, you've given up your biggest advantages by coming here in disguise. And that's leaving your friends, your horse, and the weapons I gave you on the other side."

"I'm not completely alone," I said defensively.

"You must be speaking of the Shaynee."

"And John Wesley Gardner."

Carson whistled. "That's a good one to have watching your back, so long as you stay on his good side... and don't snore. Where does he stand on all of this?"

"He's just hiding out, letting some heat die down before returning to our side and his life of crime. But I think I can count on him in a pinch."

"Then what do you need from me?"

I pulled the small bundle that was hanging out of my back pocket free and set it on the counter. The bag made clinking noises as the objects inside settled.

"I want you to remind Reydan who he messed with." Turning the bag over on its end, I dumped out the Pinkerton badges in a pile. Several were coated with blood, a couple others smeared. One of them had a bullet hole through the center. A lucky shot.

"Mary and Joseph!" Carson swept the pile of badges back into the bag and pulled the drawstring tight while glaring at me. "Don't let anyone see you with these. Where'd you get them?" He hissed.

"From the Pinkertons that Reydan sent to attack my ranch."

"I heard you killed a bunch, but I didn't realize you looted the corpses too."

"To make a point." I raised a finger into the air and shook it towards the door behind me. "I want Reydan to know I'm coming for him. Wait a day or two after we leave and drop those badges on his front doorstep in the middle of the night."

The gun salesman frowned. "He'll know you're coming for him."

"He already knows."

Carson picked up the bag and placed it under the counter. "I suppose that's true. He'd have to be some sort of fool to figure you wouldn't come after him considering what he tried to do."

"I want him worried. I want him to look over his shoulder and wonder if I'm aiming a rifle at it. Because one day, very soon, I will be."

"You'd shoot a man in the back?" He arched an eyebrow quizzically.

"He's not much of a man. So, yes."

The salesman rubbed the graying hair along his temple with a thumb. He sighed. "You know Reydan's father is a Senator, right? There will be hell to pay with a man of Reydan's stature dying. Wealthy and politically connected railroad tycoons don't just get murdered and nothing bad happen to the people who did it."

"I'll burn that bridge after I cross it."

"That's not how the saying goes."

"Close enough," I stuck out my hand. "Thanks, Carson, for everything."

He shook it firmly and looked me in the eye. "Good luck, Johnson Brown. And if you plan on dying, return the *Eighty-Six*. I don't want some asshole Pinkerton to take it off your corpse."

Giving him a sideways grin, I took my hat and walked out of the store.

***

"Johnson Brown," a soft female voice spoke from beside the door as I closed it behind me.

"Marshal Landry," I replied, turning to face my sister.

"How'd you know it was me?"

"I could smell the whiskey and tobacco on your breath from a mile away."

She hawked and spat out the plug she'd been chewing on. It splattered against the newly built boardwalk. Frowning, she stepped forward and flicked the nasty lump into the road with the toe of her boot. A smear of brown juice and spit was left behind on the boards.

"Where's your friends?" I asked her.

Leaning back against the slap board sides of Liberty Arms, she crossed her arms and jerked her head down the street. "Meeting Colonel Carver."

"Without you?"

"I told them I'd rather poke around town a bit than play politics with the Army."

"Too bad. But if you get the chance, you should meet Governor Fredrick. He is quite the charmer." I looked at her out of the corner of my eye. "And a good-looking bachelor at that."

She snorted then laughed. "I don't need a husband. There are too many bad men that need arresting and hanging."

"There are other Marshals."

"But there's only one of me," she said softly.

We stood in silence for a moment, myself keeping an eye up and down the street for anyone I might know, and I could feel my sister's eyes on me.

"What?" I finally asked.

She looked pointedly at the sign above us. "Liberty Arms," she read. "Why are you here?"

"I like guns. Always have. You know that."

"Yes, but you're not carrying anything new. No rifle case," she looked me up and down, "no obvious sign of another pistol, no nothing. Besides, from what I've heard, you've quite the armaments already... An 1886 Winchester prototype, not even released to the public yet, and a pair of matching Colt Peacemakers with an Arkansas Toothpick."

"It's called a Bowie," I corrected her.

"Same thing. You're dodging the question."

I watched the Reverend cross the street a couple of buildings down from us. I would recognize that gait of his anywhere. Without thinking, I tipped my hat lower over my eyes. He was one man I needed to avoid.

"See someone you recognize?" She turned her head to look in the same direction as I did as the Reverend entered the General Store. "Who is that? A man of the cloth?"

"A friend. Leave him alone." I turned back to her. "What do you want? To pester me to death?"

"Right now, I want to know why you were in this gun store."

"Just looking around."

She threw her head back and laughed. "You're a terrible liar."

"Actually, I'm quite good."

Pushing herself off the side of the building, she stood upright and shook her head. "See you around, Johnson Brown."

I watched as she sauntered away before turning and walking in the opposite direction.

***

"Got a couple of soldiers who want to meet you," Wesley whispered to me as I entered the stables.

Frowning, I looked around. I didn't see any uniformed men. "Where are they?"

"They just left. Said for the leader of C Troop to come find them once you got back." He frowned. "Would they know you?"

"Probably," I admitted. "They give their names?"

"Colonel Carver, Captain Hawney, and a young fellow named Lieutenant Daniels."

"I know them and they'd recognize me. And worse, the only one I trust is Lieutenant Daniels."

"Well, they're waiting on you. So, you'd best start coming up with a plan before they get annoyed and come back here searching for you."

I looked around. The Raiders looked bored. Talon was still lying in the sun and cutting notches in his rifle stock. Bart was rubbing his new horse down. A couple of men were sitting on benches playing cards and gambling with what looked like pebbles. "Let's get everyone mounted."

"We running?"

"More like trotting."

In half an hour we had everyone mounted. Ten minutes after that, we rode to the eastern gate on the same side as the railroad and portcullis to head back to our encampment.

A pair of soldiers stepped in front of me with their hands held up.

I pulled back on Bucky's reins, hoping he wouldn't start trying to throw me.

Luck was with me. He just tossed his head in disgust and stamped his hooves impatiently.

"What is it, Private?" I asked the soldier who was closest to me with a frown.

"Where you headed?" the other asked, another private, but apparently the boss of the two. I turned my frown into a glare. The uniformed man swallowed hard but didn't back down.

"To Fort York and the Shimmer."

"The Captain know?"

I shared a look with Wesley. While we'd been getting our mounts ready, I'd told him my thoughts and interactions with the officers. Of course, that power tripping fool would control who came and went in his domain.

"Captain Hawney told me it was time to leave, and none too politely at that," I said confidently.

The soldier chuckled. "That sounds like him." He stepped out of the way and extended his arm and hand towards the open gate. "Ride safe, gentlemen."

"Much appreciated," I waved at the remnants of Charlie Troop behind me to move forward.

With just enough haste to not look suspicious, we rode through the gate.

About fifty yards in front of us, the two Axemen stood beside their trikes.

I thumped Bucky's sides and rode ahead of the column to meet them. "Knud, Ulf, good to see you."

Knud tipped his tattooed head in greeting, while Ulf patted the large black single horn in the center of the face of his trike.

"You ready to go back?" I pointed down the tracks in the direction C Troop was headed.

Ulf said something to the other axeman and the pair of them laughed before mounting. As the column closed the distance between us, the Vikings began to move their horned dinosaurs down the tracks towards the Shimmer.

We fell in behind them, letting the pair of dinosaur mounted Axemen lead the way. Both they and their mounts weren't only survivors of this side, they were thrivers. They'd been born and raised in this prehistoric world. I trusted their instincts over my own.

As we rode, I looked at the Axemen's trikes, for the first time noticing the healed scars on each mount now overlayed with a few fresh cuts and gouges from trike horns and such. These trikes and Vikings had been through the wringer a time or two and lived to tell the tale.

"You forgot to say goodbye to Marshal Landry."

I adjusted the position of my latest Winchester across the pommel of the saddle, trying to make it more comfortable and balanced. "Wouldn't be the first time. But I'm sure our paths will cross again."

"Me too. She's a looker."

I gave Wesley a side-eyed glare and he chuckled with a hand raised to me. "No offense, just saying. All I've seen for female company for the past few weeks has been a few trikes."

"You'd think after a job well done, they'd turn us loose a little bit, let us get some rest and relaxation. But you know we both can't afford that."

"Such is a life in hiding. Speaking of which, you forgot to get even back there."

"Didn't forget," I told him sharply. "Just didn't have an opportunity. I'd like to find or make one where I get out alive afterwards."

"That's always the hard part of planning an assassination."

"You said it right."

Knud slowed his trike, then turned back around to face us. With a single finger, he rose it to the lips on his inked face, indicating we should be quiet. Then he jerked his head towards the front.

Standing in Bucky's stirrups, I rose from the saddle and looked ahead, noting the turn of the railroad and our distance from Whitesberg.

We were about to cross the battlefield from the previous day.

***

I passed the Axeman's warning down the column, trusting the men of my troop to keep quiet and know that their lives likely depended upon it.

And as we moved through the forest, into the opening, the first thing we saw was a fifteen-foot tall, red-feathered bird stretch its wings casually, showing off its intimidatingly large wingspread, then step on an ape corpse and rip off an arm with its beak. Throwing its pink tufted head back, the giant pterodactyl swallowed the limb whole. Its throat bobbed slightly as the hairy morsel moved into its body.

"What the hell is that?" Wesley whispered, his voice breaking slightly as he took in the sight of the gigantic bird. "Some sort of giant Breeha?"

"Nope. That… is what the Shayana call a Merhah. Irving tells me it's some sort of Quetzal. A, ah… Quetzalcoatlus." I was sure I mispronounced the name, but I was pretty certain that's what Irving said it was while we were discussing the dinosaurs I'd seen so far. "It's the largest flying dinosaur in the world."

"Should we shoot it?" Talon called softly from behind us.

"Let's not stir up any more trouble," I told him without looking back. The last thing I needed was to lose more men before I could give command back to Lieutenant Heath.

We gave the Quetzal a wide berth as we rode past. A hundred feet past the giant bird were the remains of the stagecoach.

Wesley gave a low whistle as we rode by. "Look at that."

I was already looking at it, and not liking what I was seeing. The coach had been ripped open like a can of beans. Paneling and boards had been shattered and splintered beneath the claws of some giant beast. What remained of the dead horses was only a giant smear of gore from where something... or somethings... had feasted.

Immediately, I was thinking of the Tyrannosaurus we'd killed weeks ago. Was it possible another one had moved into the area? Or could there have been more than one here? Was there a nest nearby? There was no telling without tracking the giant beast, and we didn't have time for that foolishness. It seemed like a good way to get eaten.

Ulf and Knud seemed uneasy by whatever caused the destruction, and they whispered between each other in axeman speak rapidly. After a quick glance back at the column, they urged their trikes to move faster, and we pushed our horses from a walk into a quick trot behind them.

Ahead of us was a pair of allosauruses tearing apart a dead ape between them. The hairy painted corpse was already mangled and missing chunks, but the dinosaurs seemed to be playing with it, like a dog would play tug of war with another. As we watched, a leg came off in one of the beast's mouths. In disinterest, the dinosaur opened its jaws and dropped the limb before snatching at the rest of the corpse the other allosaurus was trying to turn away with.

Without thinking, I raised a hand and grasped at where my allosaurus claw would have been hanging. But it was gone, and I lowered my hand. Skyla had it now. And she was safe, back East with her family and the Smithsonian, recuperating.

I missed her very much.

"Why the long face?" Wesley whispered as the pair of Vikings ahead crossed the steel train tracks to put more space between our column and the carnivorous and apparently bored dinosaurs.

"Just thinking."

"The men didn't die because of you. Lieutenant Heath will understand that," Wesley said, thankfully misunderstanding my visible emotions.

I didn't answer, instead giving the allosaurus one last lingering look.

I was tired of playing this game.

I wanted my revenge and then I wanted to return to my love in one piece.

It was time to find or make an opportunity to kill the bastard.

Upon our return to the Shimmer encampment, Lieutenant Heath was waiting for us.

We stopped our column and waited as the officer tried to talk to the Axemen. I knew that the Raider troop officers had been practicing their language, but I hadn't realized how poorly it was going until the Lieutenant threw up his hands in disgust and walked away from the Vikings.

The pair chuckled, turned their trikes and wandered away. Off to who knows where, they didn't have a particular place set aside for their kind in our encampment. From what I'd been able to glean, they simply showed up in pairs or small groups and helped out when needed. Other times they'd cause trouble with the Shayana or Pinkertons. The soldiers they seemed to respect to a degree, but not the detectives. They seemed to go out of their way to goad the badged turd burglars into fights or arguments.

"Johnson," Lieutenant Heath looked down the column and sighed. "Casualty report?"

I pulled the slip of paper from my pocket and handed it to him.

The Lieutenant opened the piece of paper, read it over and frowned. "Did you recover the bodies?"

"Wesley and the others did, sir. I was with Marshal Landry trying to get back one of the other Marshals the apes snatched to sacrifice."

"Which one?"

"Marshal McGibbons."

"Did you get him back?"

I nodded. "Unharmed for the most part, sir."

"Good." He looked down the column again and back to me. "I suppose you left the bodies in Whitesberg?"

"Yes, sir, I figured it would be better to bring them back on the train."

"Good thinking, Johnson. Go ahead and turn the men loose to tend to their mounts and get some chow. After that, you and I will talk."

***

"Have a seat, Johnson," the Lieutenant commanded me with a not unkind voice after I finished giving him a quick recounting of what had occurred during our escort of the US Marshals.

I sat, dreading his response to my actions.

Lieutenant Heath sat on a log across a smoldering fire from me. He patted his pockets for a moment before pulling out a pipe and tobacco. With well-rehearsed movements, he began packing the bowl.

"I want you to know, I don't blame you for what happened to C Troop while it was under your command. These men, these Raiders, they are not shock troops. They aren't trained or meant to ride headlong into battle with mounted apes. They did the best they could, with what they had, to protect their charges under an ambush. If Wesley hadn't managed to regroup and turned the men around to engage after the stagecoach crashed, the Marshals would likely have all been killed. And Irving along with them."

I swallowed hard, thinking of Marshal Landry. We had enough drama in my family as it was without my being responsible for my law-enforcing sister's death. Father would never forgive me for that. He liked me well enough, but he always doted on her. And Irving, I'd taken to the young man. He had a bright future on this side if he lived long enough to see it.

"Governor Fredrick would like to meet with you."

I blinked, trying hard not to let the surprise and worry show.

He saw it anyways and raised his pipe slightly to wave away my concerns. "Don't worry about the men, he's well aware that some of them are probably wanted for breaking various laws," he said, misunderstanding my sudden worry. "But just because he's aware of it, doesn't mean he wants the newspapers catching on and giving him hell over it. The publicity would probably ruin his chances of keeping his position as Governor, or this unit."

"Yes, sir," I said, as thoughts spun through my head of how I could avoid Fredrick. "But, perhaps instead of meeting, we could-"

"Could what?" came a booming voice from behind me as a large man stepped around my seat and planted himself before Lieutenant Heath and myself.

Together, Heath and I stood.

Fredrick stared at me for a moment, blinking, and I could see the realization dawning in his spectacled eyes.

"Lieutenant," he said slowly. "I'd like to speak with Mr. Brown alone, if you don't mind. Nothing against you, sir, or your opinion, I'd just like to hear the story direct from the horse's mouth and unencumbered by a fine officer's presence."

"As you wish, Governor." Lieutenant Heath gave me an encouraging wink and strode away, leaving me behind with my friend.

Fredrick's mouth grew into a beaming grin, raising his bushy mustache high and exposing straight white teeth. "My goodness, Jed, it's great to see you alive!"

"You as well, Fredrick." We shook hands.

He sat on the log that the Lieutenant abandoned. "Sit down, man! Tell me everything."

I sat, but before I could begin to speak, the overzealous famed hunter-turned-politician began chuckling. "I knew you were here somewhere. Wade sent me a telegram weeks ago that an old friend would be joining the Raiders but didn't wish to stand out. Right away, I knew! I knew it was you he was talking about. I've been keeping an eye out for you ever since." He looked me up and down. "Well, you certainly are disguised. Without your horse and guns, and that goatee added on your face, I'm surprised I recognized you at all."

"That was the intent. But I laid low just the same... just trying to blend in with the other Raiders... until this ape ambush."

"Yes..." he rubbed his chin thoughtfully. "Well, don't you worry, we're going to kick the apes in the groin for that. Hard."

"Fredrick," I stared at my friend and shook my head slowly, "I'm not here for the apes."

"Yes," he said slowly, his thoughtful frown turning serious. "I heard of the attack on your place. And of Skyla being shot, and Charles and your friend being killed."

"And I aim to make Reydan pay for that with his life."

"Jed, let the Marshals handle that. Reydan White is one of the men I want brought to trial once they gather enough evidence. I'm certain there are more victims of his out there than just you and Skyla."

"You and I both know that they can't do squat against one of the wealthiest men in America and the son of a Senator unless they catch him with blood dripping from his hands from a fresh murder... and even then, he'd probably still get away with it."

"We will catch him, I'm sure of it. If you'd just come out of hiding, we could lure him into going after you again and get him then!"

"No!" I stood abruptly, jerking my hat off and slamming it down. "No more! Enough of my friends have been hurt or killed because of his orders. This time I do it my way, alone."

"You aren't alone," Fredrick said softly as he rose to his feet to leave. "It's time you stopped thinking that way." He took several steps before stopping and halfway turning back to me. "Your guns are in a cabinet in my office. Otto and some of his braves snuck them over and passed them along to me." He sighed and spoke over his shoulder as he walked away, "We'll be in Whitesberg if you need us."

Lieutenant Heath appeared shortly after Fredrick left. "How'd it go with the Governor?"

"Fine. Seems like a nice enough fellow."

"He is a force of nature," Heath replied. "That man will move mountains through sheer will power. I wouldn't be surprised if he ran for President someday."

"I could see that." I chewed on my lip, still thinking over what Fredrick had said. "Anything else you need me for, sir?"

"No, go ahead and get some rest. From what I gather, Charlie Troop will be needed again soon."

"Yes, sir."

***

Three days later, the Lieutenant pulled us all together at the crack of dawn to deliver the news.

"Listen up, gentlemen," he held a stick in his hand and tapped the ground in front of him thoughtfully. "The Shayana have been keeping an eye on the apes, and they've assembled an army. A big one that's getting bigger by the day."

A low murmur spread amongst the men of my troop as Raiders began whispering to each other about the news.

"Quiet." He stared at us until only the sound of the encampment coming alive in the early morning hour could be heard.

"We've been playing soft with these damned monkeys long enough. Now we are going to hit them, hard. The aim is for all three Raider troops to hit them at the same time, all along their perimeter. We want to stir them up, make them angry, and maybe a little hungry for our blood. If we're lucky, they'll come after us in retaliation before their army gets any bigger. If we're unlucky, we'll have at least given them a solid black eye and whittled their forces down a bit."

"And if we're real unlucky, we get eaten," Wesley whispered in my ear.

I smirked, but my thoughts were racing. Perhaps in all the confusion I could slip away and go after Reydan. But what then? I'd have to get into Whitesberg somehow. Unless I could get word to Otto to open a gate for me. How would I do that?

"Johnson, are you paying attention or practicing a frown?" Lieutenant Heath asked. Apparently, he'd said something else that I hadn't heard.

The men around me chuckled and I faked a smile but didn't say anything.

"As I was saying. We want them to come at us." He raised the crooked stick and gestured at the encampment we were standing in. "Our defenses will never be stronger than they are now." He chuckled, "And if we don't hurry and engage the apes, Congress is threatening to send troops down to Texas to quell some water and grazing right issues. We need to use them while we've got them here."

"What sort of apes are we facing, sir?" Bart asked with a worried look on his face.

"Hairy ones."

Charlie Troop broke into snickers again and Talon shoved the Raider playfully as he ducked his face in embarrassment.

"I meant-"

"I know what you meant, Bart." Heath spat on the ground and rubbed it with the end of the stick. "There's at least one dragon, maybe two. A lot of trikes, and a bunch of raptor cages."

George swore loudly behind me. A couple of men chuckled at his accent.

The Lieutenant continued, "We can't hide from 'em. We've got to face them head on with gunfire." He pulled a silver watch from his pocket and clicked it open. "Governor Fredrick is giving a speech in… twenty-one minutes; I suggest you grab something to eat and ready your gear."

Wesley and I walked together back to our tent, both quiet as we thought about the task before us. I wasn't hungry, and my companion didn't seem to be either.

"You good for this?" Wesley finally asked, breaking the silence between us.

"I don't see any other choice. No way to get out of this and finish Reydan off." I spat to the side and wiped the corner of my mouth and mustache. "Reckon I'll be coming along for the attack."

"Good to have you."

Reaching my tent, I pulled the flap back and looked at Wesley. "Thanks, Wesley. Good to have you too." Dropping the flap, I stuck my hand out and he shook it while I looked him in the eyes. "You've been a good friend these past weeks. I don't know what I'd have done without you."

Dropping my hand, the outlaw-in-hiding shook his head and ducked into the tent, saying over his shoulder, "Something stupid no doubt."

Laughing, I followed him inside. I didn't have much for belongings, but I kept them neat and ready to leave in a second should there either be an opportunity to go after Reydan, or if I was discovered by his Pinkertons or some other crony. And since all my personal guns were in Fredrick's office now, I didn't have any possessions I couldn't leave behind in thirty seconds or less if I felt the heat. Just an old bedroll, saddle, and Bucky. I rubbed my backside gingerly; that was a horse I would certainly not miss.

But I suppose he still beat walking.

***

This time Fredrick stood beside a cannon atop a mound of packed dirt and a palisade built around it. Resting beside him, with its octagonal barrel leaned against the black steel of the crew served weapon, was one of his heavily customized rifles. He cut a dashing figure in the rising light of the Prehistoria sun.

His eyes cut over the crowd, and once he found me standing near the back, he gave a subtle tip of the hat in my direction.

Raising a hand, he quietened the murmur of the crowd without a loud shout, or a pistol shot.

"Raiders! Your time has come. As your commanding officers have no doubt told you, an ape army is being raised. According to our Shayana allies, they number in the hundreds and are growing larger by the day." He waited for the cursing and muttering at that enemy number to cease and then smirked from beneath his bushy mustache. "Luckily for us, we've plenty of ammunition." His smirk faded to a serious frown. "What we are short on, is men. The Encampment, as I'm told this backside of Fort York is being called, will have a hard time handling an attack by that many. We don't dare let them grow their forces further. So, we're sending you. Your task will be the same, regardless of the troop you may be in. You will seek out this army and you will hit them. Hard and brutally. You will kill as many of them as you can. And then you will lead the surviving apes back here where we will be waiting with bullets and cannon shot." He patted the cannon beside him lovingly. "I'm told this one has been christened 'Martha' by its crew. And I know that 'Martha' will do her part to blow many an ape to hell on their futile charge up this valley. But it's up to the Raiders to see that she gets the chance.

"Hit them, gentlemen, hit them hard. Then lead them back to us." He nodded savagely. "We'll do the rest after that. God bless, and happy hunting."

Captain Theo moved beside the Governor and quickly shouted at us to shut up and stay here before we could leave.

Fredrick shook the officer's hand, picked up his customized Winchester rifle, and stepped off the mound of dirt and out of sight behind the cannon named Martha.

Theo waved a hand behind him, and out came Lieutenant Heath and Lieutenant Barlow. My officer looked composed and confident. Barlow, commander of Bravo Troop, looked eager. I guess that was saying something since he'd been bloodied already by the apes and looked like he was ready for revenge. Maybe I'd underestimated him.

"Gentlemen," Captain Theo began. "The ape army is gathering two days from here. You are going to leave within the hour to begin your trek to attack. You will spend the night in the prehistoric wilderness, where there will be no campfires, no smoking, and fifty percent watch at all times. I tell you this, because you've all engaged with the apes already. You know what it's like to fight them now during the daylight, but at night it's going to be an entirely different animal. At night you will be at your most vulnerable. The apes, and believe me, they will be out there, will be able to get close to you. And when they are close, they have the upper hand with their size, strength, and weapons. We've trained you hard. But this will be your hardest task yet. You will be sleep deprived, and saddle tired from riding long hours. But you must stay ready and vigilant at all times to do battle.

"You will be exhausted by the time you hit them. And then you'll have to return here with an army of angry apes on your tail. You will be beyond tired by then and likely running your mounts to near death to keep ahead of the apes. Believe me, we are not just kicking over a hornet's nest, we're stomping on it then lighting it on fire." He paused, reached down and lifted up a bundle of dynamite overhead for everyone to see. "And this is your fire."

Talon whistled, a low and thoughtful noise.

"Hot damn," Bart grumbled. "I guess this is where we earn our pay and land deed."

"Every one of you will be carrying a bundle of this to use as your Commander sees fit," Captain Theo grinned at the crowd. "And remember, have fun."

***

Sweat trickled down my face as I lashed Bucky with the reins.

Charlie Troop had been whooped.

The damn numbers had always been against us.

"You think the Shayana knew?" Wesley called out to me as he pushed his horse to keep up with the rest of us.

I didn't bother answering, because at the moment it didn't matter. But later on, if Governor Fredrick or anyone else found out the Shayana knew and didn't tell us, there'd be another war in Prehistoria coming.

We'd lost a third of our men in the attack, and our Lieutenant was leading the column even as he bled out from an ape arrow through his side.

I didn't know where he was headed, he had the only map. All I knew was that south was the direction we were going and that was correct. That was where the encampment was located, and safety, and a surgeon for Lieutenant Heath.

It appeared we'd gotten away from the ape army. We hadn't heard or seen them for several hours.

The Lieutenant finally slowed down and passed the word for us to dismount.

We were in a small clearing lined with ferns inside the forest. Not the most defendable position, but one where we could keep an eye on each other and out for any apes sneaking up on us.

I looked at the dark faces, covered in sweat and shadow. We'd lost a lot of good men, including George. The Chinese Raider had fought like a wildcat when his horse went down. His big hat knocked aside, long black hair in a ponytail, and his custom rebel yell coming from his lips as he lashed out with the butt of his empty pistol... he'd fought bravely.

The man deserved a statue.

His loss had hit us all hard.

Lieutenant Heath coughed painfully, and Talon carefully helped him out of the saddle. Once on his feet, he stood straight, his eyes squinting in pain at the broken arrow jutting from his bloodied uniform.

"Raiders of C Troop, care for your horses and reload your weapons. We'll rest here for ten, then we move again." He leaned against a tree, then slid down into a sitting position, his face white from pain and exertion.

"Johnson, Wesley," he said to us, taking deep breaths that were obviously painful.

Tying off Bucky's reins to a nearby limb, I moved to the officer's side with Wesley.

Heath looked at the outlaw gunman, "Do you mind seeing to my horse? I don't believe I'm up to the task."

"Yes, sir." Wesley patted him gently on the shoulder, glanced at me, shook his head slightly as if to say he didn't think the Lieutenant was going to make it, then stepped away to tend to the animals.

"Johnson," Heath raised his head slightly to look up at me. I had to agree with Wesley, it appeared that death was coming for our commander soon.

"Sir?"

With the back of his hand, he wiped a trickle of blood away from his lips. "Johnson, if I don't make it, you're in charge." With a blood-smeared hand, he grabbed mine, his grip still strong. "They'll listen to you. And you get them back to safety, as many of them as you can. We kicked them in the groin pretty hard, and they're going to keep coming after us. It'll be a running fight from here on out. If I slow you down, leave me. I'll find a way back if I can."

"I ain't leaving you, sir," I said sincerely and meaning every bit of it. If I could keep him alive, I'd do so. But with his wound, things didn't look promising.

"It's an order."

"Sir, I-"

Heath pulled his pistol from its holster, thrust it outwards beside my face, and squeezed the trigger at the same moment an arrow zipped past and embedded itself in the Lieutenant's stomach.

Jerking away from the concussive boom and flare of flame from the officer's gun, I twirled with my Winchester in hand.

Apes.

Three of them.

Just dark outlines shifting in the shadows of the trees.

We lit them up with gunfire.

Within a couple of seconds, it was all over. The apes were dead, and the men were twirling around with guns pointed outwards from our position, waiting for more movement to betray any other attackers.

Turning back to Heath, I feared what I would see.

The officer clutched the arrow piercing his lower abdomen, and I could tell from the depth of the shaft that the obsidian point had gone through his body and pinned him to the tree.

"Shit, sir." I grasped for the shaft, feeling the thickness of the wood. There was no way to snap the arrow in my hands, we'd need something to cut it.

Putting both hands on it, I pulled gently. Testing it, just in case.

Nothing.

"Alright, Lieutenant. We're going to have to cut this arrow and pull you off it," I told him.

"No, no! Leave me here," he coughed painfully and with a blood-smeared smile chuckled. "I do believe I'm stuck."

"They'll kill you, sir!" Talon hissed as he looked around the darkened forest for more apes.

"They already have. Bart, fetch me some dynamite and give it here."

The Raider quickly fetched a bundle of boom sticks and handed them solemnly to the Lieutenant.

Our Commander reached into his pocket and pulled out a folded map. With his blood-smeared hand shaking, he passed it to me. "Johnson Brown, you're in charge. Take Charlie Troop home."

"Yes, sir." We clasped hands for a final time, and I stood, leaving my Lieutenant slouched against the rough bark of the great prehistoric tree. This would be his final resting place, but he would not go out of this world alone.

I walked over to where Bucky was tied off. In front of him was a dropped canteen and wet hat still partially filled with water. Wesley hadn't been tending to the Lieutenant's horse, he'd been tending to mine. He had known that the commander of C Troop wasn't going to make it... before he'd been arrowed.

"We gotta get moving," Wesley said calmly as he finished reloading his pistol and slipped it into the holster on his hip.

"Agreed. They're catching up."

The gun fighter picked up his hat and let Bucky slop more water out of it. "I think these are eager beavers. Pushing ahead of the main force to try and count coup or some ape equivalent on us."

"Let's not give them the chance." I pulled myself into the saddle of my sweat-lathered appaloosa.

"Raiders!" I glanced at where the Lieutenant lay pinned to the tree, and he gave me a weak and solemn salute.

"Let's ride!"

Talon glared at me from the back of his horse as I led the column away from Heath. He was angry at leaving our officer. I was too, but I had a new task at hand; to keep as many of the Charlie Troop Raiders alive as I could. And we were being hounded by a damnable army of apes.

I'd talk to the men when we had a chance but for now, either we rode, or we picked somewhere for a final stand that none of us would be walking away from.

Roughly five minutes had passed before we heard the dynamite go off behind us.

"A final gift," Wesley muttered as he ducked beneath a low hanging branch.

"Now we know how far behind they are, and with luck, they'll slow down a bit."

"Oh, I doubt they'll slow down."

"Way to stay positive, Wesley."

The gun slinger looked at the black sky and stars filtering through the trees that towered overhead. "Where are we headed, Johnson?"

"South to the Encampment."

Wesley twisted around in his saddle, checking on the line of riders behind us. "I don't think that's a good idea."

"Why not?"

"Before things went to hell during our attack, we watched over half the ape army leave. They were headed southwest, not southeast towards the Shimmer and Fort York."

I chewed on my lip for a moment before responding. "Maybe they're going to hit them from two directions? Or going after Novagant? If so, we'd need to warn Jarl Mikah and the Vikings somehow..."

The gunslinger shook his head. "My money is on Whitesberg."

"Whitesberg?"

"Think about it. With an army that size, they could hit both places at once with a good chance of winning. If they just hit one, the other could send reinforcements and flank the attacking army."

I shifted my rifle and stared into the darkness ahead. "You may be giving them too much credit. They are just apes."

"No, Johnson. You're not giving them enough. They've shown tactics before."

I thought about the Battle of the Apes and the Fall of Fort Jipson, both times the apes had surprised us with their cunning.

They had used infantry and cavalry tactics against us.

"Shit."

Wesley chuckled darkly. "Now you're catching on."

"Without reinforcements from the Encampment, Whitesberg would fall. They don't have enough men to defend a place that large against such an army."

"And Reydan White would fall with it," the outlaw added slyly.

"Yeah…" I rubbed my eyes. Damned, but I was tired. No fires meant no coffee, and it'd been a long couple of days. I was about to start eating coffee beans if I could find some. I sighed and turned Bucky's head towards the southwest. From behind I heard muttering from the column.

"There are other men there though, good men. I can't let them die."

"And don't forget Marshal Landry," Wesley said.

Sighing, I wiped sweat from my brow. "Yeah, her too."

A rider moved alongside me. It was Talon. "Johnson, what the hell? Where are you taking us?"

I tugged Bucky's reins to a stop and turned him around to face the other riders as they grouped up before me.

"You heard Lieutenant Heath's explosion. The apes are only a few minutes behind us. So, I'll make this quick. The apes are going to hit the Encampment, and Whitesberg. And we're going to Whitesberg to help defend it."

The men muttered and cursed amongst themselves.

Talon spit off to the side. "Shouldn't you give us a choice? Maybe some of us would prefer the safety of the Shimmer?"

"No."

"What?" He pushed his horse forward, anger etched across his face.

"I'll not give any man the opportunity to act cowardly. We ride together and we ride to Whitesberg. The Lieutenant would have wanted that."

"You left him to die!" Talon shouted loudly, startling something in the ferns nearby that skittered away. From the size, I guessed it was one of those small brown rat things.

Placing my hand on my pistol, I glared back. "He made his choice on how to die. And he died like a man, taking out those bastard apes with him and giving us notice of how far they are behind us. At the time, about five minutes. So, if you've got something you want to say to me, say it damned quick with a gun in your hand or fall in line and let's get moving before they catch up."

With an angry grunt, Talon looked down at the back of his horse and slowly nodded. "Alright, Johnson." He glanced up from under his hat with a slight grin, "Let's show the other Raiders how Charlie Troop fights."

"Damn right!" Bart called with a whoop.

"Shuddup," Wesley said quietly. "You're making it easier for the apes to find us."

I spun Bucky around and urged him into a trot. We'd lost time over this little spat, and we needed to get to Whitesberg before the other ape army did.

***

Our horses were barely able to walk when we entered the Northern gate of Whitesberg. They were lathered and beat, some wounded, and all exhausted. That was something we shared with our mounts. But unlike our mounts, our job wasn't done.

No.

It was just getting started.

One of the soldiers at the gate took my reins and looked us over in shock as the rest of the column entered.

I slipped from the saddle, catching myself before I toppled over. We'd ridden all night and day, luckily without being attacked again, and managed to beat the ape army to Whitesberg.

But now was no time to dally. We had defenses we needed to prepare.

"Where's Colonel Carver?" I croaked before twisting the cap off my canteen and taking a swig of the tepid water.

"With the Governor and Reydan White, in his office."

I gritted my teeth. It was time for this to all come to a head. "Take me there."

Wesley dismounted, more gracefully than I and stretched for a moment before adding, "Take us there."

I nodded at him. I could use the support for what we had planned.

"Talon, you're in charge," I told the Raider.

He stood a bit straighter and gave me a nod that I could trust him.

"Uh, right this way, gentlemen." A Private moved to lead the way.

We followed him; some of the soreness of my rear end started to fade away a bit while I flexed my fingers. They felt stiff from grasping the reins tightly in anticipation of having to kick Bucky and the column into a run to get away from any attackers. Hours of white knuckled gripping would make any quick draw that I had slow and pathetic.

I hoped it wouldn't come to that.

The Private stopped at an intersection near Carson's gun store. "His office is that way, five buildings down. You can't miss it. It's white and official looking, with a balcony and a big sign."

"Thanks," I told him before Wesley and I hurriedly walked down the street.

Outside of Liberty Arms lounged a half dozen Shaynee braves, talking with a few Vikings. A pair of trikes were tied to the large hitching post in front of the store. The two warrior tribes had connected well. Surprisingly, much better than then the Indians did with the Prehistoria Shayana.

One of the Shaynees stood, dusted off his hide leggings, and stared at us as we walked.

Noting the hideous scarring across his bare chest, I gave him a nod and a 'come with us' hand motion.

Otto said something to the other braves, hefted his decorated rifle, and left them behind. He quickly crossed the street, caught up with us, and flanked me on my left side while Wesley covered my right.

I felt better having another man on my side for this confrontation.

"Good to see you, Otto."

"You as well, Huck Berry," the brave rumbled back.

We reached the Governor's office a few minutes later. It was a nice-looking place, regal and stoic, whitewashed and pristine. I hoped it would survive what was coming.

A pair of Pinkertons lounged outside, enjoying the shade from the balcony above them and guarding the door. At our approach, they stood and straightened their matching long black coats. The badges on their hips reflected the sun with false authority.

The first, an older man sporting a graying mustache, held his hand out to stop us with a haughty look.

I gave what I hoped was a friendly grin. "We're here to see Governor Fredrick von Holsak."

"Mr. White is with him. You can wait over there until their business has concluded." He pointed with a crooked finger toward a row of rocking chairs. The chairs looked so new that I bet if I stepped a bit closer, I could smell the sawdust on them.

"As for the Injun, he can wait out in the street. Where he belongs," the Pinkerton chuckled and looked to his companion for agreement.

Before he could turn back, Otto'd thumped him upside the skull with his rifle. The feathered and beaded Winchester repeater dropped the Pinkerton like a sack of flour.

"I wouldn't," Wesley warned, his voice low and calm. He'd already drawn his pistol, and the barrel was pointed at the other Pinkerton whose hands were still wrapped around the front lapels of his black coat. "Now, disarm yourself... with your left hand."

The detective complied, unbuckling and letting the holstered gun fall to the boardwalk with a clatter.

"Yep. That'll do." I pointed at the fancy window paned double doors that probably cost two month's wages for a Raider. "You gonna stand there, or let us in, Pinkerton?"

"What about Old Fred?" he asked as though any of us cared about the downed detective.

"Old Fred will come around. Now open the doors. Slowly."

The disarmed man opened the doors, and as we walked through, I grabbed him by the collar and shoved him bodily ahead of us. "Where are they?" I demanded as we looked around the entry room. It was wallpapered. A pretty floral pattern of blue and yellow swirls, and trimmed out in white. A pair of long benches rested on either side of the room, a place for folks to wait their turn to see my friend.

And damned if there wasn't a painting of him.

A big one.

At the far end of the room, hanging from the wall. Right where everyone who came in would see it.

I grinned as I took in the art piece.

Fredrick smiled gallantly, from a kneeling position beside a dead tyrannosaurus while wearing his typical impeccable attire. His favorite rifle was cradled in his arms. The slain beast's mouth was open, exposing reddened teeth and a pink tongue.

Wesley whistled. "Now that's a man who's proud of his achievements."

"He sure is." I poked the detective in the back. "I asked you where they were. If I ask again, you're going to have a knot on your head that will rival Old Fred's."

Otto patted his rifle stock with an evil grin.

"I-I don't know. Honest. Probably upstairs."

"You're a real help," I muttered while pushing him towards the wrought iron circular staircase in the corner of the room.

"Shall I wait down here?" Wesley asked, peeking out the paned glass window at the unconscious detective in the street.

I tilted my head to see. An axeman was kneeling beside Fred and appeared to be robbing him while another watched.

"Naw, I'm going to need your level head to keep us all alive." I was dreading what I'd feel or do when I saw Reydan. I had a vengeful, angry streak in me. It'd kept me alive all these years. But some time had passed since he tried to kill Skyla...

I ground my teeth as I felt my blood begin to boil.

Yeah, I was going to need Wesley alright.

**

At the top of the stairs, we reached a single wide door. I didn't recognize the wood type, which meant it may have come from this side. But it looked dense.

I slammed the Pinkerton into it, knocking the door open and sending the detective sprawling onto the floor.

He landed mostly on a rug that looked like it was made of dinosaur hide.

We barged through right after him. I had my pistol in one hand and Ashley's bullet punched tomahawk in the other. Wesley had his pistol out. Otto's decorated rifle was tucked into his shoulder, barrel up and muzzle pointed ahead with his finger already caressing the trigger.

"Hands up, you bitches' sons!" Otto roared incorrectly as we lined up to face the occupants of the room with weapons drawn.

The large room was quiet.

Fredrick sat behind his desk, his fingers templed together in thought. On top of his giant desk rested a sun-bleached raptor skull. Beside him, leaning over the Governor's shoulder to look at a piece of large paper together, was Reydan White.

Cato stood motionless between us, his hands on the butts of his guns, but the pistols were still holstered.

I'd finally gotten the drop on my former brother. I met his eyes with mine and returned his glare with a wink.

"So-sorry boss, they got the drop on us," the detective on the ground said from where he lay looking up at his employer.

"No we didn't, you're just terrible at your job," Wesley reminded him. "Unless it comes to picking on small, unarmed folks or Chinese migrants wanting better pay. Then you're pretty good at being assholes in big numbers."

Fredrick leaned forward from behind his desk. "Jed, good to see you again."

Reydan's cheeks flushed red as recognition crossed his face. "You!" he growled.

My arm was outstretched towards the tycoon, pistol gripped tightly, and my finger on the trigger.

How easy it would be to end this evil, right here and right now. Just squeeze a few more ounces and send a bullet through his face.

So easy.

I thought of the people who'd died because of him. The people who would die because of him if I didn't stop him. I thought of Skyla back East, recovering from her wounds... of Charles, lying in a grave on my ranch beside Bo and Jim.

"Jed!" Wesley said sharply, cutting through my darkening thoughts that threatened to make my finger apply a few more ounces of pressure to the trigger. "We need him."

I sighed and lowered both the tomahawk and the pistol.

Fredrick sighed in relief. Cato kept his hands on his guns, and Reydan White trembled in rage at my appearance. Wesley uncocked his hammer and holstered his pistol, while Otto held on to his rifle. I realized he had the barrel pointed at Cato. Smart move.

"For the moment, we all need to band together," I glared at Reydan. "That's the only reason you're still breathing. Because Whitesberg needs you and your army of Pinkertons to survive what's coming."

"What's coming, Jed?" Fredrick asked with a frown.

"An ape army."

"Shit," the Governor swore before standing angrily. He shoved his seat against the desk with a solid thud.

Reydan barked a short laugh as he stepped around the table, picking up his ivory-handled cane on the way. "They aren't headed here. They're headed to the Shimmer and the Encampment. Don't play us for fools. We've been aware of the Army's plan to lure them there for some time now."

"Mr. White," Fredrick interjected, "Jed's been riding with my Raiders. If he says the apes are headed here, he would know first."

Reydan spun on the Governor. "Yes. Jed. And you knew he was alive all this time?" he hissed angrily.

"Steady yourself, sir," Fredrick said, staring back at the powerful rail tycoon fearlessly. "I just recently found out and he's been a blessing to our Raiders. I've no doubt many of them are alive because of his knowledge and actions." He turned to me. "Jed, where's Lieutenant Heath?"

I swallowed hard trying to suddenly find my voice.

Wesley answered before I could, "He was wounded, twice. First time when we hit the apes, second time when the apes hit us on the way back. He was pinned to a tree with an ape arrow and ordered Jed to take charge and leave him behind with a bundle of dynamite. He used the dynamite to let us know how far the apes were behind us when he blew them up with it."

Fredrick nodded. "Brave man. I'll see to it his family knows of his death... and his valor."

"So, you led the apes here?" Reydan asked.

"No. They split their forces before our attack. That's part of what ruined it and put such a hurting on us. We expect Alpha Troop to be wiped out, but Bravo Troop may have gotten away mostly unscathed," Wesley reported.

I nodded in agreement with the gunman. "Bravo Troop wasn't in position yet, I didn't hear any shooting from that area. But either way, the apes will be here soon. We barely got around them without engaging."

"Then we need to get reinforcements from the Encampment immediately. But the next train isn't due until tomorrow morning." Reydan turned to the Governor. "Will you send a man to Fort York on horseback? Or shall I?"

Otto spoke from across the room where he was inspecting the blue curtains beside the double doors leading to the balcony. "Send Shaynee." He pulled a knife from its sheath and began cutting a thin strip off the cloth.

"No, dammit. Don't do that, Otto!" Fredrick warned in annoyance. "If you want some blue cloth, I'll get you some, but don't destroy my new drapes."

The Shaynee warrior grinned and tied the small strip to his rifle's stock where it dangled alongside a raptor and eagle feather.

"I don't trust the Indians," Reydan stated flatly. "I'll send one of mine." He looked down at the detective who had moved to sit in a chair. "You, take Earl and the fastest horses you can find and ride. Now."

"Sir," the Pinkerton protested, "I'm not much of a rider, I-"

"I didn't ask," Reydan snarled. "Go."

The detective stood, looked around the room angrily as if on the verge of saying something as he chewed on his front lip. Finally, after a long moment, he nodded and stepped around us to leave.

"Sooner you go, the better chance you have of staying alive," Wesley warned him.

The detective shouldered past without a word and pushed through the door, leaving it open behind him.

"He's a dead man," I said.

"Yep," Wesley nodded.

"Very dead," Otto agreed as he looked out the window at the street below.

"You said we needed to work together. How?" Reydan asked as he fiddled with his cane. "And why should we? You killed a dozen of my detectives." He gestured at the window near Otto. "Those other detectives out there know that. They want you dead."

"And the Army wants you arrested!" a voice boomed from behind us.

Colonel Carver and Captain Hawney came through the door with rifles in hand. Behind them were a half dozen soldiers, all armed and ready.

"Nice disguise, Jed," the Colonel told me with a sly grin.

"How'd you know I was here?"

He gestured a gloved hand towards Otto. "We've been keeping an eye on the Shaynee. We figured you would need their help for whatever you had planned. And here you are."

"Here I am. But I don't think I'll let you arrest me today," I warned him.

Captain Hawney stepped forward with his rifle in hand. "Let me take him in, Colonel." He smiled evilly. "He may resist."

Wesley moved between us. "Easy, butter bars," he said in a condescending tone while mocking the officer's rank.

"Everyone! Stop it," Fredrick commanded.

"What's going on?" came a woman's voice from behind the soldiers. The uniformed men looked around, surprised at the interference.

"Move aside, gents. We'll take this from here," a familiar man's voice said as Colonel Carver nodded at his soldiers. The Army men parted to make a path through.

Marshal Landry pushed between a pair of soldiers. Following her came the other two US Marshals, Carlos and McGibbons. And Carlos' arm was still in a sling from the stagecoach ride over here.

"Well, isn't this a treat," Wesley said, winking at my sister.

I swear it looked like she almost blushed, but she caught herself and vented on everyone in the room.

"What's the meaning of this?"

"Marshals Landry, McGibbons, and Carlos... I believe you have the most authority here of any party," Fredrick said. "Do you wish to take Jed into custody?"

"Jed? As in Jedidiah Huckleberry Smith?" McGibbons' jaw dropped. "You? You saved my life?"

"At your service, sir." I looked around the room. Damn, but there were a lot of people in it with guns and a stake in me dying.

"Where's your famous guns?" Carlos asked in confusion. "And that horse of yours?"

"I'm in disguise."

"Enough of this!" Reydan slammed his fist down on the Governor's desk. "I want him arrested for the murder of almost a dozen detectives. One of them was shot in the back, and another executed with a shotgun! And then he dared to taunt me by leaving their bloodied badges on my railcar's step!"

"Mr. White, what were those detectives doing coming back from Jed's ranch? We went there. We saw the bullet holes in the burned timbers of his house," my sister murmured almost softly. Carlos nodded his head in agreement.

I knew my sister. I knew that voice of hers. Reydan was walking on dangerous ground here. If Pearl was talking that softly, it meant she was about to pounce.

"Why, I've no idea," he stammered. "Those men are dead, and I was never able to find out what their purpose was. They often went on rides to blow off some steam."

I was still holding the Smith and Wesson in one hand and the tomahawk in the other. I remembered cradling Charles' burnt body as I removed it from the wreckage of my home. The crackling of cooked flesh as it snapped and broke under my fingers. The lightness of what was once a strong and sturdy friend. The stench.

Without thinking, I hurled the Shaynee weapon at the tycoon.

It sunk blade first into the desk several inches to the right of Reydan's hand with a thunk.

Disregarding the risk of being fired upon by my sister, blood brother, and Wesley, Cato drew both his pistols and pointed them at me.

Then a couple of surprising things happened.

First, Reydan grabbed his cane with two hands, pointed it at me and damned if the end of that thing didn't blossom fire and something slam into my chest that felt like a mule kick.

Second, as all the attention was on the pair of us, Cato swung one of his pistols to point at Reydan then back at me, as if for a split-second he was unsure of who he should kill.

I staggered a half step backwards, more in shock than anything as the dragon-scaled vest absorbed the bullet impact.

"Jed!" Fredrick cried out.

"You piece of Yankee shit-" Jerking up my right arm, I aligned the sights of my gun on Reydan's face.

BAM!

My pistol flew from stinging fingers.

Shaking my hand, I glared at Cato who had shot the Smith and Wesson out of my hand. Not that impressive of a shot really, we were only a dozen steps apart. But I was lucky the bastard didn't take off any of my fingers.

The room erupted from its shocked silence.

"Jed, you asshole!" Fredrick shouted, reaching forward and jerking the Shaynee tomahawk free from his desk to shake at me angrily. "How are you not wounded or dead? And this desk is brand new!"

"Get him!" Captain Hawney yelled as he and Colonel Carver grabbed me by the arms. They pulled them behind my back as I struggled to free myself.

"He's ours!" Marshal Pearl Landry said as she shoved the rifle of the soldier closest to her down and away from pointing at me.

Otto kept calm. He fingered the wolf hide throw that was over one of the chairs against the wall and sat down in it uncomfortably with his rifle across his knees.

As for Reydan, he angrily pulled out another cartridge from a pocket and began working to open the ivory head on his cane-gun. Now I knew why he always had that damned thing with him.

"Shuddup, everyone!" Fredrick roared, slamming the tomahawk repeatedly against the top of his desk, creating deep gouges in the fine wood surface and sending splinters flying.

Everyone stopped and looked at his uncharacteristic rage.

The Governor stopped, the Shaynee weapon still held tightly in his hand. "By God." He took a deep breath to calm himself. "If you all don't start getting along, I'm going to ride away and let the damned apes have you all."

"Apes? What apes?" Marshal McGibbons asked uncomfortably.

"We came in here to warn the Governor, and Reydan White, of the ape army approaching so you could prepare your defenses," Wesley said softly as he stared at Cato. "Nice shooting, by the way. How are you at distances?"

Cato shrugged a single shoulder but remained silent.

"Consider us warned," Reydan interjected as he snapped the head of his cane shut over a fresh cartridge. He pointed the barrel end of the loaded cane gun at me. "I want this man arrested for attempted murder."

"Gladly," Captain Hawney replied, tightening his grip on my arm.

Fredrick looked at the Shaynee tomahawk thoughtfully then spoke slowly and deliberately.

"No. The Army doesn't get Jed. The Marshals do."

My sister winked at the officers holding me.

"What? This is bullshit!" Hawney cried. "We just saw him try to kill Mr. White!"

"And Reydan White just tried to shoot Jed. Tit for tat if you ask me," Marshal Landry said.

"Yes, and how is it you're alive?" Fredrick asked me.

"Indeed," Reydan grumbled. "How?"

"Call it a trick of the trade, asshole. I soak up bullets and piss molten lead."

Wesley snorted.

"The Marshals have got nothing to do with this," Captain Hawney protested again.

"Silence," Colonel Carver warned his subordinate. "Let's hear the Governor out."

"Captain Hawney, I fought with your predecessor at both the Battle of the Apes and the Fall of Fort Jipson." Fredrick pointed the tomahawk at him. "Captain Brandthorn was a warrior with honor and integrity, and above that, he knew when to speak and when to remain silent. That is a skill you've yet to learn." He turned the Shaynee weapon towards the trio of US Marshals. "You will take Jed into custody. Then you will use him to help prepare the defenses of Whitesberg of the impending ape attack. And once the apes attack, you will release him to do that which he does best... kill apes."

"What?" Reydan roared. "This is MY town! I built and paid for it! I'll not have an attempted murder on myself go unpunished and this man go free! What is to keep him from attacking me again?"

I looked from Fredrick to Reydan, then back to Fredrick.

The man did have a good point. I had every intention of killing him once the opportunity presented itself. Too many had died or been wounded because of him. He was too dangerous to let live, even if it cost me my life.

But I wasn't fool enough to say that.

Instead, I just jerked my arms free from the officers, raised my empty hands helplessly, and made a promise I wasn't sure I could keep. "Reydan and I will settle our scores after the battle. Assuming the apes don't slaughter or sacrifice us all. I promise. Honest Injun and all that."

Otto grunted in disgust from where he was now leaning against the wall behind the Governor. I swear he was moving around just so he could be the first to kill someone if a lethal fight commenced.

"This is preposterous," Captain Hawney grumbled.

"Mr. White," Fredrick stared at him through his spectacles, "you may have helped build this town, but you've had the Army's assistance in its protection as well as financial subsidies from the United States Government. And the President has put ME in charge of this territory and as such, this town. Now, unless you wish for me to take the Army and depart, leaving only yourself and your hired detectives to combat the apes, you will do as I command." He turned his attention to me. "Jed, after the battle, assuming you survive, you'll go back into the custody of the US Marshals until we can get a judge out here. And I have to tell you, there are a lot of witnesses in this room who saw you throw this weapon," he hefted the Shaynee tomahawk, "at Mr. White."

"My only regret is that it missed," I mumbled under my breath.

"We also witnessed Mr. White shoot Jed with a cane gun, albeit uselessly," my sister smiled evilly. "Perhaps we should take Mr. White into custody as well until this can be sorted out by a judge."

"Like hell!" Reydan roared.

Fredrick slammed the tomahawk into his table again, this time leaving it embedded with a loud thump.

"If you all don't knock it off, I'm not going to have a desk left!" he shouted.

The room grew quiet as the Governor took a deep breath.

"Marshals McGibbons, Carlos, and Landry, Jed is to remain in your custody yet still tasked with running Charlie Troop of the Rough Raiders. I want him supervised at all times, he is never to be left alone without one of you by his side. Colonel Carver, I'm sure that a man of your rank and ability has thoughts on how to prepare Whitesberg for an attack. I'd like to hear them. Mr. White, we'll need your army of detectives as well as any more Maxim machine guns or anything else you may have up your sleeve."

"Preferably something better than that cane gun," I smirked at the tycoon who twisted the ivory handle on his cane like he was thinking about trying to beat me with it.

The tycoon glowered at me.

"Jed!" Fredrick sighed. "If you will shut up long enough to listen, I need your assistance. We have a group of both Axemen and Shayana here in town doing some trading and whatnot. I need you to ask them to stay."

"Hmm. Who's leading them?"

"Jarl Mikah for the Axemen, and Afton for the Shayana."

Gritting my teeth, I frowned slightly. Damn the luck of getting Afton.

"Is there a problem?" Colonel Carver asked.

"Jarl Mikah is a good one to have, I've dealt with him some. Shoot, Otto over there exchanged blows with him at their last Jarl's funeral.

They're best buddies now. But Afton," I shook my head as my eyes met Wesley's, "he's something else."

"Make it work, sir," Carver told me.

"Agreed. Make it work, Jed," Fredrick repeated.

"Fine." I turned to go as Otto jerked his tomahawk free of the desk and slid it into his belt.

"Wait." Fredrick stepped around Reydan, then Cato, as he crossed the room to where a pair of tall cabinets stood against the wall. Opening them, he gestured at me to come look.

Inside was the *Eighty-Six*, my holster and matching Colts, and Bowie knife.

With a grin that threatened to break my face in half, I pulled the prototype Winchester model 1886 rifle's sling off the hook it was hanging on and cradled it lovingly in my arms. "How I've missed you," I whispered.

Setting it aside, I unbuckled and tossed the empty holster and old gunbelt aside. Grabbing the wrapped-up belt and holstered pistols, I slung it around my waist and quickly buckled the belt together. Flexing my fingers, I practiced drawing the Colts.

They felt like they practically leapt into my hands.

Sliding them back in their holsters, I picked up the *Eighty-Six* and turned around, feeling properly armed once again.

"Governor, you just happened to have his weapons in your office?" Reydan asked coldly.

"Did you think they were destroyed in a fire?" Fredrick winked at me before turning back to the railroad tycoon. "I understand how much a man's weapons mean to him and was entrusted with Jed's long before I knew of his subterfuge."

"This is all very interesting, but we've defenses to prepare," Colonel Carver said. "I recommend we get on with it."

"I'll go deal with the Shayana and Axemen," I told the group before spinning about, walking past Cato without acknowledging his presence, and then through the throng of soldiers gathered in the hallway.

Battle was coming.

***

With Wesley and Otto by my side, and Marshal McGibbons following a respectable distance behind, we headed to find the Shaynee.

Otto had mentioned that they were camped next to the Axemen in the southeast corner of Whitesberg, and I wanted to see Jarl Mikah. No particular reason to see him first, except that I didn't care for the Shayana leader, Afton.

This particular corner of Whitesberg was the last to be completed and on the other side of the western wall was the ocean hills leading down to the beach and lapping waves. The packed sand and rock inside the wall also made this place the least desirable.

Which meant it was perfect for the Vikings and Indians to camp at and be left alone to their own devices.

When we reached the Shaynee camp, there was no telling where theirs began and where the Axemen's ended. The sun was burning down hot on my Stetson, shoulders, and back of my neck as I took in the sight.

There were painted ponies and trikes intermingled in large makeshift pens. As I watched, an axeman grabbed the mane of a pony and tried to jump on its bareback. He lasted about two bounces before being dropped on his face to the roar of the mixed crowd watching. A pair of Shaynee braves rushed into the pen and helped the sand-covered Viking back to his feet.

"I reckon you take to the Axemen, huh Otto?" I asked him wryly.

"Good people," he replied as he pointed at Squatting Bull racing Horny Devil against an axeman mounted on a gorgeous red and black streaked trike. This ceratopsid had two spikes rising vertically off its bone shield and several smaller ones fanning out along the sides. Its sloping face had only a single black horn above its beak.

"Asger," I chuckled as I watched his mount, Slepinir, easily beat Horny Devil across a line marked in the sand.

Otto huffed. "Horny Devil still weak from wounds of Toothed One."

"Yeah, yeah, I know. He got bit by a Tyrannosaurus." With that comment, I walked towards where the pair of trike riders were slowing their mounts to a stop.

Squatting Bull was closest, and I looked over his trike. The Toothed One, or a Tyrannosaurus as we called them, had taken a savage bite out of Horny Devil's bone shield before being disemboweled by Sleipnir and shot to death by Fredrick.

"Looks like he's healing nicely," I told the young Shaynee brave.

"Jed?" Asger squinted at me. "I heard you were dead."

I clasped wrists with the big bearded axeman. "Not yet," I told him with a grin.

"Good! When do we kill apes?"

"Tonight! And that's what I'm here about."

"Who is that?" Asger pointed a finger at Marshal McGibbons who was trying not to stick out like, well, a dark black man surrounded by white and brown savages.

"A friend, he's been told to keep an eye on me."

"Hmmm," he grumbled thoughtfully but didn't offer any other words.

"Where's Jarl Mikah? I need to speak to him."

Asger pointed a finger in the air. Following it, I saw where he was pointing. The one-armed Viking leader was standing along the top of the wall, staring out to sea at something unseen by those of us below.

The big axeman slid down from his trike. "I'll get him."

"No, no need. I haven't been on top of the walls yet; I'd like to see what he sees. Does he speak English yet?"

"A little."

"If you don't mind, Jed, I'm going to see if I can't find another pistol," Wesley said softly.

"Good idea. Ask Carson over at Liberty Arms, I bet he'll have something for you. And what about you, Otto? Care to join me on the wall?"

"No. I get Shaynee warriors ready."

Tipping my hat at the group, I walked to the nearest staircase.

With my foot on the bottom step, I motioned at McGibbons to come closer. "No point in lurking around me, I'm only up to good at the moment."

He grinned and began walking up the stairs beside me.

"Tell me, Marshal, you regret coming out here now?"

"Because of the apes?"

"Well, because you've already survived one attack, and now you're about to be under a much larger one."

He shrugged. "Before I joined the Marshals, I was in the Army."

"That's good, that'll come in handy tonight. Who'd you fight against?"

"Confederates."

I internally kicked myself for not realizing just how old he was. McGibbons was probably close to my father's age so it would stand that he'd been in the War Between the States.

"Don't worry, I won't hold you being a Southerner against you," he chuckled. "War ended long ago."

I stopped, turned to face the man, and frowned at him.

"For some. I'm sure you've heard the rumors about Reydan White though, haven't you? He fought for the Union and raided the South after the war."

McGibbons nodded slowly while chewing his lower lip. "I never heard that until I came out here. But some of the Pinkerton detectives have spoken of it."

"That's because it's true. I'm living proof of it and the scars I carry on my back remind me every day that the war may have ended, but some battles go on."

"I don't believe in vengeance righting any wrong."

I turned back to the stairs in disgust. "I do."

Reaching the top of the wall, I was surprised to see another man walking away from the Jarl.

With a grin, I shook the newcomer's hand. "Reverend, how are you?"

"Jedidiah. How delightful to see you alive." The man of faith frowned. "I heard of what happened. I want you to know, I made a trip through the Shimmer to pray over your friends' graves."

"Thanks, Reverend, I tried… but didn't have the words."

"They don't always come easily."

I nodded at Jarl Mikah. "Converting the heathens?"

Reverend grinned. "That's the plan. But for now, I've just been trying to teach the Jarl how to speak English."

"Asger said he'd learned some."

"I think he understands more than he speaks," he leaned forward conspiringly and whispered, "He's a smart fellow. Tread carefully if you plan on using him as part of your plan for vengeance."

"Shouldn't you be trying to talk me out of it?"

"Vengeance is mine, sayith the Lord," he quoted before frowning. "That doesn't mean he won't use human hands to carry it out."

"Mine are willing."

He patted me on the back with the hand holding his battered black leather-bound Bible. "Good to see you, Jedidiah."

"You as well."

He walked away; a tall figure dressed in black with a mysterious past. Watching him descend the stairs, I shook my head. I'd never fully understand the Reverend. But I was appreciative of his understanding and companionship.

"Strange fellow," McGibbons muttered to me.

Ignoring him, I moved towards the Axemen's leader who stood still, his hand resting on the sharpened palisade while he watched the ocean's waves lap at the shore.

Jarl Mikah was an interesting fellow. For one thing, he only had one arm. And to lead a warrior clan such as the Axemen with only one arm to wield a sword, I'd expect he was pretty damn good with it. For another thing, he was ambitious. Upon his ascension to Jarl, he'd promised to cross the ocean and conquer new territories. I expected that was part of his reason for working with us, he wanted to be better armed and equipped to challenge the unknown for ownership.

Mikah turned to me as I approached, and I tipped my hat. "Jarl."

"Jed," he said simply before turning back to face the ocean.

"The apes are attacking us tonight. With an army." I wasn't sure how much English he could speak, so I just figured I'd spit it out and hope for the best. "We need the Axemen to fight with us."

"Ja. Yes. This we do," he said, before pointing a finger at the partial construction of a dock leading out into the now low tide. "For help."

"With boats?" I asked.

"Yes, and," he pointed at my rifle, "these."

I smiled to myself. Everyone in Prehistoria loved guns.

"Ja. Sounds like we have a deal," I offered my hand, and he shook it with his.

"How many men do you have?"

He said something I didn't understand. Seeing the confusion on my face, he flashed the fingers on his hands at me, twice.

Twenty, then.

That'd have to do.

Resting my forearms on the palisade, I leaned forward and looked down. Damn but we were high up. Reydan had brought in men from California who were used to cutting redwoods, and then he used them to cut and maneuver these prehistoric trees into usefulness. I wasn't sure how deep the ends of the trunks were buried in the sand, but the tops stood a good twenty to thirty feet high on this side depending on the slope of the ground below. It was an impressive feat, but for men used to moving redwoods, what were the Prehistoria trees but smaller versions.

"Thank you, Jarl Mikah."

"Do the Shaynee fight with us?"

"They do."

Jarl smiled. It was an unsettling sight and one I'd never seen before. But it gave me the impression of a raptor snarling before shredding you apart with fang and claw.

"Good. Let the hairy men come. They shall break themselves on our shields and die upon our swords. And we will remind them of why they hide from us."

"Hell yes," I told him. "And we'll do it together."

Turning to go, I ignored McGibbons and crossed the platform to descend the steps. With the Vikings on our side, we'd give quite the account of ourselves to the apes.

"Do we really need these savages?" McGibbons asked from behind me as he hurried to catch up.

Stopping abruptly, I turned to face him. "The apes aren't messing around. And contrary to the ability of modern firearms and Maxim machine guns, we're outnumbered. Our goal is to survive as long as possible and win if we can. But it's going to be a brutal fight to the end."

The black Marshal gulped hard. "I didn't realize it was that bad."

"They mean to wipe us out, McGibbons. And this is their chance."

***

Wesley and my sister caught up with me as I walked down the streets between the partially constructed bank and saloon. The sign above the saloon said, "Crystal Palace". Nice sounding place, but I doubted we'd have time to visit.

The outlaw was wearing two Colt Lightnings now in a holstered setup similar to how he'd fought before at Granite Falls. Marshal Landry on the other hand, was openly chewing her tobacco and glaring at McGibbons for giving her a dirty look.

"I've got this scum," she told the black Marshal jokingly.

"Thanks. I'm going to find a drink, then catch some shuteye before tonight," he replied before walking into the saloon.

Pearl spat a brown stream onto the broken gravel underfoot and looked back at Wesley and I. "Well, they've got something of a plan," she said.

"What is it?"

"Basically, we fight as long as we can and hope that the Encampment is able to defeat their army and come to our aid."

I stopped in the middle of the street and looked around. Word must have gotten around, because soldiers and Pinkertons were moving in a hurry to various positions. "They say how many men we have?"

Pearl chewed for a moment thoughtfully. "About two hundred soldiers, Pinkertons, and your Rough Raiders. Maybe fifty of the Shayana, Shaynee, and Viking men. About two dozen shop owners or carpenters and such that are stuck with us. And one woman who's worth a dozen men." She pointed at herself.

"You're worth that much, are you?" I teased.

"Try me and find out."

Wesley grinned.

"Hm. So about three hundred total. That ain't much." I glanced at Wesley, an idea forming. "Pearl, where's the jail at?"

"Oh, Jed," he said, shaking his head.

"What? It worked with you last time."

"Yeah, but do you remember that big dumbass, Little Timmy? He tried to kill you during the battle."

Pearl Landry shook her head. "That's the one they tried to hang you for killing in return, isn't it?"

"You heard about that?" I asked her.

She spat another stream of tobacco, then reached into her jaw with her fingers and flung out the chewed up wad. "I've heard a lot about you lately. But the Sheriff's office and jail is over there," she pointed at a building set off by itself, with the backside backed up against the palisade. It was an unsightly building and stood out from the rest with its plain looks. But it did look fairly solid from this distance.

We walked to the building, and I hammered a fist against the closed door.

A Pinkerton peeked out, his eyes were rimmed in red, and he stank of booze and sweat.

I shoved the door open and shouldered him aside.

"What a mess," Wesley muttered as the three of us looked around the room.

There was trash and garbage spread all over the floor and desk. Empty glass whiskey bottles rolled underfoot. Another detective stirred from a pair of cots behind the desk. As he sat up, a bottle fell to the floor and rolled under the desk, gurgling whiskey, as the detective chased after it.

Three iron cells lined the far wall against the palisade, and next to the last one was a crudely drawn bullseye on the wall. I walked over to it and fingered one of the numerous bullet holes thoughtfully.

"We, ah, we're supposed to be here. Keeping an eye on the prisoners."

"And shooting up the inside of the building?" I growled. "Where's the Sheriff?"

"We don't have one yet," the Pinkerton mumbled almost apologetically.

I eyeballed the men inside the cells. There were four of them, two in one cell and a single man in each of the others.

"What are they in for?"

"Ah, drunk and disorderly."

"Let them out," I said.

The Pinkerton who chased the bottle under the desk rose up with it in hand and took a swig. "And who the hell are you?"

"Jedidiah Huckleberry Smith."

"You!" shouted the one who'd answered the door in recognition. He grabbed for his pistol, but Marshal Landry slapped his hand away and shoved him against the log wall. With a single finger pointed at his face, she froze him in place.

"See this?" she lifted her badge from where it was pinned to her coat. "This means I can kill anyone who crosses me with impunity. Including Pinkertons."

The other detective set the partially filled bottle down carefully and kept his hands away from his pistol.

Wesley leaned closer to me and whispered, "I'm glad she's on our side."

"What's your name, Pinkerton?" I asked the one farthest away from my sister.

"Madison, and his is Casey."

I pointed with the *Eighty-Six* at the cells where the prisoners watched us with interest. "Okay, Detective Madison, I said to let them out."

He picked up a large ring of keys from the desk and moved to the cells, unlocking the doors one by one. The men inside shuffled forward and looked at me suspiciously.

Wesley spat. "Gentlemen, what do think of your two slothful Pinkerton guards right now?"

One of the inmates stepped forward. He was a little fellow in stature, but from the bend in his nose and the scars around his face, I could tell he was a brawler. "I reckon they're drunk and disorderly, sir."

"Yup."

"Get in the cell," Landry said, shoving Detective Casey towards them. The former prisoners moved aside and watched with amusement as she herded both the Pinkertons into the same cell close to the bullseye on the wall and locked the door. The ring of keys she hung on a peg behind the desk, well out of their reach.

"Alright, listen up. Word is spreading, but I'm going to go ahead and tell you. An army of apes is going to attack us, probably tonight. And we need your help."

One of the former prisoners, a lean fellow with a wicked scar across his cheek, laughed. "Mister, you've got to be shittin' us. Hell, we're just lumberjacks. We cut trees. And I ain't stayin' for no battle. I'll take the train and be shed of this place just as soon as you let me out the door."

"There ain't no train," Pearl told him. "You're stuck."

"No... No... what do you mean no train?" he asked, bewildered.

"Next train isn't due until tomorrow. If it can even get through the apes."

The short inmate who spoke earlier picked up the partially drunk bottle of whiskey and took a swig. "I reckon we're in for a fight then."

"Yup," Wesley said calmly.

"Reckon we'd best go get some guns," he said, leading the men past us and out of the office. The man with the scarred cheek glanced back with a look of despair, but followed his friends out anyways.

"Wait! What about us?" shouted Pinkerton Casey as both of them gripped the iron bars hopelessly.

"Someone will be along soon enough to let you out. Until then, sober up," my sister told them.

We turned to go.

***

I sent the former prisoners with Wesley to where the remaining Raiders of Charlie Troop were resting. They were going to join my little band of misfits. I figured they owed me now, and it might come in handy later.

Marshal Landry and I walked around, trying to figure out where the Shayana leader was when we ran into Lieutenant Daniels.

The young officer grabbed my hand and shook it enthusiastically. "Jed! It's good to see you! And if it weren't for your weapons, I wouldn't have even recognized you. You've cleaned up, man!"

I scratched my goatee and slicked down my mustache as I cut the pleasantries. "They burned my house, killed Charles, and shot Skyla. If we survive this fight, I'm going to kill Reydan."

His eyes grew large, and his jaw dropped slightly. "Well don't go around advertising it!"

"I need to know whose side you're on."

"I'm on the Army's side, Jed. You know that. And you're wanted for questioning by us about a dozen dead Pinkertons."

I gnawed on my bottom lip while staring at him. "Did you not hear me? They burned my house. Killed my hired hand and Charles. And shot Skyla."

"I know what they did!" He dropped his voice to an angry whisper as he jabbed a finger at me. "I was with the party that went out to bring back the bodies after they were discovered. I went to your ranch. I saw the torched house and fresh graves. I also picked up the mutilated bodies. Don't tell me you didn't kill them, it had you written all over it. You shotgunned one man to death, shot another in the back as he ran away, and ripped half of one's face off somehow! And then you looted the badges."

My sister looked at me sharply. I shrugged indifferently. "They didn't need them, and I needed to send Reydan a message."

"Dammit, Jed! But you make it hard to be your friend."

"So, you are on my side."

"Shit!" He kicked a chunk of large gravel in the street. It bounced against a watering trough next to a hitching post. "You know I'm on your side. But I'm not helping you murder anyone!"

"I just want to make sure that if Captain Hawney asks you to shoot me in the back or arrest me, you'll give me some sort of chance first."

"He's not that bad of a man," Daniels said defensively.

"Yes, he is. And would be worse if he weren't held back by Colonel Carver."

"He is my superior."

"By rank perhaps, but not in morals."

The young Lieutenant shook his head, as though giving up on the argument.

My sister saw a chance and cut in. "We're looking for the Shayana leader, Afton. Have you seen him?"

"He's been hanging out around the Crystal Palace lately."

"The saloon?" she asked. "I thought it was closed."

Daniels scoffed. "Please. It was probably the first place opened. But the Army has barred us from it, and Reydan has barred the Pinkertons. He doesn't want any of us drinking when we should be protecting his precious town. Only the workers can drink, or the natives."

Marshal Landry laughed.

"What?"

"We caught a couple of drunk detectives in the Sheriff's office. We had them swap places with the inmates."

"Oh hell, you two..." He turned and started walking. "I'm going to go let them out. Try not to piss off any more people before the apes get here."

"Yes, sir!" I called after him with a smug grin.

The Crystal Palace was a couple buildings down, and a short walk.

When we got there, we realized it was a mighty nice place as we pushed through the double doors and entered. The floor was smooth and didn't creak, fancy leather chairs were set around the room, leather bound barstools lined the polished bar, and a man in a dark suit with a white handkerchief thrown over his arm was serving drinks to a pair of Axemen who were chanting what sounded like Viking drinking songs.

And right away we noticed Afton, surrounded by a dozen of his men, staring up at the crystal chandelier that the saloon was named for. The necklace of severed ape ears rested on his scarred armor breastplate, and somewhere along the way he'd picked up a pistol that was holstered on his side. Against the chair leaned his bow and quiver full of arrows. His blue eyes darted towards us as we entered, and he leered at my sister as he rose to a sitting position.

"Has thou come to offer me a wife?" he asked with a smirk. I could practically smell the whiskey on his breath from a dozen steps away.

Pearl drew her pistol and pointed the barrel at his face.

"No. We come to offer you a fight," she said as his smirk turned to a frown and the other Shayana jerked or staggered upright. Various weapons were drawn; swords unsheathed, pistols unholstered, arrows nocked, and a pair of rifle levers were worked.

"Whoa," I muttered to my sister as an awful lot of hardware was pointed in our direction. She slowly lowered her pistol but didn't holster it.

"And what fight is this?" Afton asked as he struggled to stand upright. He swayed slightly, burped, and wiped his mouth with the back of his hand. His feet bumped into several empty bottles which went rolling across the polished wooden floor.

"Apes. A bunch of them."

"No." He took a step forward. "We've bled enough for you'ns."

Marshal Landry raised an eyebrow at me, and I had to frown to keep from grinning. I'd told her about the exchanging of lingo between our two groups, and how the Shayana were turning into Americans.

"You don't have a choice. There aren't enough breehas here to fly you all away, and the apes are surrounding us."

I wasn't sure of that, but I suspected it was true. It's what I'd have done, and the apes certainly had the numbers to send plenty of trike riders ahead to keep any of us from escaping. And besides, we needed the damned Shayana to help us stay alive.

"Breehas," Afton laughed joyfully, his necklace of ears bouncing against his breastplate. He spread his arm to show the tribesmen around him. "Apes are no threat to breeha riders."

"They have a dragon also, asshole. A couple of them," my sister told him. "And where do you think this ape army is going to go after us? Probably to your mountaintop hideaway. You think they can handle dragons better than we can?"

We were making a lot of assumptions, but it seemed to be working. Afton straightened and his jaw set as the men around him muttered angrily.

"This we cannot have. We shall fight here."

"Good. We need Shayana help. Keep your Breehas for the dragon, and any other men you can spare we need on the northern wall."

Afton shouted at his men, and they lowered their weapons. "We go!" He waved his arm forward and stumbled out the door surrounded by his men who appeared to be only slightly less intoxicated.

"Have you seen the breehas' perches?"

"No, but I've heard the danged things making their racket a few times."

"South wall. When they built the palisade there was a large mound of rocks and junk and since they couldn't bury the bottoms of the poles in it, they built around it. It makes kind of a natural squared off area that the giant pterodactyls love. The Shayana land and fly off from there, and the birds just hang out until their rider comes back. And now I think I'll have a drink."

I followed my sister to the bar. "How have you learned so much about this place?"

"Men like to talk."

The bartender quickly walked over to us before we raised a finger. He ignored me, gave my sister an appraising glance that lingered on her badge, and asked, "What'll it be?"

"How about a pair of whiskeys?" Pearl asked as we sat on the leather-topped stools.

"For you and your… charge?"

"No, he's not under arrest. And those whiskeys are just for me. He can order his own."

"I'll just have a water," I told him.

"We don't serve water."

Pearl slapped me on the back. "Jedidiah Huckleberry Smith doesn't drink water! He'll have a beer."

The bartender's eyes about popped out of his skull. "The Heart Eater of Granite Falls?"

I sighed. "That's me."

He slapped his hand on the polished bar. "Drinks are on me!"

My sister grinned at me as the bartender rushed away. "This is going well. We should hang out more often."

"I'd have preferred a water, you know."

"I know, but I just wanted to, for once, declare my brother to be the legendary ape slayer."

"I'm not legendary."

"Like it or not, you are. You should learn to use it to your advantage."

"I was." I rested my elbow on the bar and leaned aside to look at her. "Skyla's father was working on getting me a pardon. That's why I went with Fredrick and the others to find the Vikings. Trying to do everything I can to help my case."

She nodded thoughtfully. "Killing a dozen Pinkertons probably didn't help that pardon any."

"Pardon or not, they asked for it."

"Yes, they did," she said softly as the bartender set a pair of shot glasses filled with amber liquid in front of her, and then he set a bottle in front of me.

"If you need anything else, just ask," he said excitedly before one of the Vikings shouted something and he ran over to see what the bearded man wanted.

I took a swig of the beer. It was warm.

Marshal Pearl Landry downed her first shot glass with a large swallow. "Ah. Been a long time since we've drunk together, little brother," she said slyly.

"I remember." I smiled at the memory. Cato, Pearl, and I had been hiding in the calving barn, passing around a bottle of Father's, pretending to be more drunk than we really were. We'd been laughing hysterically, until Cato threw up and Father caught us. After that, we sobered up quick with a switch to our rear ends.

As we both remembered, we grew quiet, and I sipped on my warm beer again.

Pearl rolled the empty shot glass between her fingers. "Do you think Cato can be saved?" she asked softly.

"I don't know. Reydan has twisted him up something awful, I think."

"Father hopes, though."

"Yes."

I pushed my beer away. "Enough of this. Let's go kill some apes."

"Damn right," she knocked back her other shot and smiled.

***

Governor Fredrick found us as we stepped outside onto the boardwalk.

"What are you two doing? Drinking away the day? We've a battle about to commence."

I scoffed at the famed hunter-turned-politician. "I'm betting you've already had a drink too."

"Danged right I have. How else am I to handle all this pressure of being a politician?" He tipped his hat at my escort. "Marshal Landry, how are you, ma'am?"

"Miss," she said with a flirty smile. "And I'm well."

I rolled my eyes.

"Miss," Fredrick corrected himself. "Do you mind if I borrow Jed?"

"You told me not to let him out of my sight."

"Agreed, I did. Well, let me show you both from the wall."

Together we crossed through the street, behind the Crystal Palace, and climbed the staircase by the Sheriff's office. I suspected, thanks to Lieutenant Daniels, the building was now empty of drunk detectives.

Along the platform walkway, we encountered a Maxim machine gun. The strange, boxy contraption was emplaced near an opening notched into the palisade. Fredrick nodded to the group of soldiers lounging near it. "Any signs of apes yet?"

"None yet, sir."

"Keep an eye out." He leaned forward and looked through the opening by the fat barrel of the Maxim.

Since Whitesberg had been built on a large hill, it had a commanding presence on the area around it. And with the deforestation of trees needed for the large wall that encircled it, there was a large field of view. The problem was, there were also a lot of leftover giant stumps out there that could give shelter to apes.

"Sir, I don't see how they can attack us," one of the soldiers said. "Shoot, we'd just slaughter them as they tried to climb these walls."

"Jed, how many do you think are in the ape army approaching us?"

I spit off the edge of the palisade wall and watched it fall about twenty-five feet to the ground. "I'd reckon…five, maybe six hundred."

The youngest looking soldier in the group gasped.

"Surely you jest?" said another.

"No. I do not jest. And there are at least two dragons. But I don't know if the dragons are coming for us or the Encampment."

"Johnson? Johnson Brown?" came a voice from behind us.

Turning, I saw Irving reaching the top of the stairs, his journal in hand and a boyish grin on his face.

"I thought you'd returned to the Shimmer!" I told him as he stopped in front of us.

"No, well, not yet. I saw a pair of ankylosaurus yesterday near the wall and spent the evening watching and drawing them. Amazing creatures, Johnson!"

I raised my hand. "Alright, alright. You might as well know my name isn't Johnson Brown."

Marshal Landry and Fredrick shared a grin.

Irving looked at me peculiarly. "What is it then?"

Sighing, I admitted, "It's Jedidiah Huckleberry Smith."

"No. NO! You can't-" his eyes dropped to my matching Colts and *Eighty-Six* rifle I carried in hand. "You ARE!" He clapped his hands in glee.

"Yes, he is," Pearly Landry said with a grin.

"You… you taught me how to shoot! And the whole time you were the Heart Eater!"

"I didn't eat it, I just took a bite," I protested.

"Well," Irving looked at the soldiers suspiciously. "You know you have a lot of enemies in here, right? There's a ton of Pinkertons."

"I know. Fredrick, what are we going to do with him?" I asked pointedly.

"I'll keep him with me, Colonel Carver is running the show. I'm just going to pick a nice spot and pot shot at some apes from the wall."

"Excellent!" Irving shouted.

"Is that what you brought us up here to show us? Your pot shotting position?" Pearl asked.

"No. I just wanted to show Jed where the Rough Raiders and some of the Shaynee would be positioned. And that's beside this Maxim, protecting it from any apes that try to climb the wall or sling arrows or whatnot at it. This, and the cannon further down, is your position and we expect the apes to attack from this direction. We've got to protect the machine gun and cannon at all costs." He looked at me sideways, "Which means if Otto wants to repeat that trick of his to kill a dragon, he's welcome to it."

"I'll tell him, but I doubt it."

"I heard about that! He jumped onto the back of it and smashed its head open with a tomahawk," Irving said excitedly.

"He got lucky, kid. Very lucky."

"Was it the same tomahawk you were carrying earlier?" He looked me up and down. "Where'd it go?"

"It wasn't, but the one I was carrying is back with Otto where it belongs for now."

Marshal Landry coughed. "Can we get back to the battle plans? I'd like to stay alive."

"Right," Fredrick muttered. With his finger, he pointed down along the palisade. "We'll have other men stationed at each of the cannons and Maxims. We aren't going to move the other crew-served guns from the other walls because we are worried we might get flanked and have nothing to fight with. That means we'll be stretched thin along this wall."

"Okay, I'll-"

"APES!" The soldier manning the Maxim let off a small burst of bullets, then another, and another.

Spinning, I jerked the *Eighty-Six* up and looked for a target. Irving jerked his pistol out and ducked below the palisade wall, peeking between the logs for targets.

There was nothing that I could see.

"Where?" Fredrick shouted.

"I saw them, I swear. There was a white and brown one that just ducked behind that tree stump over there."

"Which one?"

The soldier fired another burst and we watched the bullets impact against the side of the large stump with a spray of splinters. "Right there. I swear, sir!"

"Okay," Fredrick patted the soldier's shoulder. "I believe you. Keep an eye out for more. But conserve your ammunition the best you can; don't go wasting a bandoleer of bullets where a single cartridge will suffice."

I snickered. The Governor was notably horrific at aiming his own weapons when he started shooting.

Landry peered over the edge at the stumps that dotted the field in front of us. "Damn the lumberjacks for leaving those things standing up, they've got to be a good four feet tall, thick as hell, and ample protection from bullets and probably even cannon balls unless you get a direct hit with one."

"It's going to give the apes lots of cover to get close. But they won't be riding trikes through there easily."

"Yeah, not there." I pointed to our west. "They'll ride the trikes up the beach to get to us. Give them a nice low tide, packed sand, and they'll be on us before we know it."

"Reydan White told Colonel Carver the same thing," Fredrick said.

"Hell of a thought for a supposed 'quartermaster' from the war."

"That's what I thought," Fredrick said wryly as he looked around. The entire town was coming alive after the firing of the Maxim. Men were moving into position and looking for things to shoot. Captain Hawney was running towards us, and he looked displeased.

"Well, that got them going."

"Hurry up and get your men up here, Jed. I'll feel better with some protection on this gun. And I'll handle Hawney, he's probably angry at someone shooting."

The soldier who had fired gulped loudly.

"Yes, sir," I told the Governor before spinning on my heel and jogging down the steps with Marshal Landry behind me.

***

Wesley had the Rough Raiders waiting for me outside of the stables. Sheepishly, I removed my hat and slapped it against my leg. Pearl was kind enough to stand back and give me some space.

I sighed and spoke, "I suppose word has gotten around now. You know who I am."

"The Heart Eater of Granite Falls!" Talon whooped, followed by several others.

"I prefer Jed... I'm sorry I lied to you men. And I'm sorry I ah, haven't been forthcoming about who I am or what I know of this side."

"Did you know about the turtle?" Bart asked with an arched eyebrow and a frown.

"No, I'd never even heard of anything like that before. Much less seen one. I couldn't have saved Jethro, nor could I have saved George, Lieutenant Heath, or the others."

"You saved me," a Raider said softly.

"And me as well."

"Same here."

"You shot that ape off me, I was sure I was a goner."

I dipped my head, nodding slightly as the Raiders spoke of what I'd done. It choked me up. And for a moment, I didn't trust my mouth to speak.

Finally, I glanced back up at them. "Look, gents, I'm just a man put in some awful damn situations that I've come out ahead on. And I tell you now, we're in one together. These apes are coming to wipe us out. Our place is going to be on the northern wall," I pointed at the wall towering over us. "Right there, protecting the Maxim and cannon on the left side. I can't tell you what is going to happen, but you saw the ape army the same as I did. You know what's headed this way. And you know Whitesberg needs us or it's going to be wiped out."

"Why you fighting to protect those bastard Pinkertons? Didn't you just kill a dozen of them?" a Raider said, spitting to the side in disgust.

"And I heard rumors about Reydan White torturing you back after the war. That true?" another asked.

Gritting my teeth against the barrage of questions, I handed the *Eighty-Six* to Wesley then removed my dragon-scale vest and shirt.

Turning my back on the Raiders, I let them see the whip lash scars that crisscrossed my back and sides.

They quieted down and I spoke firmly.

"This is what Reydan White and his men did to me when I was a kid. They tied me to a tree, whipped me, and left me for dead as they torched and looted my home."

Turning back to face them, I stood there, suddenly angry with the memories of what'd been done to me.

"Listen to me now. I did kill those Pinkertons. Like the Yankee Raiders of my childhood, they killed my friends, burned my home, and left me for dead again. I slayed those Pinkertons with a rightful vengeance. Every damned one of them." I pulled my arms through my shirt and began to button it back up. "So, now you know what Reydan and the Pinkertons deny. You've seen it with your own eyes. And since I'm standing here, telling you that we've got to fight with them to defeat the apes, you know I'm serious. And I'm not doing this for Reydan White or his bastards for hire. I'm doing this for the soldiers, and the townsfolk, and the three poor fools that I let out of the jail. It's that bad.

We're facing extinction on this side. And if Whitesberg falls, the ape army will link up with the one attacking the Encampment and combined they will wipe them out as well. This is our only chance. We've divided their forces and now we've got to destroy them both or suffer the consequences. And those consequences, you should know full well by now. Death if you're lucky. Mutilation and sacrifice if you're not. And if that's not enough, remember that if Whitesberg and the Encampment fall, Fort York will be ripe for plucking along with Granite Falls. And those hundreds of women and children in that town are counting on you to fight so they don't have to." I took the *Eighty-Six* back from Wesley. "We're going to fight and we're going to win. Because there ain't no other option. Now follow me; it's time to find our places on the wall."

***

I'd no sooner gotten the remaining Rough Raiders into position, along with Otto and his Shaynee, plus the inmates, than the apes appeared in the distance.

I watched them through a borrowed collapsible telescope, as mine had burned in the house.

They were painted for war, and they moved at an easy step in long lines forward towards us. A bunch of them were pushing carts, that I knew to hold raptors, and others carried long poles between them as they moved.

"Damn, but I wish Ashley James was here," I said. "She'd have a field day with them in the open like that, even at this distance."

The apes flowed through the field of stumps, and ferns, until they assembled in a long, ragged line in front of us. No sign of any trikes or dragons.

"Oh shit," I muttered as a pair of painted apes dragged a man from between their lines and into sight. He was battered and bloody, his clothing little more than rags wrapped around his body, but it was unmistakable. "It's George."

"No!" shouted Talon. "Dammit, no!"

I sighed and ran my fingers through my hair. There wasn't anything that could be done.

From below I heard one of the gates open. Peeking over the edge I watched Colonel Carver ride out with Sergeant Gibbons at his side and an ape stumbled along behind tied to a rope. Gibbons held a pistol in his hand, but Carver rode fearlessly forward.

"Oh no. They're going to try and negotiate."

"How?" Landry asked.

I pointed at the black Sergeant. "He speaks ape." I didn't bother telling her that he only spoke a little.

"Is that the ape they tried to scare us with when we enlisted?" Bart asked.

"Looks like," Talon said. "Maybe we'll get little George back after all."

Watching through the telescope, I could tell the apes were confused. I reckoned negotiation was a new thing to them.

The ape leader moved forward from the line. He was a head taller than the others, a plain brown color fur, with a green swirl circled around on his chest with a pair of yellow lines below his face.

Stepping beside George, he lifted his obsidian club and bellowed at the pair of riders approaching. Our men stopped their horses. They were probably fifty yards from the line of apes. I felt my heart hammering in my chest as I watched. This was dangerous as hell and I certainly wouldn't have picked this course of action, but Carver was in charge. And he seemed to be a smart fellow.

I could hear Gibbons shouting faintly in the apes' guttural and rough language. Through the telescope I saw him point at George, and then gesture with his pistol at the ape they had brought with them.

A prisoner exchange.

The leader ape pointed his club at Colonel Carver and a pair of arrows sprouted from the officer's chest.

As the man toppled backwards on his horse, Gibbons pulled the trigger and shot the ape prisoner through the skull.

Dropping low over his saddle, Gibbons jumped his horse forward towards the line of apes, firing his pistol and hitting the brown ape leader. The ape dropped his club, and I could hear him screaming angrily from our position on the wall.

"Don't," I shouted, even though I knew it was impossible for Gibbons to hear me.

The Sergeant shot the ape on the right, holding onto George's arm.

And fell from the saddle as an arrow dropped his horse.

The ape leader picked up his club, limped over to where Sergeant Gibbons had fallen out of sight, and smashed the obsidian rock down over and over.

I shook in helpless rage as the leader finished savaging my friend's body.

Another ape had grabbed the Chinese Rough Raider's arm and was holding him in place as the lead ape snatched a bowl of smoldering prehistoric herbs from another.

He inhaled deeply, hurled the bowl down, and jammed a knife into George's belly.

His piercing screams carried over to us as the ape sawed the blade upwards and pulled out George's heart. The Chinaman flopped lifelessly to the ground while the ape leader ripped a chunk of flesh off the heart, then hurled it into the army of apes where they fought for the bloody organ.

Lowering the telescope, I moved to the cannon and kicked the cast metal tube helplessly. "Fire, damn you!" I shouted at the soldiers manning it.

"We can't! We haven't been given orders," the Corporal in charge protested.

Drawing one of my Colts, I cocked the hammer back.

"Colonel Carver and Sergeant Gibbons are dead. Avenge them or get out of the way."

"Yes, sir!" the Corporal decided quickly as he looked in wide eyes at my pistol. "Fire! Fire! Fire!" He screamed at the top of his lungs as the cannon fuse was lit.

Two seconds later, the cannon boomed, billowing a plume of smoke out the barrel and sending a lead ball flinging across the field of stumps. The ball hit fifty yards to the right of the ape leader and our dead friends. But it was a solid hit just a few yards short of the army, sending an explosion of earth and dirt into the air and into the front ranks of apes. From my view in the telescope, over a dozen were knocked down and at least six didn't rise again.

"Keep it up!" I shouted at the crew as they began to reload.

A hand jerked me around.

Captain Hawney.

"What the hell do you think you're doing? You're not in charge here. I am!"

"Then lead!" I shoved him out of my way as I stalked back to the Maxim machine gun where Wesley and the others waited by the top of the palisade wall.

Behind me I heard him shouting at the other cannon to begin firing. Whether he liked it or not, the battle was joined.

Reaching my old position, I watched through the telescope as the ape army began to move forward.

***

Both cannons on this side of the wall fired. Great gouts of earth and blood sprayed as the 12-pound cannon balls found their targets. I remembered from what seemed like years ago, standing in Granite Falls as our lone cannon was fired and my long-deceased friend, Captain Brandthorn, telling me about how the 12 pounder was one of the best cannons ever created.

Once again, they were earning their due.

"Maxims! Open fire!" shouted Hawney. The call was repeated along the wall by the men that lined it.

The Rough Raiders, plus a few others, stood on the western side of the northern wall watching the apes get chewed up as they charged uphill through cannon ball and now machine gun fire.

Vikings stood ready in the center of the wall, prepared to sling arrows when the distance closed between us. Mounted Shayanas were well behind us, on their giant mound of rocks near the southern wall, waiting for a dragon to appear. Those unlucky enough to be on foot were on the northern wall with us, stationed with the Vikings.

Through the telescope I noticed an ape take a bullet through the chest and fall, dropping his long pole. The group around him paused for a moment, with another picking it up and then running in unison towards us.

I realized what they were carrying.

"They've got ladders!" I shouted. "Shoot the ones with the ladders!"

The Rough Raiders rose from behind the palisade, rested their rifles between the sharpened points of the wall, and opened fire.

But the apes were seemingly endless. With each one we dropped it seemed like another two took its place. The army grew closer and soon were taking up positions behind the stumps and firing arrows at us.

The thick shafted ape arrows thunked into the wall below us.

And we kept shooting the bastards.

It was Wesley who realized what they were doing. "Shoot the bow and arrow apes! They're firing handholds into the wall!"

As he shouted that down the line, I realized very few of the arrows they'd fired had gone over our heads. They were all embedded into the wall below us. Some were close to impaling men, but many were obviously hitting low.

"You didn't tell me they were such smart sons of bitches," Marshal Landry yelled at me as the cannon down the wall boomed again.

"It's like they're getting smarter!"

The apes hit the wall in a rush.

Long ladders were lifted high and set against the towering palisade. Other apes grabbed the thick shafted arrows and began to climb.

Now arrows began to zip around us, shooting overhead, embedding into the pointed tops of the logs, and hitting a few unlucky men in the face, chest, or shoulders.

I ducked as an arrow flew past my head, nearly taking my hat with it.

"This is bullshit!" Talon cried out as he raised himself up, leaned over the wall slightly, and fired down into the apes climbing the closest ladder.

"Do it for George!" I screamed as I knelt behind the wall and began reloading the *Eighty-Six* while wishing I had a lit bundle of dynamite to throw over the wall.

"For George!" the Raiders repeated in a shout.

With my rifle reloaded, I worked the lever to send a round into the chamber. While bent in half, I moved down the wall to the Maxim machine gun that was still firing. Steam was coming off the fat round barrel end.

"More cartridges!" the Private shooting shouted. The Corporal dragged over another wooden crate and ripped the lid off. As he loaded the weapon, I used the machine gun opening to target the apes climbing up the ladders.

"Defend the Maxim!" I shouted at the three former inmates who were taking potshots over the wall with pistols.

They moved closer, still keeping their heads low as arrows zipped past overhead.

The inmate with the scarred face reached his arm up, pointed his pistol over the wall, and fired several times downwards.

"Try aiming!" I told him as the *Eighty-Six* knocked another ape off the ladder to my right. Bellowing, the ugly painted monkey fell backwards into the mix of apes fighting to get to us.

Jerking his head, the man looked over the wall to shoot and took an arrow through his left eye.

His body collapsed on the platform and the pistol fell from an open hand.

An ape face lurched in front of me suddenly.

Before I could work the lever on my rifle, it grabbed onto the glowing hot metal barrel of the Maxim and screamed in pain as hair burned and flesh cooked from the steaming metal. Flipping my rifle around, I thrust the metal buttplate into the monkey's mouth and knocked him out of sight.

"Defend yourselves!" screamed Captain Hawney as apes began clambering over the tops of the palisade. Grabbing rifles and men, they flung them over the wall into the seething mass of hairy bodies below.

The Vikings began screaming incoherently and began slashing and hacking with swords and axes. The Shaynee, not to be outdone, went hand to hand with the apes. Their lithe bodies grappled with the larger and stronger apes, maneuvering them into a position to stab with knives or hack with tomahawks.

Wesley dropped his rifle, drew both pistols and began shooting apes left and right as they climbed over the wall.

The Maxim began firing again, chattering as the soldier gripped the pair of D handles on the weapon and pressed the trigger.

"Just shoot them all!" I told him as he fired the weapon into the field of apes in front of us. "We'll keep them off you!"

Pearl moved by my side, a Winchester rifle in hand. She fired, cussed, spit tobacco, and fired some more as the Rough Raiders and such tried to keep the apes from overtaking the wall.

"Look!" Talon cried out, pointing to the west.

An ape climbed onto the platform, and with my *Eighty-Six* in my left hand, I drew a pistol and fired twice into its painted chest. The big monkey fell, grasping at the oozing holes, before toppling off and falling twenty feet or so inside the town.

Shoving the pistol back in its holster, I turned to see what the Rough Raider was alarmed about.

Trikes. Probably forty or so, with apes riding double on their backs racing down the flat, packed sand of the beach towards the western wall.

"Shit, shit, shit," I muttered as I tried to think of what to do. The apes were tying us up on the northern wall, and now their small force was going to flank us where we didn't have but a couple of undefended Maxims and cannons.

"Rough Raiders!" I screamed to get the men's attention. "West wall! West wall!"

And without waiting, I took off at a run, dodging the swing of a stone axe from an ape eager to join battle with a human.

Pearl shot that one with her rifle, and we shared a look as I ran past her.

"Watch your back!" she shouted after me.

I didn't realize what she meant until I turned the corner on the wall and reached the first Maxim machine gun.

This wall's crew-served weapons were manned by Pinkertons.

Not many, only a small group around each cannon or machine gun. Certainly not enough to prevent eighty to a hundred apes from climbing over the wall and wiping us all out.

As before, the apes began firing arrows into the wall as the trikes closed the distance.

Between explosions of meat and sand from cannon balls, and the impact of bullets from the Maxim, the apes charged fearlessly at the wall.

I turned to face the Rough Raiders as they stumbled to a stop in front of me. "Once the apes get within fifty yards of the wall, the cannons can't hit them, and I don't think the Maxims can either. That's where we'll shine. Repel the bastards!"

"Repel the bastards!" the men repeated in a shout.

I noticed that the two remaining inmates were still with us; I grabbed one and pushed him ahead of me. "Both of you, get to the other Maxim, protect it at all costs."

"Just us?" He gulped and looked in terror at the number of trikes running towards us.

"We'll be strung out along the wall with you. Aim for the apes, the trikes can't hurt us up here."

"Yes, sir!" He grabbed his former inmate buddy and jogged down the platform with his head ducked down.

The inmate he pulled with him took an ape arrow through the skull and dropped, then slowly fell off the platform.

"Shoot," I muttered. "Hey Talon! Bart! Go with him!"

The two Rough Raiders didn't acknowledge me except to fire a couple more shots then jog down the wall after the lumberjack.

Mounted trikes slammed into the wall. The platform rocked and I grabbed a sharpened point to steady myself.

Below, apes began to climb, using arrows and gripping whatever handholds they could find in the logs to move up the palisade towards us.

Slinging the *Eighty-Six*, I drew both pistols, leaned forward and fired downwards into their scowling, angry, howling painted faces. Within seconds my Colts were empty, and I was kneeling behind the wall reloading them painfully slow with a single cartridge at a time.

As I reloaded with my fingers, I looked to the northern wall that we'd left.

It was hand to hand fighting still. From what I could tell, the closest Maxim and cannon were down, their crews tied up with trying to stay alive in the moment. But more and more apes were clamoring over the wall.

"Fall back! Fall back!" I heard vaguely being shouted above the sound of gunfire and explosions.

Captain Hawney was waving his hand for everyone on the northern wall to retreat down into the town. I wasn't sure what plan he had but letting the apes into the town seemed like a really bad situation.

People began moving backwards towards the various stairs. Luckily, they had three sets of stairs per wall. One at each corner, shared with the other wall, and one in the center. That gave everyone plenty of room to begin retreating.

I snapped the cylinder gate shut on my second Peacemaker and rose.

An ape grabbed me by the shoulder, her fingers digging into my flesh like sharpened iron hooks. Stabbing a Colt into her face, I pulled the trigger and sent a spray of mush and gore onto the ape behind her.

And with that, the apes were climbing over our wall. A Rough Raider was bashed down with an axe in front of me, his arm nearly severed at the shoulder from the chipped stone.

Bullets hit the wall beside me.

Dropping to the ground, I pointed my pistol inside the town to see who was trying to kill me during the battle.

From the Governor's office balcony, Fredrick waved his hat at me, then lifted his rifle and fired again in my direction. This time he actually hit, and a small spray of blood splashed onto my shirt as he dropped an ape off the wall.

I waved a hand at him as Irving appeared on the balcony beside him. The kid was armed with a rifle, most likely one of Fredrick's customized Winchesters. I never taught him how to shoot a rifle, but I guess it was sink or swim now.

The Governor fired again, and the bullet sent splinters flying near my face.

Damned if I wasn't going to get killed by my own friend.

Apes from the northern wall were moving towards us, cutting down men as they cleared the walkway. Others were slinging arrows at us, making us pinned between an attacking force climbing the wall and hitting us from behind simultaneously.

"Rough Raiders! Retreat! Retreat!" I shouted and the call was repeated by the others as they began to try and disengage and escape down the stairs.

An explosion of flames burst from the far end of the northern wall followed by the ear-piercing scream of a dragon.

Moments later, the gunpowder stacked by the cannon blew. The explosion sent a tremor through the entire wall, shaking us all to our core, and created a twenty-foot gap of fallen and damaged timbers. Pinkertons went flying through the air, some on fire, others already mangled.

Now the damned apes were going to pour into the town.

Scrambling to my feet, I rushed for the stairs, gunning down apes with my Colts as they appeared before me.

A female ape leapt off the wall and landed on the walkway in front of me. Canines bared, she thrust a spear at my chest.

Throwing myself against the wall to avoid the obsidian tip, I pulled the triggers on the Colts and was rewarded with a pair of dry clicks.

No more bullets.

Without pause, I hurled myself at her and tried to bend the barrel of a Colt over her forehead.

The hard blued steel gashed her open, sending blood running down her painted face and into her eyes.

Shoving her with my shoulder into her waist, I pushed her off the platform.

She grabbed my arm on the way off and pulled me with her.

I landed on top of her, and from the gasping sounds she was making, she'd busted some ribs and such when we hit the packed and rocky ground.

I went to town on the ape with both Colts. Beating and pistol whipping her until her hairy black skull cracked and she stopped twitching.

Exhausted from the effort, I rolled off the dead ape and staggered to my feet.

Above me, with loud screeches, the breehas attacked the dragon in mass. There were only seven riders, Afton included, and I prayed it was enough to take down the dragon.

Around me, it was chaos. Apes and men were everywhere.

I watched Jarl Mikah cut an ape down with his sword while a Pinkerton was stabbed through the chest with a spear. Beyond them, a Shaynee brave took a moment in the fight to place his foot on the back of a dying ape and quickly scalp him.

Marshal Landry ran into the Governor's office with a pair of apes on her tail. On the balcony above, Fredrick and Irving waved at me to run to them.

Snapping a quick shot at the closest ape chasing Pearl, I ran after them and into the building.

By the time I hurled myself into the office and kicked the door shut behind me, there was a pair of dead apes in the entryway and Pearl standing over them reloading her revolver.

"Holy-" at a loss for words I just shook my head.

"Yeah, we didn't plan on this, did we?"

"If so, no one told me."

"Let's get to the balcony and kill some apes."

Without answering, I ran past her and up the stairs.

***

Irving was sitting behind the balcony rail, reloading rifles, and passing them to the Governor when I burst through the double doors.

"Fredrick!" I shouted.

"Jed! And Marshal Landry, I see! Welcome to the brawl," he called over his shoulder before firing another shot at an ape climbing over the western wall.

"He seems rather excited," Pearl muttered as she took up a position between where the building met the balcony. From there she was partially covered on the left side and had a large field of view to fire into it.

"He's an optimist," I told her.

The door behind us burst open, and spinning about, I nearly pulled the trigger on Wesley.

The gunfighter was out of breath and panting hard. He bent over at the knees, raised a hand at us, and sucked in deep lungfuls of air.

"So... damned... many," he said breathlessly.

"Yeah, and we lost the Maxims and cannons!" Irving cried out as he passed another rifle to Fredrick.

"But we're still alive, boy, and very much in the fight!" the Governor replied with a toothy grin.

Pearl ducked back as an arrow zipped past her and embedded itself in the building siding. "Got any ideas, Jed?"

"Nope. We're just going to have to kill them all."

A breeha fell from the sky. Smoking and burning, it crashed into the partially constructed building across the street. Within seconds, the flames were spreading.

"We need to kill that dragon!" Fredrick shouted.

"The Shayana are supposed to do that," Wesley called back while reloading his Winchester.

I looked into the sky, the breehas' riders were still in the fight. The giant pterodactyls were mobbing the dragon like a pack of crows attacking an eagle. One breeha swooped low and came up sideways to the dragon. I saw the fading sunlight flashing off a sword as a cut was made towards the dragon rider.

"We need to kill the rider," Pearl yelled.

"Done!" Fredrick twisted around, pointed his rifle in the direction of the dragon and began sending round after round into the sky.

"Don't!"

"What? I can hit it!"

"Fredrick," I grabbed him by the shoulder. "You've many astounding qualities, but accuracy is not one of them."

He shook free of my hand. "That's why I carry so many guns!"

Irving shouted for help from behind us.

Twisting, we saw an ape crawling over the balcony. Before we could react, the kid had pulled the rifle he was reloading into his shoulder and fired a round into the monkey's chest.

The dead ape slumped over the rail.

"Well done, kid!" I called out with a grin. He'd do just fine.

Turning my attention back to the western wall, I peered through the smoke billowing from the burning building and realized that the apes coming over had nearly stopped. The platform was cleared of living humans, having all retreated into various buildings and positions inside the town.

A pair of apes grabbed the cannon and rolled it backwards off the walkway. It toppled over and thudded hard to the ground inside the wall, upside down and unusable.

The same apes moved towards the Maxim.

Flipping the peep sight up on my *Eighty-Six*, I fired a round into one of the ape's backs. He arched at the impact then dropped. The other, suddenly aware that he was in the open and being fired upon, leapt off the platform to the ground some twenty feet below.

From the way he landed and fell, I'd say he broke a leg.

I let the ape crawl a few yards as I lined up the sights again and put a bullet through him.

"Alright, there's a machine gun on the wall that's still good. If we can get to it."

"Then what?" Pearl asked.

"We can turn it around and start shooting apes."

"Why can't we stay here?" Irving asked as he finished reloading the rifle and set it aside.

"The faster we kill them, the better," I told him then pointed. "And look! Turn it around and you've got a straight shot down the center of Main Street."

The doors burst open again, this time with Reydan rushing through them. Cato was behind him, backing through the doorways with both his pistols firing into Fredrick's office. Wesley moved beside him and fired a couple of shots into the room.

"You!" Reydan and I both shouted as we saw each other. I swung my rifle barrel to cover him.

"No!" Marshal Landry stepped between us. "None of this shit. We need every gun we can get to survive this."

"Fine," I said bitterly, lowering the *Eighty-Six* and glaring at my enemy.

The railroad tycoon was carrying a rifle now and wore a pair of pistols strapped around his waist.

"That's quite the outfit for a former quartermaster," I snarked at him while recalling that he'd been armed the same way on the day he torched our home, kidnapped Cato, and whipped me.

From the street below, I heard a loud shout of excitement and peeked over the railing.

Carson Skinner was mounted on the back of a big black horse and racing down the street with a pistol in his hand. As we watched, he worked the horse, zig zagging between apes and men as he fired shot after shot into them. Emptying the pistol, he holstered it and drew another from a brace that hung from the pommel of his saddle.

Twirling his horse below us at the end of the street, he looked up, grinned as happily as I'd ever seen him, and shouted, "You going to join the fight or just watch?"

Before I could think of something clever to reply, he'd kicked his heels to the horse and rode back the way he came, once again dealing death to the apes on a grand scale.

Across the street the burning building collapsed, and the scent of cooking pterodactyl was strong from the dead breeha inside.

In front of the roaring flames, several Rough Raiders and a Pinkerton detective were using a wagon and a water trough for cover as they fired over and around the obstacles at approaching apes. Several monkeys lay dead in front of them already.

"We need that Maxim!" Reydan said, pointing at the western wall.

"No kidding," I grumbled as I shot an ape that was sneaking up behind a pair of Axemen down the street.

"Cato and I will get it firing, but we'll need protection as we work it," Reydan glared at me before looking around at us.

"I'll go," Fredrick said over his shoulder.

"Me too," replied Irving as he finished loading another rifle.

"And I," said Wesley while peeking into the office for any more apes sneaking through the building.

They all looked at me.

"I need to rally Charlie Troop," I told them, heading towards the double doors and the dead ape lying between them. Past that corpse were four more stacked up almost neatly on the dinosaur hide rug.

"The Rough Raiders are gone," Reydan said in annoyance.

I jabbed a finger across the street as the Pinkerton took an arrow through the throat and fell behind the wagon. "There's a couple over there that ain't. You go do what you need to do, and I'll do what I need to."

With that, I spun my back on my enemy and friends and jogged through the Governor's office, down the stairs, and to the door looking out at the street.

The street was a blood bath. There were bodies everywhere, I was thankful to see more were apes than men. But at the same time, there was an awful lot of shooting going on around me. The battle for Whitesberg was still fully joined, it had just moved from the walls into the buildings and streets.

Ducking my head, I ran across the street to the burning building as arrows and stray bullets zipped past around me.

Reaching the trough, I skipped on my knees to a stop behind it.

Both Raiders looked at me like I was nuts.

"Gentlemen," I said, "I'm here to lead you to victory."

They looked at each other and laughed. Then I laughed as well.

We were up a serious creek in a bad way.

***

The first thing I did was loot the dead Pinkerton.

Not for money, but for the ammunition he might have. As I unfortunately suspected, he did not have any .45-70 for the *Eighty-Six*, but he had plenty of cartridges for my Colt Peacemakers. If I wanted more bullets for my rifle, I was going to have to fight my way to Carson's store.

As soon as I thought of that, I realized it'd be a great place to fight from.

But first we had to get there alive, and there were an awful lot of apes running around.

I was about to step onto the street when the recognizable sound of heavy trike feet echoed down to us.

Peeking around the trough, I saw Wesley and Pearl making their way up the staircase towards the others at the Maxim machine gun on the wall. And I saw a stampede of trikes rushing down the street towards them.

The breeched northern wall must have finally collapsed to the point where the apes could bring their heavy mounts in.

And then I saw them.

Raptors.

Racing down the streets alongside and between the trikes, spreading out as they saw people and attaching in flying leaps of claws and teeth.

Great.

Just great.

A Shayana went down beneath the gnashing teeth of a raptor.

An axeman leapt off the roof of a building onto the backs of one of the trikes, smashing the blade of his axe into the back of the ape riding it.

A soldier didn't get out of the way in time and was trampled beneath the heavy running feet of a trike.

It was violent pandemonium.

"Alright, listen up. Building by building, we're going to make our way to Liberty Arms and grab anyone we can on the way."

"Why can't we just wait here? Wait for reinforcements?"

"No one is coming anytime soon."

Pop! Pop! Pop! Small divots sprouted from the street as Reydan and Cato got the Maxim firing. The bullets strung along, running up the streets, and then hitting the charging trikes right in their horned faces.

Dead mounts tumbled over and fell as they died, blocking Main Street off from the others that pushed and milled around behind the fallen.

"Now's a good time! Let's go!"

With a very real fear of Reydan putting the sights of the Maxim on my back, we crossed the alleyway and stopped at the corner of the building next to ours.

Near us lay a group of dead apes around several Axemen. One of the apes still had an axe jutting out from her chest. A Viking ran down the street, pausing only to step on the dead ape and wrench the axe out, before carrying on.

I called for him to come with us, but he either didn't hear or didn't understand and went on his own merry way.

From the window behind us came the shattering sound of glass followed by a rifle barrel sticking out. The gun bloomed fire as a shot rang out.

"Hold your fire!" I called out. "We're coming in!"

"Come on then!"

One of the Raiders grabbed the door handle, turned the knob and ran into the room as an arrow thunked into the building where he'd been standing moments ago. We followed him in, and I slammed the door shut behind us.

Captain Hawney stared at me. His eyes were wide, part of his hair was singed, and ash was smudged on his face and tattered uniform.

From the looks of things, he must have been near the explosion on the wall.

Now he sat curled against the corner of the building, with his knees pulled against his chest and pistol held tightly in both hands in front of him.

Shooting out the busted windows was Talon and a few soldiers.

The Rough Raider saw me. "What the hell is going on, Johnson? And who's manning the Maxim? Lord bless them!" He was shooting out the window into Main Street where a steady stream of bullets from the machine gun was keeping the dead trikes piling up in front of the buildings as the mounted apes kept trying to push through town.

"The Governor, plus a few others." I wasn't about to tell him my nemesis was up there saving all our lives.

"Well, he's a goner!" Talon pointed at the Captain who was now trembling and muttering what sounded like a prayer. "I dragged him out of the blast debris like that, and he hasn't been any help since."

"Where's Lieutenant Daniels?"

"I don't know who that is?"

One of the soldiers turned to reply. His mouth opened, but an ape reached through the window, grabbed him by the shoulder and dragged him kicking and screaming over the broken glass and outside.

I ran over, jerked the *Eighty-Six* into my shoulder, and peeked through the open window. The ape jerked a spear out of the soldier's stomach and turned back to face me as I pulled the trigger.

The large round hit the monkey a bit high, blasting through where his neck and shoulder connected. The ape screamed and thrust the spear through the window at me.

Batting it aside with the barrel of the rifle, I stepped back, worked the lever again, and fired without aiming the sights. This time I connected with a better placed shot and the ape dropped from sight.

From the front of the building came a shout followed by a heavy thud.

"Trike hit the building!" Talon cried out; he looked shook up but quickly went back to firing out the window.

I glanced from my Rough Raiders to Captain Hawney. I couldn't just leave the man. Glancing around the building, I saw what looked like a closet near the back.

Kneeling next to the officer, I slowly reached out and began to take the pistol from his clenched hands. He jerked away instinctively. "Captain," I said. "I've got somewhere safe for you, but I'm going to need that pistol first."

Hawney shook his head back and forth as his eyes searched mine.

"It's empty, anyways," Talon said between firing and racking the lever on his Winchester.

"You certain?"

"Certain as can be."

"Okay," I motioned to the other Rough Raiders. "Help the Captain into the closet."

The two men gently placed their hands under his arms and helped the shook man onto his feet, then helped him stumble back to the closet. Once they had him set inside, I told him as gently as I could, "We'll be back for you. Just stay here and stay quiet."

He didn't respond, but a tear trickled down his soot-covered cheek.

I closed the door with a click. There was no lock or anything on it, he'd be able to get out or an ape able to get in, but he was a liability in this fight.

We'd taken a couple steps away when a loud BAM came from the closet.

Swearing, I leapt over and jerked the door open.

It was as I feared. That pistol hadn't been unloaded after all.

I closed the door gently and hardened my face before turning back to my men. "Lieutenant Daniels is in charge now, if he's alive or we can find him."

"And if he's not?" one asked.

"Then I reckon I am."

**

"Everyone ready?" I called out to the men behind me.

They nodded but they didn't look happy.

I didn't blame them. But all I could think to do was seek out that blasted leader ape and kill him. And hopefully that'd break the apes' spirit and attack.

"Remember, we're looking for a big ape. About a foot taller than the others. He's got brown fur and a green swirl circled on his chest with a pair of yellow lines on his chin. And if he's leading this army, you know he's a badass. Keep your eyes peeled. You see him, you shoot him, immediately."

"Yes, sir," the Rough Raiders and surviving soldiers said in unison.

Grabbing the handle of the door, I jerked it open.

A raptor stood on the boardwalk in front of us. Its reptilian mouth was blood stained and we were close enough to see bits of flesh in its teeth.

With my left hand, I quick drew my Colt Peacemaker and hit the raptor before he could move. All that practice paid off as the lethal little dinosaur collapsed and kicked is clawed feet in death spasms.

"Let's go!"

We ran around a dead trike and rider, keeping our heads down low as the Maxim continued firing. Bullets cracked by overhead as they shot at targets further down the street from us.

I was certain they'd run out of ammunition soon. Unless they were able to steal some from one of the other positions. I hoped it was Reydan who went on that task, his skill at pillaging would come in handy for once.

A trio of apes burst from the alleyway to our right, charging across Main Street with spears and stone axes in hand. One of them leapt over a dead ape while another slowed long enough to stab his spear into the back of a wounded axeman.

"Shoot them!" Talon screamed.

Leaping to our nearest bits of cover, I ended up standing behind a thick post that wasn't thick enough to actually protect me. Using it as a rest, I pinned the *Eighty-Six* against it with my left hand and fired. My bullet hit the lead ape along with several others, and within a second or two, all three apes were dead.

The building we were at was locked, and even though I banged on it with my fist and rifle butt, no one answered from inside.

We kept moving.

After a handful of steps, an arrow hit a Rough Raider in the leg and dropped him.

"Roofs! They're on the roofs!" one of the soldiers shouted as he fired upwards.

I couldn't see anything up there from my angle, but I did see a ladder leading to the top of the partially constructed building in front of us. Running to it, I slung the *Eighty-Six* across my back and climbed hand over hand. Talon followed me as the others kept firing at whoever was above us.

There were four of them.

Apes.

Two on top of this building and two on the other one across the alley.

They'd lean over, fire an arrow, then duck back as my men tried to shoot them.

Staying low, I ran behind the closest one and slammed the buttstock of the *Eighty-Six* into where his kidney should have been. Letting out a bellow of pain, he dropped the bow, grabbed at his back and fell off the roof.

Talon shot the other with his pistol, then began shooting at the two apes across the alleyway.

He killed all three before I managed to turn my rifle around.

"Good shooting," I told him.

"Thanks."

We peeked over the edge. The Rough Raider who'd taken the arrow through the leg was dead, his body pin cushioned with several other arrows. The other men appeared fine and unwounded as they peeked around the corners of the buildings and shot at whatever they could.

It was nonstop.

"Grab his ammunition!" I called down to them. "We can't afford to run out."

I patted my pockets; I only had a few cartridges for the *Eighty-Six* on me, but plenty of .45s in the loops on my gun belt.

I needed to get to Carson Skinner's store.

Luckily, it was just a couple buildings over.

Unluckily, there were a lot of monkeys, raptors, and trikes between us and it.

Splinters flew as a trio of bullets hit the flat rooftop beside me. Hurling myself to the right, I came dangerously close to falling off the edge.

The bullets hit with such accuracy and speed, that there was only one place they could have come from.

Twisting my body, I looked back at the western wall.

Sure as shit, Reydan White was working the Maxim.

My friends around him were defending the position from a large group of apes working their way up the stairs. It took me a minute to locate Cato, he was over at the other machine gun, picking up a pair of heavy cartridge boxes to feed the Maxim with.

I swear even at this distance I could see the sneer on the railroad tycoon's bearded face as he adjusted the large, barreled rifle.

Talon kneeled beside me, "They're going for the machine gun!" he shouted as he lined his sights up on the group of apes moving up the stairs to get to my friends.

"No! Get back!" I tried to tell him as he fired.

The spray of blood from Maxim bullets impacting his body was devastating. It splashed onto my face and arm.

Without thinking, I rolled off the edge of the roof as more bullets impacted where I'd been a split-second ago.

***

I fell on an ape. He broke my fall with his hairy body. The pair of us tangled under my weight and to the ground in the alleyway.

Before I could move or draw a pistol, an obsidian-tipped spear point was placed against my neck.

Looking up in shock, I saw the young female ape that I'd previously saved holding the weapon at my throat. Her missing ear had been bandaged with one of the dried fern poultices from this side.

Gulping hard, my hand slowly moved towards my pistol as the male ape with her pulled himself out from under me and growled in anger.

He spoke to her roughly, but she snapped something back and moved the spear point away from me. I could feel a small trickle of blood from the tiny slash she'd given me with the weapon.

Grunting angrily, he growled louder at her and jabbed his stone axe at me.

She seemed to shrug at me, as if to say, 'sorry' and pulled her spear back to thrust.

Instinctively I drew, flipped the barrel of the pistol upwards, and fired a shot into her stomach. Thumbing back the hammer, I hit the male ape as well, dropping him where he stood.

The one-eared female dropped her spear and stepped back, staggering to a knee.

She looked at me pitifully.

A shot rang out and she toppled forward onto her face. From behind me, around the corner came the others in my small group of Rough Raiders and soldiers.

"Got her!" one of the privates said with a grin.

I stared at him for a moment, unsure of what to say. Then I looked back at the dead female. I'd saved her for nothing, possibly killed a Shayana tribesman for nothing, and almost died… for nothing. Why'd I even bother setting her free?

"We need to go," one of the Rough Raiders said hurriedly.

A pair of mounted trikes ran by the back street, and one of the apes loosened an arrow down the alleyway at us but missed by a good fifteen feet.

"Yep. Let's go find the leader," I said finally, pushing what had just occurred to the back of my mind.

A screech came from overhead, and we ducked as a stream of fire filled the sky between the two buildings as an obviously wounded dragon chased after a breeha. Seconds later a trio of mounted pterodactyls flew after it, close enough and low enough that I could tell one of them was the Shaynee leader, Afton.

We moved to the back street. It seemed safer without as many apes and trikes, and most importantly, Reydan behind a Maxim. The buildings and their false fronts should hide me from him as we moved, but I needed to find a way to shoot the bastard.

Before he killed me, or the apes killed him.

"Over there!" a soldier shouted beside me, pointing at the Crystal Palace down the alley and across Main Street.

"What?" I asked as I checked my *Eighty-Six*. I was down to just what was in the magazine tube.

"I saw him, brown fur, green circle on his chest, all that. He went inside the saloon!"

"Let's go get him."

I ran down the alleyway with my group close around me. We reached the edge of the building. From the sign on the boardwalk, it was a General Store and there was a backdoor leading to the alley we were in.

Grabbing the door, I jerked it open, and we rushed inside.

Otto and a mixture of axemen and Shayana and Shaynee were inside.

We looked at a lot of gun barrels for a moment before they were lowered.

"Guess I should have knocked first," I quipped jokingly.

The scarred Shaynee brave rolled his eyes.

From the number of shell casings scattered about on the floor and under tables and shelves of dry goods, it appeared like they'd been holding down this fort for some time. All the windows were shot out, and the front door was barricaded shut with an overturned table. A couple of dead apes lay strewn on the floor in pools of blood. From the looks of their wounds, the Vikings had taken those out.

"Rough Raiders, this room appears full. Get to the roof and provide covering fire."

"What about you, Johnson?" one asked as he grabbed a strip of jerky from an unshattered glass jar by the checkout table.

"I'm going after that ape."

"Which hairy man?" Otto demanded.

"Brown one, green circle on chest, yellow on face. He's their leader."

"I go with you then."

I nodded without even thinking. "Okay." It may be a wild goose chase, but if it was the lead ape, we needed to kill him. And two were better than one. And believe me, I did not want to go into the Crystal Palace by my lonesome.

"Ja!" cried a Viking as he shot his bow through an open window. Beside him a Shayana fired his flintlock, and a massive cloud of burnt black powder billowed into the street.

Otto and I moved to the side door and opened it cautiously as the Rough Raiders followed. The alley was empty except for the dead, and I stepped over a soldier, then an ape, and moved to the edge of Main Street.

There was an ear-piercing roar of pain, followed by another bout of flame overhead. Then the dragon came falling to the ground.

But not directly.

No, the crazy dragon riding ape landed it on top of Reydan White and the Maxim machine gun.

With a thunderous boom, the dragon smashed through the small group standing by the weapon and wiped the walkway empty as it toppled off the backside of the wall.

"No!" I shouted as I found myself standing in the open street trying to see if any of my friends up there were still alive.

Otto grabbed me by a shoulder and jerked me behind a wagon. The harnessed horses were dead, arrowed through in multiple places. One looked trampled, like a trike had stomped over its corpse.

Shaking free of the Indian, I leaned over to see.

Fredrick, Pearl, and Wesley were still alive; they'd been protecting the stairs when the dragon hit.

As I watched, Fredrick and Wesley raced to the top of the empty walkway, leaned over, and pulled Irving up from where he must have been hanging from the outside of the wall.

But there was no sign of Reydan, or Cato.

And now we'd lost one of our most valuable weapons in this fight.

Carson Skinner raced by again on the back of his black horse. He didn't seem to notice us as he twisted about in the saddle and shot at the mounted trike chasing him.

"Okay, Otto. Let's go get this ape."

We ran at the same time, side by side, across Main Street, onto the boardwalk, and through the double doors of the Crystal Palace.

***

Skidding to a stop, I dropped the *Eighty-Six* to the floor and drew my Colts.

The ape leader was standing before us, with a pair of raptors.

I fired both guns as fast as I could. We were close enough that I didn't need to aim, I just needed to pull the triggers as quickly as humanly possible.

The four-foot-tall dinosaurs shrieked and screamed as tufts of feathers flew off their bodies.

Even after taking a couple of bullets, one leapt at Otto. The Shaynee brave lifted his rifle horizontally to fend off the little beast's attack. It bit the rifle, teeth scratching the blued metal and gouging into the decorated wood stock.

I fired a bullet into the raptor's head before both guns went empty and clicked as I rotated the cylinders on already fired cartridges.

Both dinosaurs were down, but the lead ape was not.

He moved for us with long loping strides.

Otto jerked his tomahawk free and threw it.

End over end the blade twirled, only to be knocked out of the air by the big hairy monkey's hand.

As the weapon clattered to the floor, the ape grabbed Otto by the throat and lifted him kicking and struggling into the air.

Scooping up the *Eighty-Six*, I swung it like a bat by the barrel and cracked the walnut stock against the towering ape's skull.

He didn't let go of Otto.

I swung again and the ape caught the bat in his free hand, jerked it from mine and tossed it aside like a child's toy instead of the almost ten-pound rifle that it was.

Then he lunged forward and grabbed me by the throat as well.

Lifting us both in the air, he roared victoriously. Bits of spittle flew from behind his canines as my windpipe felt like it was being slowly crushed.

But I'd been in this situation before.

Reaching behind my back, I pulled the long-bladed Bowie free from its sheath and rammed it upwards into the ape's hairy armpit. The blade sank half its length into flesh and blood oozed down to my clenched fist on the handle.

The big monkey bellowed in pain and dropped me as I jerked the blade free.

With a step and a half twist, he hurled Otto against the bar where my blood brother hit with a bone jarring thud and crumpled.

Holding nothing but the blood-covered Bowie knife in front of me, I thought for a second about how screwed I was facing a monstrously beast of an ape one on one.

Then I remembered George. Sweet Chinese George. Charlie Company's mascot. In that big dumb hat of his, always making rebel yells and being excited about whatever miserable or repetitive training we were about to do.

It made me angry.

And before the ape could react, I charged.

Slamming my shoulder into the eight-foot-tall ape, it was like running into a brick shithouse. But I wasn't there trying to topple him over.

No.

I was slashing with my blade and cutting everything that was between us.

The ape grabbed me in a bear hug and bit into my shoulder with its yellowed canines.

Screaming from the pain, I jabbed my large Bowie into the ape's side over and over, praying that I'd hit something vital.

I must have finally hit something important because my flesh ripped as he pulled his teeth free and let me go.

I dropped to my knees in front of him, my blade still jutting out from the ape's side.

Lots of blood was pouring out of the slashing wounds on its green painted chest and stomach, but the big hairy ape was still standing strong.

I looked up just as the ape kicked me in the chest.

Flying backwards I slammed into the very same table that Afton the Shayana had been drinking from earlier that day.

Bottles fell to the ground about me, and one rolled against me as I grasped for my breath.

Looking across the room I saw Otto stirring slowly, and knew I needed to buy some time. If anything, to give my blood brother a chance to finish the job.

Grabbing the bottle beside me by the neck, I stood and smashed it against the tabletop. Jagged glass edges were left behind, and I took a staggered step towards the ape.

"C'mon, you ape," I told him, and held the broken bottle before me.

The ape pounded his fist against his chest, roared, and drew a chipped obsidian blade from the belt at his waist.

The very same blade he'd gutted George with.

Snarling like a rabid animal, I leapt at him with every ounce of fury I had left in my body.

The jagged glass bottle went into his throat.

As the ape staggered backwards, dropping his knife and falling, I fell on top of him.

Like some sort of possessed beast, I jerked the broken glass free and ripped it back and forth across the green painted swirl on his chest. Red blood flowed freely from the sliced open black skin, mixing with the paint.

The ape leader once again grasped me into a bear hug, and I cried out in pain as his grip began to tighten.

We were staring at each other, face to face. His brown eyes were boring into me with a depth of disgust that one only held towards an inferior creature. He was dying, we both knew it. But he was going to kill me on the way out.

My spine creaked under the force being applied to my back.

Breath expelled from my lungs.

Tears sprang to my eyes as my vision began to go dark.

This was it.

Skyla, I thought. I've failed you.

The ape's head disintegrated in an explosion of blood and gore as a loud boom threatened to destroy my hearing.

The grip on my back ceased and I rolled off the corpse, gasping for breath and trying to make sense of what had just happened.

Otto stood over me, my broken *Eighty-Six* in his hands and a faint trickle of smoke coming from the barrel.

"Oh, thank God," I wheezed.

"Not god; Otto," my blood brother grinned before helping me stand.

"Yes, Otto." I wiped the brains and bits of skull off my face and slapped him on the back with the same hand. "I'm grateful for you."

The Indian looked in disgust at the gore that smeared onto his bare back.

I picked up my Colts from where I'd dropped them and sat in one of the leather-bound chairs beside the bar. Outside, a trike bellowed and we saw Asger ride past on his magnificent black and red beast.

As I reloaded the Peacemakers, I looked at the ape leader's corpse sadly. "I was going to suggest we cut his head off and give it to Carson to ride up and down the street with... but I guess that's not possible now. There's not enough left."

"We could drag the body?" Otto said matter of factly while picking up his tomahawk off the floor.

"It's a big damn body and no one would recognize it." I snapped the gate shut on the first Colt and accepted my broken rifle from Otto. With sadness, I sat the once mighty *Eighty-Six* on the bar, and reloaded the other pistol.

"No, we're going to have to do this the old fashioned way." I stood, holstered my second pistol and picked up my broken stocked rifle. "By killing them all."

We moved to the double doors. Apes, raptors, and trikes were every damn where now and most of the living men were holed up in various buildings, fighting them off one by one.

I looked forlornly at Liberty Arms, it was so close but so far away.

Screw it.

"Get ready to run," I told Otto.

"Shaynee braves no run. We fight!"

"Not run from it, run towards it." I pointed out the door. "That big building that looks like a jail. We're going there."

"Okay, Huck Berry."

"Ready, and-"

Otto knocked the door open and took off running. A few steps behind him, I came out with broken rifle slung over my back and a Colt Peacemaker in both hands.

I fired at everything. Blood sprayed as some shots connected, others missed.

But after what felt like a really, really long run, Otto beat me to Liberty Arms and tried to open the door.

I skidded to a stop beside him, firing at a pair of apes running across the street towards us.

"No open!" Otto shouted as he fought the heavy set door.

I fired and fired and then both guns went dry at the same time. The last of the two apes was really close now. Sensing victory, he roared and lifted his stone club up to smite me.

The door swung open, and Carson blew the ape nearly in half with a scattergun.

"Get in!" he shouted.

We pushed by the man and into his store.

Otto screamed and sunk his tomahawk into the head of the raptor mount, then paused, looking at it oddly as he tugged the blade free.

"Dammit! That was NEW!" Carson shouted as he shifted over to a window and picked up a Spencer repeating rifle he had laid beside the door. Boom! He fired through the iron bars.

Otto moved to the other window and began firing a pistol through it.

"Well don't just stand there, grab some guns and get to killing!"

I realized the tables that'd formerly held leather and shooting goods were now emptied of everything but guns and ammunition.

Holstering my empty Colts, I unslung the *Eighty-Six* and laid it gently on one of the tables.

Carson saw the rifle and his eyes widened. "What the hell have you done to it?" he shouted before turning back to the window and firing the Spencer rifle again.

"Long story," I muttered as I quickly looked at all the weapons.

There were so many choices.

"Got any Gatlings?" I asked sarcastically and wishfully at the same time.

"No! Hurry up and get to shooting."

I grabbed a model 1873 Winchester off the table, it was a spitting image of the one they'd given me when I'd enlisted in the Rough Raiders.

Scooping up a box of .44-40, I began thumbing them into the magazine tube under the rifle as quickly as I could work the cartridges in my fingers.

"Jed, Otto and I will hold them off down here. You get upstairs and see how the rest of the town looks," Carson demanded. "There's more guns up there if you need them!"

I ran to the back of the store, up the staircase and to the second floor. My early assumption had been correct; this was his living quarters. Several large trunks were lying open along the walls, and as I made my way across the large room towards the window overlooking Main Street, I noticed one of them held a gray confederate uniform and cavalry sword.

Reaching the window, I peeked through the unbroken glass outside.

Apes and men were still clashing in the open, but it appeared that most men were holed up in the buildings.

A faint piercing scream came to my ears. Uncertain of what I heard, I pressed my ear against the glass and listened again.

Over the screams, bellows, gunshots, and roars, I heard another scream.

I looked towards the eastern wall. It was still intact, but devoid of men or apes. The crew-served weapons that'd been mounted there had been thrown over the wall by apes it appeared. But the giant portcullis that covered the train tracks was still down.

Another scream.

This one closer.

I noticed the glass pressed against my face was beginning to shake slightly. I placed a hand against it.

A breeha flew by, swooping down the large street, picking up an ape in its claws and carrying it high aloft to be dropped to its death.

The glass trembled more.

I looked at the portcullis as it blew inwards from the force of a steam locomotive hitting it at full speed.

The bottom of the giant iron gate was ripped out of the ground by the pointed cow catcher guard on the train, and the top fell onto the locomotive, knocking the steam turret off before sliding to the side.

The train kept moving, brakes screamed in protest now as they were applied to the steel wheels.

Black smoke poured from the top of the locomotive.

The train smashed into several trikes and apes who had the lack of luck to be standing on the rails in the street.

Blood splattered as the locomotive was knocked off its tracks.

It slid forward with one set of wheels digging into the gravel as the other set of wheels tore up wooden rail ties between the tracks.

The entire gun store shook as the train slid to a stop in front of us in a cloud of dust and earth.

Behind the steam engine, passenger cars disembarked dozens upon dozens of men.

Gunfire erupted along both sides of the cars as men began firing through the windows while others pushed and jostled to get off and into the fight.

Apes dropped in droves.

I smashed the window out with the barrel of the Winchester and began shooting at anything hairy.

A raptor raced out from an alleyway, leaping into the air, screaming and clawing at the side of one of the passenger cars until it was killed.

The tide was turning.

Apes began to run back towards the northern wall that'd exploded apart.

I watched as Lieutenant Barlow and his remaining men of Bravo Troop fired into their backsides as the surviving apes tried to escape.

The battle turned into a slaughter.

I stopped shooting once I ran out of targets.

Suddenly weary, I crossed the room, walked down the stairs and checked on Carson and Otto.

The pair of them were sitting in chairs beside the mounted and now damaged stuffed raptor, sipping from a whiskey flask.

Carson took the flask from Otto, took a sip, noticed me crossing the room and held it up.

Accepting the whiskey, I took a drink and let the burn clear my parched throat.

The shooting going on outside was becoming more sporadic.

I pointed at my *Eighty-Six* on the table. "Can that stock be fixed?"

Carson shook his head, "No, it's ruined. We'll need a new one. But luckily for you, I know Mr. Browning. I'm certain I'll get it fixed once I regale him with the adventures you've used it for. He's been very curious about the events of your discovery of Prehistoria and speaks of them often in our correspondences."

"Thank you, Carson. I've a task I need to tend to, but I'll be back."

"Ah yes, you've come for revenge, and it appears revenge you shall have."

"One way or another, yes. Mind if I borrow this Winchester?"

"Be my guest, and good luck, sir."

I tipped my hat at the unlikely pair of Southern aristocrat and savage Indian, then stepped out into the fading sunlight.

Night was approaching, and I was glad this battle was ending before it arrived. Stepping over an ape corpse and around the derailed locomotive, I ran into Lieutenant Barlow of Bravo Troop.

"Mr. Johnson Brown," he beamed at me. "I'm glad that Bravo Troop arrived in the nick of time to save Charlie Troop. Thanks to our decimation of the ape army that attacked the Shimmer, we were able to ride to your rescue. And we slaughtered them by the bushel, those poor ape bastards never had a chance. Now, where might Lieutenant Heath be?"

I looked around. There were a lot more soldiers and Pinkertons that'd disembarked the train than just his troop, but all I said was, "Dead."

The young Lieutenant frowned but quickly recovered. "A shame then. Captain Theo and Alpha Troop has been wiped out as well; it appears that I am in command of the remaining Rough Raiders."

"Reckon so."

"Then you need to bring the remaining men of C Troop to me, Mr. Brown."

"Would, but can't. My name is Jedidiah Huckleberry Smith and I'm looking for a Marshal to turn myself in to. Seen any?"

"Ah..." his mouth froze as his eyes took in my twin Colt Peacemakers strapped to my waist. He unfroze himself and reached towards his flap-covered pistol. "As you are a wanted man, I shall take you into custody and see to it that you are delivered to the proper authorities for questioning."

I dropped my hand to the grip of my Colt and shook my head slightly. "No, you won't. I've business to attend to first. But if you see a Marshal, send them to the western wall. That's where I'll be. But if you try to arrest me now, you'd better be a faster draw than what that flapped military holster will allow you to be."

"Cer-certainly," he backed away a step then turned and yelled at some soldiers to hurry up and help the wounded in the nearby buildings.

Walking away, I headed down Main Street, stepping around and over the dead and hoping not to see anyone I cared about on the ground.

Pushing open the gate in the western wall, I stepped onto the beach battlefield and headed towards the dead dragon. The giant beast was lying where it'd fallen, partially impaled by a couple of the giant logs the wall had been built with.

My footsteps made no sound as I walked across the sand and rock-strewn beach. Several men were out here, having been thrown or jerked over the wall by attacking apes. All of them had been cut down or crushed beneath the waves of trikes and apes attacking this side.

From what I could see, nothing lived on this side. But I kept my hands near my Colts, just in case. And I also recalled the wretched giant crabs that liked to inhabit these shallow waters and had a taste for flesh and blood.

The partially constructed dock along with the few small boats that'd been built had been all put to the torch by the apes. They'd burned down to the waterline.

I reached the dragon corpse and while there was no sign of Cato, only a set of boot prints from where someone had staggered away, I did find my nemesis still alive.

***

Reydan lay pinned underneath the Maxim, a bloody froth covered his gray tinged beard and neck as he raggedly coughed.

"Looks like you're dyin'," I told him as I raised my Colt and pointed the muzzle of the Peacemaker at his face.

"Do it," he snarled.

I cocked the hammer back and looked down the sights that were lined up on his forehead.

A simple squeeze. That's all it'd take to avenge a ten-year-old boy who'd been tied to a tree and whipped until he turned into a man.

"Do it!"

I savored the moment.

Then, I uncocked the hammer and holstered the pistol.

He looked at me in disbelief before shaking and coughing up another wad of bloody phlegm.

"No. I don't think I will."

I sat beside my dying mortal enemy as his final minutes drained from him. Stretching slightly, I looked up and saw Wesley, Pearl, and Irving on the wall. A moment later, Governor Fredrick appeared and gave me a slight wave that I returned with an easy smile.

"Like I said, looks like you're dying. I think I'll just sit here a while and wait on it."

"You... bastard..." he wheezed.

"Yup. I'm gonna sit right here and tell you what I'm going to do once you're gone." I looked him in the eyes. His were full of anger and hatred, but I also saw the fear in them of his imminent death.

"I'm gonna live, you sonuva bitch. I'm going to go find my horse, then go find my woman back East, and we're going to come back to Prehistoria and make a home and keep livin'. It may or may not be for long, but it will be longer than you. And without you, this world is going to be a nicer place."

He coughed, then his body convulsed, shuddering for a second under the weight of the heavy gun.

"You done?" I waited a moment for his eyes to fix back on me. "As I was saying, we're going to have us a nice little family over here. And if anyone like you ever rears their ugly head, or tries to take from me what's mine, I'll make sure they suffer a similar fate as you." I chuckled. "Maybe I won't drop a Maxim on them though, but I'll find a way."

I glanced down at him to see if he was still listening. He was, but it appeared his death was moments away.

I patted him on the shoulder.

"So long, you cretin."

His eyes narrowed at me, then relaxed, unmoving, unblinking, and unwavering in the setting sun.

***

Snow was falling as I walked down the covered city streets of Washington. It crunched slightly under my boots as I followed the shadowy figure. They carried a lantern and appeared to be in a hurry to get home. I didn't blame them; it was cold after all. The brick-and-mortar buildings that lined the gas lantern lit streets reeked of money and power. Christmas trees and lit candles burned through the windows.

It was a wonderful time of year.

The flickering light turned right, moving down an alleyway.

I quickened my steps to close the distance.

The figure paused, then hurried up a staircase to a door to a building that could only be described as a mansion.

Reaching the bottom of the staircase, I reached under my coat and drew my pistol.

"Senator White?" I called softly.

The figure paused at their task of unlocking the door and turned, raising the lantern. His face was familiar. The grey beard, the suspicious eyes, and a hardened, cold face of a man who'd eagerly lust for revenge. The apple hadn't fallen far from the tree.

"Yes? Who is it?"

I shot him.

***

The Stratten family residence was several blocks away. I walked, quickly at first to get some distance between myself and the dead Senator, and then slower as I savored my newly found freedom.

In my pocket was a letter from Skyla that had been waiting for me at Granite Falls after I returned from Prehistoria. Wolverine Wade and Ashley James had it.

On the envelope was her address and folded with the letter was my Presidential pardon.

In my other pocket was a wedding ring for my Skyla.

The future was bright, and ours.

***

My fiance slipped her hand into mine as I stared at the bright bit of metal in my hand and squeezed gently.

"You certain about this?" I asked Governor Fredrick skeptically.

"Can't think of a better man," he replied, standing before me with a large grin under his mustache.

"That's sad," I mused thoughtfully while turning the Sheriff's badge over in my hand.

Carbine nickered from the corral. I looked at my dun mustang. "What do you think boy, are we up to the challenge?"

He pawed the ground, his hoof digging a furrow in the gravel.

"I reckon that's a yes... from both of us."

Wolverine Wade Mackin drew and fired his pistol in the air, as Ashley James hooted in glee. Otto slapped me hard on the back.

Skyla leaned close, her shoulder resting against mine. "This is a good thing, Jed. You'll be a great law man."

"Shoot, great? More like magnificent. Because he knows both sides of the law," US Marshal Pearl Landry laughed then spit a stream of tobacco juice off to the side. "My brother will do just dandy."

Taking the tin badge from my hand, Skyla stepped in front of me and gently pinned the metal piece to my checkered shirt. She patted it gently, then stepped aside as Governor Fredrick moved before me.

He gripped me by the shoulder and leaned in close. "Your entire life has led you to this point, Jed. Reydan White is dead, Prehistoria is.. mostly... secured for humankind, and you've a Presidential Pardon in your pocket. I know you won't let me down." With his fist, he smashed the tin badge, pressing it hard into my chest. "So, it'll stick," he explained with a grin.

I looked at my friends gathered around me in front of the Sheriff's office in Whitesberg.

"Thank you. All of you, for this. I never could have come so far without you all." I glanced behind me with a wry grin. "And I suppose a Sheriff will be needing deputies."

Eugene Landry and Wesley Clemmons met each other's eyes then mine.

"I ah, suppose I'll be needing a job." my father said, speaking slowly. "A man's got to eat and according to Fredrick, I'm only a wanted man on the other side of the Shimmer. I suppose that means I'm stuck on this side."

"What about you, Wesley?" Governor Fredrick asked.

"I do believe I'll burst into flames should I wear a badge. But I'll be around if you need me."

Looking back at the Sheriff's Office, I watched as Sara pranced around the corral with a new saddle on her back. A gift from Jarl Mikah after the battle ended. "Well, everyone, I do believe this will be a whole 'nother sort of adventure for us."

The End.

***

Jedidiah Huckleberry Smith will return....

***

An open letter to my readers from an eternally grateful author.

Five years ago, my wife told me to write a book. I arrogantly told myself it'd be done in six months and began writing a book about cowboys and dinosaurs. Eighteen months later and after a helping of humble pie, I managed to finish the book and began passing it around to everyone I could find who was willing to give a wannabe author a chance while I began pursuing the ever-elusive publishing agent or press who was willing to print my book. At the time, the working title was actually 'RAWR! Pew Pew Pew!' because while I could write a book, I couldn't write a title that I liked.

From gun and four wheeling forums across the internet, people came willing to take this creation of mine and give it a read. And they liked it! They wanted more. But at the same time, I was being turned down by dozens of presses and agents. (I'm going to share one beautiful and well thought out rejection letter I got at the bottom without giving away the printing press who sent me it because it's quite tickling.)

But for every rejection I received, two more strangers on the internet would tell me how awesome it was and that they wanted more. It kept me going and it kept the book that would morph into 'West of Prehistoric' from being shelved forever on my thumb drive. Eventually, I found a home for it at Severed Press, an adventure/horror publisher that was willing to take a chance on a newbie author and give me a contract for this book plus any others that stemmed from it.

And as requested, I kept writing. Churning out about one book a year for this series until Raiding Prehistoric which took exactly 340 days to finish. (Woo!)

And this entire time, I have felt such gratitude and thankfulness toward all of the people who have helped me. From my beautiful, yet naïve, wife who I based Skyla on, to my annoying but loveable English Mastiff, Bear, that I based Carbine on, to all of the strangers across the internet who became confidants of my fears and worries about my books not being up to snuff that basically told me to shut up and keep writing.

I never would have made it this far had it not been for all of you.

I wish I had the words to express how thankful I am for you.

But since I do not, all I can say is that I promise I will continue to write and continue to entertain you to the very best of my ability. Be it with dinosaurs and cowboys or WWII Marines stranded on an island in the Pacific facing down fearsome sea creatures with M1 Garands, Thompson submachine guns, and flamethrowers... (oh yes, this book has been coming for years...), or any other story that my brain provides... I will do it to the best of my ability.

Thank you all, God bless, and may fortune always favor the bold.

***

Rejection Letter
Book: West of Prehistoric.
Wed, Sep 11, 2019, 2:52 PM

Erik,

At this time, we will not be moving forward as your publisher. We wish you the best of luck in your future writing and your publishing search.

Acquisition Reviewer Notes:

Zane Grey meets Sir Arthur Conan Doyle when prehistoric beasts, including myriad dinosaurs under the control of a race of huge, carnivorous bipedal apes, living in a parallel world, discover a portal into the human world where they proceed to wreak unspeakable and savage havoc in the Wyoming Territory of 1885, beginning with the spread of outlaw cum respected rancher, Jedediah Huckleberry, and gradually moving to a tense showdown in the little town of Granite Falls.

To be successful, any book, I think, must create a world in which the reader is able to suspend disbelief, if only within the pages of that book. Obviously, the farther the subject is from the known world, the more difficult it is to create that acceptance, and with a book that is this far from the "known," the task is huge. It simply doesn't work for me. While the characters are, to some degree, compelling (Jedediah Huckleberry makes a very good anti-hero), the author just tries to do too much, and it's just too hard for the reader to buy in. The ending, which leaves so many loose ends tangling, makes one think that the author finally grew just as weary of the whole thing as his reader does.

It would appear that the author here is striving to occupy a niche, and in that, he is surely successful. The problem is that he is alone in that niche. I simply can not imagine a reader group who would join him there.

Sincerely,
REDACTED.

***

Erik Testerman is a veteran grunt of the glorious Marine Corps, a 'faster than he is accurate' competitive shooter, and an admirer of fine arms and armaments out of his financial reach. He lives in the mountains of North Carolina with his lovely wife, two rambunctious children, and a slobbery English Mastiff.

To learn more about Erik Testerman or to follow his exploits as he navigates the world of the written word, visit http://GunPowderAndInk.blog or on his Facebook page at http://www.facebook.com/AuthorErikTesterman

SEVEREDPRESS

CHECK OUT OTHER GREAT DINOSAUR BOOKS

FLIPSIDE
by JAKE BIBLE

The year is 2046 and dinosaurs are real.

Time bubbles across the world, many as large as one hundred square miles, turn like clockwork, revealing prehistoric landscapes from the Cretaceous Period.

They reveal the Flipside.

Now, thirty years after the first Turn, the clockwork is breaking down as one of the world's powers has decided to exploit the phenomenon for their own gain, possibly destroying everything then and now in the process.

A MAN OUT OF TIME
by Christopher Laflan

Five years after the Chinese Axis detonated an unknown weapon of mass destruction off the southern coast of the United States, Special Ops Sergeant John Crider and the members of Shadow Company have finally captured what they all hope will lead to the end of the war. Unfortunately, the population within the United States is no longer sustainable. In an effort to stabilize the economy, the government enacts the Cryonics Act. One hundred years in suspended animation, all debt forgiven, and a chance at a less crowded future are too good to pass up for John and his young daughter.

Except not everything always goes as planned as Sergeant John Crider finds himself pitted against a land of prehistoric monsters genetically resurrected from the fossil record, murderous inhabitants, and a future he never wanted.

CHECK OUT OTHER GREAT DINOSAUR BOOKS

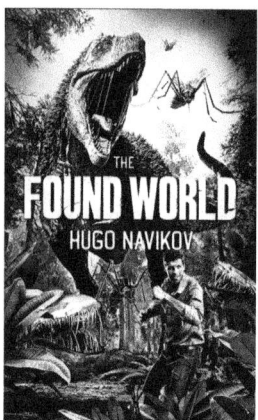

THE FOUND WORLD
by Hugo Navikov

A powerful global cabal wants adventurer Brett Russell to retrieve a superweapon stolen by the scientist who built it. To entice him to travel underneath one of the most dangerous volcanoes on Earth to find the scientist, this shadowy organization will pay him the only thing he cares about: information that will allow him to avenge his family's murder.

But before he can get paid, he and his team must enter an underground hellscape of killer plants, giant insects, terrifying dinosaurs, and an army of other predators never previously seen by man.

At the end of this journey awaits a revelation that could alter the fate of mankind ... if they can make it back from this horrifying found world.

HOUSE OF THE GODS
by Davide Mana

High above the steamy jungle of the Amazon basin, rise the flat plateaus known as the Tepui, the House of the Gods. Lost worlds of unknown beauty, a naturalistic wonder, each an ecology onto itself, shunned by the local tribes for centuries. The House of the Gods was not made for men.

But now, the crew and passengers of a small charter plane are about to find what was hidden for sixty million years.

Lost on an island in the clouds 10.000 feet above the jungle, surrounded by dinosaurs, hunted by mysterious mercenaries, the survivors of Sligo Air flight 001 will quickly learn the only rule of life on Earth: Extinction.

CHECK OUT OTHER GREAT DINOSAUR BOOKS

PRIMORDIA
by **Greig Beck**

Ben Cartwright, former soldier, home to mourn the loss of his father stumbles upon cryptic letters from the past between the author, Arthur Conan Doyle and his great, great grandfather who vanished while exploring the Amazon jungle in 1908.

Amazingly, these letters lead Ben to believe that his ancestor's expedition was the basis for Doyle's fantastical tale of a lost world inhabited by long extinct creatures. As Ben digs some more he finds clues to the whereabouts of a lost notebook that might contain a map to a place that is home to creatures that would rewrite everything known about history, biology and evolution.

But other parties now know about the notebook, and will do anything to obtain it. For Ben and his friends, it becomes a race against time and against ruthless rivals.

In the remotest corners of Venezuela, along winding river trails known only to lost tribes, and through near impenetrable jungle, Ben and his novice team find a forbidden place more terrifying and dangerous than anything they could ever have imagined.

PANGAEA EXILES
by **Jeff Brackett**

Tried and convicted for his crimes, Sean Barrow is sent into temporal exile—banished to a time so far before recorded history that there is no chance that he, or any other criminal sent back, has any chance of altering history.

Now Sean must find a way to survive more than 200 million years in the past, in a world populated by monstrous creatures that would rend him limb from limb if they got the chance. And that's just his fellow prisoners.

The dinosaurs are almost as bad.